Beautiful Disasters

An Other Girls Romance

Avery Brooks

Bywater
BOOKS

2025

This book is dedicated to my family.
Thanks for being there for me.

"Dance until you shatter yourself."
                                        —Rumi

Chapter 1

Drea Cordeira glanced at the early morning sun filtering through her floor-to-ceiling curtains and the interplay of light and shadows throughout the spacious bedroom of her loft. The softness of her sheets against her naked body reminded her that she was not alone, and she turned to see who her companion was today.

The blonde from the club stretched and smiled at her. "Good morning."

The greeting always scared Drea a little, somehow feeling more intimate than what had transpired the night . . . and early morning hours before. A feeling of mild panic gripped her chest, maybe at the idea that this could be her life, a million mornings waking up to someone expecting her to be something she wasn't.

But as Drea smiled at the woman, she felt a calm return to her, easing the tightness in her chest, allowing her to breathe again. She knew what to do. She'd done it many times before. No woman would ever truly shake her again—she'd vowed that to herself many years ago.

"Heey," she dragged out the word, coating it with her southern drawl, knowing the effect it had on women.

The woman's sleepy yet hopeful eyes turned more sensual as

Drea leaned in and kissed her, long and slow. And even though the kiss and the night before had been pleasant, Drea knew that she and the woman were having very different experiences in this moment. Drea just had to make sure the woman didn't start thinking this was something it wasn't.

When Drea pulled back from the kiss, the woman opened her mouth to speak, but before any words were formed, Drea jumped in. "Last night was . . ." Hope returned to the woman's eyes as Drea spoke, but she pressed on. "Fun." When understanding dimmed the woman's expression, Drea felt torn. She always was at this moment. Part happy that they were on the same page, but also panged that she caused that brightness in someone's eyes to disappear. But it was better now than later. At least now there were no expectations, no arguments to be had, no hateful judgments to spew. It was easy and fun and that's all she needed. All she would ever need. Still, the look on the woman's face didn't sit well.

"I'll make some coffee," she added quickly and kissed the woman's cheek before hopping out of bed, grabbing the robe draped over the latest painting she'd been working on, and heading for the kitchen. Pickles, her rust-colored tabby, appeared at her heels, meowing along the way to the kitchen, just in case Drea had somehow developed amnesia over the past few hours and had forgotten it was breakfast time.

She poured food into Pickles' bowl and gave him a quick pet before grabbing the tin of Café Du Monde chicory coffee. As she opened the lid, she took a deep breath, inhaling the familiar nutty and earthy aroma, letting it fill her lungs, awaking her body while calming her soul. Was it telling that she was more excited waking up to this coffee than to the woman in her bed?

As the coffee brewed, Drea rushed through the motions in the bathroom, grateful she had a very simple morning routine. She grabbed a black T-shirt and pulled on the jeans that had been tossed to the floor the night before. After a glance at the woman who had fallen back to sleep in her bed, she made a bit more noise pulling on her black calf-high boots and stomping back to the kitchen. Sam Parker, her boss who also happened to be her best friend since middle school, had implored everyone to be on time for the Monday morning meeting. So she couldn't be late. She had taken a few sips of coffee, letting it surge through her veins and blow away any cobwebs of sleep that still remained, when the woman, thankfully already dressed in her clothes from the previous night, joined her in the kitchen.

Pickles jumped up on the white marble island and watched the woman for a moment, and Drea wondered what he must think. It wasn't every night that she had company, but enough that he had seen a fair share of the queer female population of New Orleans. She handed the woman a to-go cup of coffee and quickly filled her own thermos.

"I'm running late for work, so I'll walk you out," Drea said as she grabbed her leather messenger bag from the counter.

The woman's face fell. "Oh, okay," she said in a voice clearly indicating it wasn't okay.

Drea turned to Pickles and scratched under his chin for a moment before leaning in. "Don't judge me, mister. You'd do it too," she whispered into his ear. Pickles gave the little purr-meow he did when he was happy, and Drea couldn't help but plant a kiss on his furry little forehead.

She smiled to the woman and placed her hand on the small of her back as she started to walk toward the door. "Shall we?"

As they walked out of Drea's apartment building into the bustling Central Business District, people rushed by them on their way to work as a line of cars rolled by and a few horns honked in the distance. The woman hesitated before saying, "Well . . ."

The mix of sadness and bewilderment in the woman's eyes stirred something in Drea, so she did the only thing she could, wrapping the woman in a hug, hoping that could be enough.

When she let go, she placed her hand on the woman's shoulder. "Take care of yourself," she said, and then turned on her heel to hurry to her car.

When the engine roared, a sense of power ran through Drea. Freedom and control. She felt most like herself when she was driving . . . and painting . . . and more sensual pursuits. She lowered the top of her convertible as the hot, sticky September air enveloped her and headed down the street, letting the wind tear through her hair. As she pressed the gas pedal further, any lingering feelings from the morning drifted from her mind, lost in a blur with the passing scenery.

As Drea entered Uptown about twenty minutes later, the colorful shotgun houses with remnants of Mardi Gras beads from the previous year's festivities still draped over wrought-iron fences, and the neighborhood bars and restaurants nestled amongst the houses, felt like home. She had moved downtown a few years ago, wanting a change, and a bit more distance from her family, but as much as she loved her loft with its view of the river, nothing held a candle to this neighborhood. She had spent most of her childhood here with Sam. The thought shook Drea from her nostalgia, and she took a hard turn as her car squealed around the final corner. She parked in front of the office, took a quick sip of coffee, and ran up the stairs, wondering what news Sam had to share with the team.

Drea entered the office like a whirlwind, her gait confident and sure, on the edge of on-time. She sat at the rectangular conference table, a bit large for their small team, and ran a hand through her dark, curly hair, a little wild from the drive over. "Good morning, y'all," she said to the half-full table.

Sam was pointing out some items on the paper in front of her to Cassie Sullivan, her administrative assistant, as they mumbled a few words back and forth. When Sam looked up, a warm smile spread across her face. "Heya, Drea."

Drea couldn't help but smile at the rhyme Sam had coined

during their younger years. The pulse of nostalgia warmed her.

The last stragglers filtered into the conference room, the only room with a door in the large, open-concept office that had been the site of a former chicory coffee house. They joined the table as Drea spun around in her chair, sipping her coffee.

As everyone got settled, Sam cleared her throat and began the meeting, covering various projects for the coming week, who was doing what, and upcoming deadlines. Drea couldn't help but smile to herself at seeing Sam in this role.

Through over twenty years of friendship, she had watched her best friend struggle through obstacles, assholes, and, as a result, self-esteem issues, but Sam had finally taken the risk of a lifetime by investing in herself, leaving her job, and starting her own marketing firm.

It wasn't easy and Sam had put in some very long days in the beginning, but Drea could now see the beginnings of the woman she had always seen in Sam, even more obvious those rare moments in the past when Sam got out of her own way and believed in herself a little.

Despite the stress and chaos of a new business, there was a peace to Sam now that Drea had never seen before. The worry line between her brows had faded, and there was a glimmer in her eyes that Drea hadn't seen in years.

Sam interrupted Drea's thoughts. "Drea, you're on Daily Bread's new logo. I told Jody we'd have it to her by Friday."

"On it, boss." Drea nodded.

"Also . . ." Sam clasped her hands together with a hopeful grin on her face. "I have two exciting things to share with you all."

The pleased look on Sam's face calmed Drea, realizing the news was going to be good. At this early stage of the company, they needed everything to go well.

"After a lot of hard work by Cassie," Sam gestured at Cassie with a warm smile, "I'm very happy to say we have landed Beau and Lorna Rush and their restaurant, The Well, as our newest clients. Cassie will serve as the lead on the account. Drea, Beau and Lorna are coming to see the mock-ups on Thursday morning. Cassie can walk you through the plans for The Well after we finish."

Drea lifted her silver thermos to Sam, then took a sip as her focus drifted from Sam's hazel eyes to the brown eyes next to her. She knew Cassie had been Sam's right hand at McGrady Marketing, the firm where Sam had worked before starting her own company, but she couldn't help but feel the tiniest twinge at someone else being so close to her best friend, even if it was just at work.

There had been so many changes over the past few months, Sam falling in love with Ash, Ash moving in with Sam, Drea joining Sam's company as the head graphic designer. Drea and Sam had been inseparable since they were kids and she was grappling with where she fit into Sam's life now. So much of her existence had centered around Sam and Jake, Sam's six-year-old son, but with everything changing, Drea felt a bit left behind.

She still saw Sam nearly every day at work, but it wasn't the same. She'd just started getting accustomed to sharing Sam's attention with Ash and now she had to deal with Cassie taking even more of it. Sam was beginning new chapters in her own life, whereas Drea felt as if she was losing everything she had known. And at thirty-five, she felt a little old to start all over.

Drea took a breath to center herself and pasted on a warm smile for Cassie, which Cassie returned. She knew Cassie wasn't to blame for anything. Drea was merely feeling insecure about all of the changes and needed to figure out how to roll with them. She and Sam were best friends. When everything settled down again, they'd be fine. Tight as ever.

A young brunette woman entered the conference room with a hesitant expression. "Hi, sorry I'm late. I had some trouble finding the place."

"No worries," Sam said. "It's perfect timing actually." Sam turned to the rest of the team. "I want to introduce you all to Erin, our new intern."

Drea recalled Sam outlining her vision and mission for the company and how important it was to her to give back to the community, including training local university students in marketing through internships. The fact that Sam had managed to move forward with that goal so soon after launching the firm was further testament to how hard she was working and how much her company meant to her.

Drea tuned back in as Sam continued. "I know it's been a little crazy getting Crescent City Marketing off the ground these last two months. And I truly appreciate all your hard work. Now that we're starting to hit stable ground, I reached out to Tulane University so we can give local students some firsthand experience. Erin is our first intern and I hope she will be the first of many over the years. Erin, do you want to introduce yourself to the team?"

Erin looked a bit surprised and nervous, but smiled at the faces around the table. "Sure. Hi, everyone. I'm really grateful to be here and honored to be your first intern. I'm a junior, majoring in marketing . . ." When Erin met Drea's gaze, she seemed to lose her train of thought for a moment and tucked a strand of shoulder-length hair behind her ear.

Drea registered the slight change, something she was used to by now. Women and men, but especially women, tended to falter when she was around. It didn't always mean something. Though it usually did.

Drea broke eye contact and took a sip of coffee, letting Erin find her words again.

"So, I'm really excited to learn from you all and apply what I've learned in the classroom to real projects." She turned toward Sam with a smile.

"Great, well, we're happy to have you. And I'm sure the team will be nothing but welcoming." Sam locked eyes with Drea for a moment, managing to pass a warning stare without breaking her smile. It took skill to master that expression, but Sam had a lot of practice. It was a combo Drea had received often during their many years of friendship.

As Drea and the rest of the team filed out of the conference room, Sam laid her hand on Drea's shoulder and whispered, "No pranking."

Drea smiled warmly at her. "You got it."

Sam held her gaze. "I mean it, Drea."

Drea saluted and headed to her desk. Sure, Drea had a . . . *history* of pranking interns and new employees at her previous position, but did Sam really think she'd do that here?

That young girl she'd duct-taped to a rolling chair was a classic story, although she still thought it was largely that girl's fault for not even trying to put up a fight. Maybe Sam was right in her concern . . . at least a little.

Drea dropped her bag on her desk and took out her laptop. As the screen awoke and the files she'd been working on the previous week stared back at her, she grabbed her thermos, suddenly needing some extra encouragement to get started. She couldn't pull nearly as many all-nighters as she used to.

"They're looking for crisp, modern, industrial, and natural tones—browns, grays, and blues—but also inviting."

Drea nodded and typed notes as Cassie sat across the desk from her and filled her in on their new client. Beau and Lorna Rush were a husband-and-wife team from Savannah, Georgia, who had relocated to New Orleans two years ago. Their farm-to-table restaurant, The Well, had one of the city's most creative cocktail lists—and was even more impressive than their food, which had garnered them several local awards during their short existence.

"Okay, any preferences on the content?" Drea paused typing and glanced at Cassie.

"They're pretty open to whatever we come up with." Cassie swept the strands of the lilac-tinged hair dipping over her eye to the side of her face. "Going off the farm-to-table idea, maybe some sort of inviting table with a throwback to the nearby land? Or a group of people with cocktails at the table? They're big into creating community. Or maybe Beau and Lorna with their dog, Rex, at the farm? He's a super cute doodle mix."

Design ideas ran through Drea's mind, and she typed a few quick notes for later. When she looked up, she met Cassie's gaze. Drea's eyes fell to the bold lipstick, several shades darker than her hair and in stark contrast to her smooth ivory skin. But as the corners of Cassie's lips turned upward, Drea caught herself and turned back to her laptop, typing a nonsensical stream of letters to let the moment pass.

"Not a huge well in the middle of a field or anything?" Drea quipped. She didn't look up as she joked about the restaurant's name but smiled to herself. Okay, she was back.

"Um, no." Cassie laughed. "They might be open to some ideas, though, to better align the restaurant name with their campaign."

"All right. I'll have some options for you to look over tomorrow morning." Drea was normally a bit more friendly with people, but there was something about Cassie she knew she wanted to keep at arm's length. She wasn't sure if it was Cassie's role in the company or something else, but she was a bit wary of letting her in.

"I look forward to it." The warmth in Cassie's smile and eyes pained Drea a little. Cassie's friendliness was disarming, but Drea wasn't in the market for new friends. She didn't like building walls, but everything had been shaky the past few months, and she was trying to protect herself. From what, she wasn't sure.

As Cassie walked away, Drea scanned the room for Erin, who was pouring a cup of coffee in the break area. When Erin turned around, Drea waved her over.

"Hi Erin, we haven't been formally introduced. I'm Drea, the graphic designer." She held out her hand to Erin, who took it with a noticeable gulp. "Ready for a shot at designing a campaign?"

Erin's eyes lit up. "Yes!"

"All right, pull up a chair."

Drea spent the rest of the morning covering the basics of campaigns and graphic design along with the specifics for The Well campaign. Like many Gen Zers Drea had worked with, Erin was a whiz at anything on the computer, especially graphic design. Drea had always been good with art, but she was old enough that it had taken a bit of training to learn the software and make it work for her particular artistic style. She admired how easily Erin took to it.

"Why don't you come up with an ad idea and we can discuss it this afternoon? It doesn't have to be fancy, just enough of a sketch to give me an idea of what you're thinking for copy and design."

Erin's eagerness was palpable. "That would be great. Thank you!"

Cassie, normally an expert multitasker, felt like she was slogging through mud, and it was only early afternoon. She had a knack for staying on top of things and getting jobs done. It was her nature—partly due to her strong work ethic, learned from her sister, and partly due to her minor need for perfectionism. She never let the balls drop. Other people might slip, but she always finished the job. It's why she often gravitated toward project leader positions, if only unofficially. Sam was the first boss who truly saw what she had to offer and gave her the title to match the expectations. For that, she was grateful. And determined not to let Sam down.

As the head project coordinator, she was the lead for most of the campaigns, at least the ones Sam didn't take under her wing, but, due to the small staff, she split her time between that and being Sam's admin. She liked the hybrid position because it gave her direct access to Sam, and together they could get ahead of most issues before the rest of the team ever knew about them. It felt like a partnership, one that made her feel seen.

Cassie tried to focus on the schedule for next week, but a burst of laughter drew her attention to Drea's desk where the giddy intern seemed to be hanging on her every word. *Poor sap.* She was falling under Drea's spell, like everyone else it seemed. Except for Cassie, of course.

Cassie had heard of Drea's reputation long before she ever met her. New Orleans was a surprisingly small city, especially the queer community. Pretty much every woman who set foot in the queer clubs in NOLA had either hooked up with Drea or wished they had.

Drea was a player, but somehow managed to charm everyone enough not to create hordes of irate women. Nobody had anything bad to say about Drea, which was . . . kind of impressive.

Well, nobody but Cassie. She didn't dislike Drea; she was just confused. After hearing about her charm and seeing it with the others at the office, she felt there was something different when Drea interacted with her. She wasn't rude exactly, just not friendly.

At first, she thought it was because they didn't know each other well, but after two months of working together, she had watched Drea be friendly with everyone else in the office. Just not her. She couldn't think of anything she had done that might have upset her, so she chalked it up to different personalities that didn't click. But if she was being honest, it bothered her. Cassie wasn't going to become another in a long line of conquests for Ms. Drea Cordeira, but she could be her friend. Except Drea apparently didn't want the friendship. And Cassie didn't know what she had done to make Drea behave so . . . well, so politely.

Cassie looked back at her computer screen. Another burst of laughter. She steeled herself and tried to focus on the calendar in front of her. But eventually her eyes wandered back to Drea's desk and the smile on Drea's face, subtle flirtation, and inviting body language. The ease that she had with Erin after only a few hours irked her.

Cassie's mind flashed back to her talk with Drea this morning. Drea hadn't been rude per se, but she definitely wasn't inviting or warm. Curt, to the point. A weight landed in Cassie's chest. Why was she the only one Drea didn't like and, more importantly, why did it bother her?

The blank schedule on her screen grabbed her attention once more. She adjusted in her seat and made herself focus.

When she finished, she walked over to Sam's desk. "Here are the potential dates for the new client meeting next week with Pawper's Pups." The windows behind Sam's desk peered onto Tchoupitoulas Street, and the view of a live oak's winding branches always grounded Cassie.

Sam stopped staring at her computer and eagerly accepted the paper from Cassie. "Great. Hmm. Let's do Tuesday."

"Okay," Cassie said cheerily, starting to walk away.

"Cassie, hang on. I'm trying to figure out what to do with Erin, and I could use your opinion." Sam motioned for her to come look at her monitor.

Cassie bent over Sam's shoulder as they stared at the intern schedule Cassie had made for Sam the previous week. She had put a lot of effort into making a rotation system for Erin to get an idea of the different roles in the company and see what she liked best, which she would then focus on for the rest of the year. Sam had seemed excited when Cassie went over the plan with her last week, so Cassie wasn't sure what had changed.

"I was going to have her start with Tom like you had planned," Sam started, but the sound of Erin's laughter caught both of their attentions. They turned toward Drea's desk in one synchronized movement. "But it looks like Drea is already working with her." Cassie couldn't take her eyes off the two of them but still managed to notice the slight tension in Sam's voice, gone almost as quickly as it appeared before Sam continued. "So, might as well start there."

Was it just her or were Drea and Erin sitting really close?

"Cassie?"

"Sorry, what?" She turned to Sam, who was staring at her.

"You okay?"

"Yes . . . yes, sorry." She shook her head as she let out a small laugh. "I think that plan sounds great." She turned to get out of there fast, not sure if she was more embarrassed by how easily Drea had entered her thoughts or that Sam might have noticed it too.

Sam stopped her. "Can you get me the final designs and marketing plan for Uptown Grocery before I pick up Jake today? I'll work on it tonight and make sure everything's ready for next week's pitch."

Though they had all been working nonstop the past couple of months to launch the firm and make it a success, no one worked harder than Sam. The bags under her eyes worried Cassie, and she hoped that as the team built a rhythm, she would take more time for herself. But she couldn't say that to Sam. They had been pretty close at their previous firm, but always professional, and everything was so new now as they were all figuring out their new roles. So she did all she could do and smiled at Sam. "Absolutely."

"You seem to have hit it off with Erin quickly." The mix of concern and curiosity with a side of hesitation in Sam's voice wasn't new to Drea, but Drea couldn't decide if it was because of her history with pranking interns or her history with women . . . or both.

She eyed Sam, who had asked for a chat before Drea headed home. Drea thought it might be about the new intern, and judging by Sam's statement she decided to settle into the comfy office chair a bit more, preparing for a lecture on professionalism in the office. "I figured she'd enjoy working on a campaign rather than standing around, but it's not a big deal if you have other plans for her."

"No, I appreciate you taking the initiative and showing her what you do. That's why I wanted to chat with you. I'm going to have Erin do rotations to get some experience in each role in the office and then have her choose one to pursue for the rest of the year."

"Solid plan, boss."

"Cassie worked up a whole schedule already and I meant to go over it with everyone before Erin started, but you know . . ." Sam gestured her hand at the office.

"Yeah," Drea said. Of course Cassie had made a schedule. Cassie always made Sam's life easier. Drea knew how harried Sam was. The pace had been frantic since the company launched, and as much as Drea had needed time to de-stress and add some work-life balance, she knew Sam needed it even more. Though she was pretty sure that opportunity hadn't come yet.

Sam ran her hand through her hair as if trying to wipe away the stress. "Anyway, I was going to start her with Tom to learn about slogans and ad copy, but I'd like you to be her first rotation."

Drea felt her brows raise. Maybe she had misjudged the purpose of this meeting.

"But I want to make sure we're on the same page about a few things," Sam continued.

There it was. Drea crossed her ankle over her knee and got comfortable.

"Drea, I need you to be professional with Erin. I know you enjoyed pranking interns at your previous position, but there's a lot riding on this right now . . . for me."

Drea was silently nodding along, but the way Sam said those last two words stilled her. Sam had rarely asked her for anything over their twenty-plus years of friendship, but the tone of her words held a pleading to them.

Sam's eyes held her. "This company is everything to me right now and I need all of us putting our best foot forward to establish it as a solid firm with integrity. I see big things in the future. And if things go well with Erin, I envision having regular interns from Tulane and UNO. So, the pranking can't happen."

"I got it, Sam. You don't need to worry." It was true, she loved pranking interns. Something about their innocence mixed with an eagerness to please made it too easy. But she would never jeopardize Sam's company or well-being. "Is that all?"

The look of discomfort on Sam's face gave her chills.

"What is it?" she asked warily.

"There can't be any . . . funny business."

Drea squinted at Sam, trying to understand her meaning.

"I saw how she was acting around you. It's how most women act around you. But that can't happen either."

"I didn't notice." Her smirk betrayed her and Sam rolled her eyes.

"This is too important, Drea. I can't risk a lawsuit from some girl who misunderstood your attention."

Drea scoffed. "I have never had any woman upset with my attention."

Sam looked to the ceiling. "And that still baffles me." She blew out a breath. "It's also not the point, Drea. It can't happen."

The rigidity in Sam's tone quelled any further jokes. "I know. I won't do anything, Sam."

There was still hesitation in Sam's expression.

"Hey." Drea held her gaze. She already knew how important this company was to Sam. To both of them. "I promise."

Relief washed over Sam's face.

Drea couldn't blame Sam for worrying, but it hurt that Sam didn't trust her to know enough not to jeopardize Sam's company. But Drea was used to her reputation preceding her in this city, and even with Sam occasionally. "Anything else?"

"Nope, that's all I got." Sam's warm smile returned as she exited strict boss mode.

Drea stood and started for her desk before turning back. "Charlie's Friday?"

Sam frowned. "I can't. Ash has some work function she wants me to go to with her. I'm sorry."

"You need me to watch Jake?" Drea asked, trying to sound unfazed despite the disappointment.

Sam shook her head. "My mom's been missing quality grandson time, so she offered to watch him." Sam's voice lightened. "But if you could watch him next week, that would be a huge help."

"No problem. Have a good night, Sam." Drea strode confidently back to her desk despite feeling like the wind had been knocked out of her. She slid her laptop into her bag and, grabbing her tumbler, headed for the door.

Everyone was packing up or had already left for the day, except for Cassie as usual. Drea glanced her way and realized Cassie was watching her. A faint smile appeared on Cassie's face before she looked back at her computer. Drea didn't smile back, suddenly irritated with Cassie for everything: making the intern schedule that Drea had apparently disrupted, being Sam's right-hand woman. Everything.

She pushed the door open, heading down the stairs and out the exterior door, letting the warm evening air wash over her. The sweet, citrusy scent of jasmine from a nearby yard wafted through the air as summer fought to hang on a while longer before giving in to autumn.

The rev of her car's engine reverberated in her soul. Driving always freed her. She ran her hands through her hair, shaking the curls as if it would remove the stress as well. She squealed out onto the road, the wind whipping at her hair as she sped through the streets. The pleasure she took in the act of driving let her leave Cassie where she belonged—at the office.

She passed people milling around at the shops and restaurants on Magazine Street, before heading up to St. Charles Avenue where there were fewer pedestrians and she could breathe a little. She drove alongside the grassy median with the steel rails of the streetcar tracks. Towering live oaks and magnolia trees bordered the road, the setting sun glinting off the Spanish moss draped over the oak limbs. It was Drea's favorite time of day.

As she neared downtown, she turned toward the river and pulled into her building's parking lot. She said hello to Earl, the doorman, who was always grinning and had the air of a distinguished gentleman, even beyond what would be expected for an octogenarian. When the elevator dinged at the tenth floor, she walked down the hallway adorned with fleur de lis wallpaper. The iconic symbol of New Orleans always gave her a sense of home.

Pickles greeted her with meows and lots of cheek rubs against her legs. Drea poured his food into his bowl and let him eat on the marble island in the kitchen, stroking his fur as he crunched away.

"You'll be my date on Friday, won't you, Pickles?"

Pickles finished his food and purred as Drea scratched his chin.

"That's what I thought."

Chapter 2

Outside the high school gym, Cassie heard the blaring whistle followed by Janay Jeffries' powerful voice barking out commands. She smiled at the sound of her best friend's voice and swung open the heavy metal door as the sounds magnified ten times. Thirty girls, assembled into rows, stomped and clapped out choreography in unison, punctuated by Janay's whistle and shouts. Cassie loved coming here. The infectious energy in the room felt more like home to her than any place she had ever known.

Sweat dripped from the faces of the girls and young women, ranging in age from thirteen to twenty-five. Their strong, muscled thighs rippled underneath tight dance shorts with each assertive stomp to the floor. The power emanating from their bodies was only dwarfed by the power of their collective mission and determination to fulfill it.

The whistle sounded. "Okay. Shantal, much better on that last round. Y'all keep it up. From the top. Energy. Go!"

Cassie stopped a few feet from where Janay stood. Janay nodded recognition with the whistle firmly planted between her lips before turning back to her team.

It had been too long since Cassie had made it to practice.

The launch of Crescent City Marketing and being Sam's go-to person at work had overtaken her life for the past two months, but now there was finally time to breathe and get back to her own life a little.

Cassie still knew all of the moves the team had been working on since the summer. She mimicked the steps with the team, occasionally catching the eye of one of the girls and silently emphasizing a slight change to their movement. Janay was the boss, but everyone, including Janay, saw Cassie as a sort of assistant step coach—the friendly, softer side to the disciplined, no-excuses, bootcamp-style attitude of Janay. Janay was a softie at heart; all the girls knew it too, but she could front the drill sergeant hat effectively for the most part.

After a few more rounds and deafening blows of the whistle, Janay called it. "Almost there. Good work. Go get some rest and see you tomorrow."

As the girls sighed in relief, wiped sweat from their faces, and hustled to grab their stuff, they all ran by Cassie, giving her high fives and some hugs as they passed.

Cassie's encouraging words followed them out the door, "Y'all look amazing. Killin' it!"

"He-ey," Janay sauntered over, wearing her typical uniform of baggy basketball shorts and a T-shirt, and wiping her face with a hand towel. It felt like a sauna in the space, the smell of sweat, mildew, and dampness filling the air, and Cassie hadn't even done anything yet. Janay wrapped her arm around Cassie's shoulder and squeezed gently, but Cassie pulled her into a real hug. "I'm all sweaty," Janay protested.

"I don't care. Just hug me." Cassie needed to feel her friend's embrace. To be centered. Janay was family and the closest thing Cassie had to a soulmate, other than her sister, Molly. Janay never needed Cassie to explain anything. She always "got" Cassie. It had meant everything to find someone who saw her, the real her.

"They're looking great," Cassie said.

"I know." Janay shrugged her shoulders up and down a few times in a confident move.

Cassie laughed and shoved her arm, but she knew the proud smile on Janay's face was genuine. Janay gave everything to her girls, though she'd be the last to say so.

"I haven't seen you in forever. Girl, what's up?" Janay asked.

Cassie wiped a bead of sweat from her forehead. "Work, work, and more work. Let's get some air."

Janay grabbed her bag and locked up as they walked outside.

"Much better." Cassie shook the front of her T-shirt to get some air underneath it. They sat on the concrete stoop, warmed by the sun, and she filled Janay in on her work situation and new coworkers as Janay sipped from her water bottle.

"Dang. You've been busy."

"So have you, as usual." Cassie tilted her head at the gym.

"Girl, they are running me ra-gged." Janay tilted her head from side to side to emphasize the last two syllables.

Cassie laughed. "You love it."

Janay scoffed, but a grin broke through the cool demeanor.

The sound of a distant band practice rang out and Cassie took a moment to let her surroundings sink in. The large, sturdy oaks lining the street gave a sense of strength and stability. Mardi Gras beads hung randomly from the trees and along the wrought-iron gates surrounding the creole cottages along the street.

The city was always one step away from a party. A light breeze blew and Cassie watched as the Spanish moss hanging from the tree limbs lifted gently, aglow from the late afternoon sun. She closed her eyes for a moment, letting the faint breeze and calmness of the moment sink in, the intoxicating aroma of the last magnolia blossoms of the season hanging in the air. Moments like these were what New Orleans meant to her— peace, sitting with her girl, just being, something she hadn't felt in nearly two months with all the work chaos.

Cassie turned back to Janay who seemed to be taking in the scenery as well. "There is one other thing."

"Shoot," Janay said, taking another swig of water.

"Drea's one of my coworkers."

Janay's eyebrows rose as she cocked her head to the side. "*Drea* Drea?"

Cassie nodded.

"Damn . . . has she hit on you yet?" Mischief twinkled in her eyes.

"No. She barely acknowledges my existence."

"What?"

"I'm serious. She's cool with everyone else, but with me . . . it's like I offended her in a past life or something. I thought maybe I was just being sensitive and it was because she didn't know me well, but then a new intern started this week and she's buddy-buddy with her day one."

"That's weird. I figured she sweet-talked every woman on the planet."

"Not every woman." Cassie shook her head, still frustrated by the situation. "I mean . . . I'm nice."

"Absolutely."

"I'm friendly."

"Mmhmm."

"People like me, damn it." She inflected the last two words bitterly.

"They do."

"I don't get it."

"Maybe she's *too* into you. Intimidated by your awesomeness." Janay nodded as if it would convince Cassie to believe her words.

Cassie shot her a look. "I don't think any woman intimidates Drea." She shook her head again. "I don't know why I even care."

"Because she's being a dick for no reason."

Cassie raised her palms to the sky with the acknowledgment. "She *is* being a dick." She blew out a breath. "No. The worst part is she isn't being a dick. She's being unfailingly polite. Civil. Distant." She shrugged. Drea treated her like someone's boring, old great-aunt. "Whatever. I don't need to be friends with everyone I work with."

Janay bumped her shoulder. "You always got me."

Cassie smiled and bumped her back. "I know." She didn't know where she'd be if Janay hadn't come into her life. She took a deep breath at the thought. "You down for Rosie's on Friday? I could use a night out."

"Yes, ma'am."

A wave of relief washed over Cassie at the thought of going out for fun for the first time in too long. Screw Drea, anyway. Cassie was done wasting her time thinking about that woman. She didn't need Drea to like her to do her job. She was a boss at work. Cassie turned her attention back to Janay and pushed Drea Cordeira out of her mind.

It had only been a few days since she started working with Erin, but Drea already felt behind on her deadlines. She enjoyed teaching Erin, but with only one laptop between them, her productivity felt like molasses. If they were going to keep hiring interns, they'd have to invest in a laptop for the position to save employees from having to share. Otherwise, they were going to get way behind on work.

She tried to work out a mix of teaching and supervising while Erin practiced what she had just learned, giving her small assignments that gave Drea a few minutes to catch up on her own work.

During those times, she would escape to the break area for some quiet and work on her tablet to try to catch up. She had never spent much time in the break area other than a few minutes here and there to grab coffee. The huge windows gave her an incredible view of the Mississippi River, rivaled only by the view from her own balcony. The lower section of the windows was cranked open to let the breeze in while the weather was still pleasant.

She sank into the plush purple velvet chair against the brick wall so she could glance out the window as she worked, and folded her legs under her. There was a hum of chatter from colleagues and the clicking of computer keys. She had never really noticed it from her desk, but being set off from the rest of the office, even by only a few feet, created more distance than she would have imagined.

"Drea."

The voice a few feet away startled her and she blinked to adjust her eyes, seeing Erin staring at her. Drea glanced at her watch to see that it had been almost thirty minutes since she had left Erin working on the last project. *Damn it.* She had hoped to get so much more done before Erin needed her again.

"Ready?"

Erin nodded.

"All right, let's see it."

As Erin turned to head back to her desk, Drea frowned at the half-complete design on her screen, realizing she needed to find a way to get her work done while still being present for Erin. It mattered to Sam and she wouldn't let her down.

Cassie envied Janay's ease in crowds and her love of social interactions. Cassie wasn't sure how much of it was Janay's innate personality and how much was her being born and raised in New Orleans, probably a bit of both. No one was ever a stranger in her presence. Cassie, on the other hand, was originally from Boston. And though she had lost much of the harsh accent over the last fifteen years she had lived in NOLA, it was not the smooth Cajun lullaby of accents from this region. But what she lacked in smoothness in tone, her personality made up for in its jovial, welcoming acceptance. Others always assumed it was a natural ability, but it took a lot of work some days.

Rosie's was packed. Other than a few clubs with an occasional LGBTQ+ night, Rosie's was the constant, the only queer club in the city catering to women. It was primarily a dance club with a huge dance floor surrounded by a bar that ran the length of one wall and booths for people to sit down. A couple of pool tables along one of the walls were for those who didn't enjoy dancing or who needed a break between songs. The lights throughout cast a pink glow, creating even more of a sultry ambience than a space full of women dancing with each other. The smell of sweat, perfume, and alcohol seemed as permanent a fixture as the furniture around them.

"I wanna dance." Janay pulled Cassie's hand, leading her through the sweaty mob to the center of the dance floor. She raised Cassie's hand and twirled her. "Dance with me, Cas!"

Cassie laughed and flung her free arm in the air "Stayin' Alive" style before Janay twirled her back and dipped her. As soon as Cassie was back on her feet, Janay moved on to dance with the people around her. When Janay danced, people were drawn to her. She allowed everyone around her to let down their guard, let go, and just live. Even if only for one dance.

Cassie loved to dance and was generally okay with being on her own on the dance floor. She didn't have the magnetism that Janay exuded, but she was chill enough that she could enjoy herself almost anywhere.

As the night wore on and Cassie became increasingly hot and sweaty, she caught Janay's eye. She waved her hand in front of her face like a fan and Janay nodded, returning a sign for a drink.

Off the dance floor, Cassie found a somewhat quiet area near an empty booth in the corner of the room. The tabletop held several abandoned drinks, some with napkins tossed haphazardly inside them, so Cassie stood as she waited for Janay.

"Hey!" Janay appeared through the crowd of women and handed her a glass of ice water. Janay somehow still looked fresh and vibrant, her rich umber complexion barely glistening in the lights from the dance floor whereas, Cassie was pretty sure she looked like a drowned rat.

"Oh my god, thank you!" Cassie grabbed the glass and gulped nearly half of it immediately.

"Sorry I took so long. I ran into . . ." There was no need to keep listening. Janay always ran into someone and always took longer than expected as a result. Even as she was telling the story, more people interrupted Janay and dragged her back to the dance floor.

Cassie took a few moments, enjoying the break from sweaty bodies bumping into her and the hot cloud of sweat and body odor enveloping the dance floor. She took one final sip of her water and bopped back to the dance floor.

She searched for Janay as she danced her way past people. Most people jumped around and matched the fast tempo, except for the few who were grinding their way to a more sensual experience, unaware of the song or people around them.

Cassie found a spot behind a group of people and swayed to the tune. She raised her arms in the air, closed her eyes, and for a moment, despite the crowded room, she felt free. As the song ended, her eyes opened once again and she watched several people leave the dance floor. It was past 1 a.m. and the room was emptying slowly. Janay usually closed the place down, and Cassie normally went home before her, but tonight she wanted to keep dancing.

The DJ played a slower song with a heavy beat as Janay appeared and slow danced with her. A group of women cleared out behind Janay, and Cassie's eyes fell on the woman beyond them. She took in the skintight leather vest with nothing underneath and the leather pants, the way the woman moved to the music and against the woman in her arms. She was intriguing and sexy as hell, and though Cassie could feel herself staring, something wouldn't let her look away. The woman whispered something into her partner's ear that made her smile, then ran her hand through her own wild hair, revealing her face. Drea. Before Cassie could look away, Drea's eyes lifted and caught Cassie watching.

Cassie let go of Janay, horrified at the thought that Drea had caught her drooling over her. Well, a hot woman who was moving sensuously on the dance floor. Not Drea. If she had known it was Drea, obviously she wouldn't have watched.

Janay didn't even notice something was wrong, a dazed smile lingering on her lips from a few cocktails earlier in the night. She took Cassie's hand and twirled her around, the move pulling laughter from Cassie as she smiled at her ridiculously adorable friend. Her worries calmed as she felt the joy and freedom that she always felt dancing. It was her happy place. Even more so now than when she used to drink. She connected even more deeply to the music without alcohol as a numbing agent.

When the music stilled, she risked a glance in Drea's direction, but she was gone. She scanned the room and saw Drea leaving with the woman from the dance floor.

The tinge of disappointment in the pit of Cassie's stomach surprised and alarmed her. This ridiculous jealousy over watching Drea leave with some hottie would be unbearable if they were dating. Thank god they never would be. She knew Drea's reputation. Tonight was par for the course where Drea was concerned. And Cassie was definitely not that kind of girl.

Chapter 3

It was odd how something so tiny managed to irk Cassie, but the sound of Drea's typing across the otherwise silent room somehow seemed as jarring as a jackhammer.

Click. Click. Click.

Cassie took a deep breath, trying to steady herself. It wasn't like this was her private office, but she had grown accustomed to having the space to herself after everyone had gone home each day. The lazy evening sun cast an almost romantic haze across the desks, and she usually used the quiet to decompress while preparing everything for the next day.

Click. Click.

She glanced at the clock on her computer screen. Five thirty. She silently willed Drea to finish whatever the hell she was working on and quit encroaching on her space.

Cassie mentally shook herself. It wasn't her space. Drea had every right to be there. In fact, Cassie was somewhat happy to see that Drea had committed wholeheartedly to training Erin, which was probably why she was staying late. And as much as Cassie would like to pretend that anyone's presence in the office would have bothered her equally, it would be a lie. She didn't like to admit it, but Drea had an effect on her. One that made her second-guess herself. And that scared her. It had been several days since she had seen Drea at the club, and Drea had seeped into her thoughts more than she wanted to admit to anyone, but especially herself.

The wheels of Drea's chair rolling across the hardwood floor snapped Cassie back to the moment. She tried to focus on the summary she was writing from the client meeting earlier that day rather than what Drea was doing by the printer, but after a few minutes of listening to every beep possible emanating from the machine and pretending not to watch Drea open every door in an effort to remove whatever jam was halting progress, Cassie finally gave in.

She walked over to Drea, who was squinting at the LCD screen full of error messages. How could someone look so sexy in a white T-shirt and jeans? Drea pushed a button, followed by a beep, then pushed another, followed promptly by another beep.

"Can I help?"

Drea looked up, seeming shocked that Cassie stood next to her before her face returned to frustration. "Sometimes I hate this fucking machine."

Cassie smiled. "I absolutely agree with that statement. Can I take a look?"

Drea stepped back and gestured at the machine. "Be my guest."

As she scrolled through the error messages, she could feel Drea's eyes on her. Not in a creepy way. Drea had a presence about her. You knew when she was there. And when she wasn't. Drea's crisp, intoxicating perfume hung in the air between them. Cassie wasn't sure what it was, maybe a white musk or something like that. It was as cool and sure as Drea, and Cassie hated to admit that the smell alone had started giving her butterflies.

Cassie's mind kept drifting back to the image of Drea in a leather vest, so she bent down and opened a series of doors, lifted handles, and removed three different sheets of paper. She lost herself in the workings of a machine she knew well, distracting herself, before returning everything to its normal position in an intricate order of operations that would annoy most people but made sense to her.

The machine took a moment before a new, more positive beep sounded and the printer resumed its task.

Cassie turned to Drea and smiled. "All good."

"So you moonlight as a miracle worker?" The warmth in Drea's voice was eclipsed only by the smile playing on her lips.

The change in Drea was so surprising that Cassie lost herself for a moment. Those blue eyes with that smile, damn. Cassie felt herself rooted to the spot, unable to do anything but respond with a slight chuckle. Then she felt the heat up her neck and knew she was blushing. *Oh, come on. Drea shows a little acknowledgment that you're awesome and this is how you react? You're better than this.* She pretended to cough and flicked her head to the side to get the bangs out of her eyes, anything to get out of this trance. When she met Drea's eyes again, the moment seemed to have passed.

Drea raised an eyebrow. "It must just hate me."

Cassie laughed, feeling more like herself, and patted the machine. "We've worked through our issues and have reached a place of mutual respect." She put her hand to her mouth as if sharing a secret and leaned closer, pretending to whisper. "It wasn't always like that."

Something passed through Drea's eyes. And as much as Cassie wanted to know what it was, it was gone almost as quickly, replaced by Drea's typical wall where she was concerned.

"Thanks for your help." Drea took the crumpled pieces of paper from Cassie and the finished pages from the paper tray.

Cassie caught a glimpse of *The Well* on the top page in Drea's hand. "Can I see?"

Drea nodded and handed her the pages.

The first one had a cocktail on a wooden table with a farm in the background. The second page was a bit less put-together but had similar elements. Cassie glanced at Drea. "Erin's?"

Drea nodded.

She flipped to the final page in her hands and paused. The watercolor effect was different from the company's typical design aesthetic, but the artistry and color were breathtaking.

"You made this?" Cassie asked.

Apparently Drea noticed the shock in her voice because a blush formed on her olive skin. "I did."

Cassie wasn't sure which surprised her more, the bold and artistic move from Drea or that she seemed almost shy about it.

"I knew you were good, but this is, like, gallery level."

Drea's eyebrows raised briefly at the compliment before she shook her head, brushing it off. "You think they'd go for it?"

Cassie felt like she had entered a parallel universe for a moment, finally breaking through Drea's wall. There was a vulnerability there and a seriousness that she had never experienced with her. "There's only one way to find out, but I definitely think you should pitch it to them."

Drea nodded again, seeming to ponder the words, before shrugging and taking the designs from Cassie. "Well, have a good night."

"Good night." Cassie watched as Drea walked back to her desk, put on her leather jacket, and slung her messenger bag over her head. She couldn't help but stand there for a moment after Drea was gone wondering if something important had just happened.

Drea was excited to hang out with Jake and eagerly opened the door when Sam stopped by to drop him off so she and Ash could have a rare date night. Though Drea was glad that Sam had found Ash and seemed happy, now that Ash had moved in with Sam and Jake, along with the chaos of Sam opening her company, Drea wasn't sure where she fit. Or if she did. Their usual Friday drinks at Charlie's had all but disappeared. It might not have been an issue if they had just been friends, but Sam and Jake had always felt like family. This was especially true after Sam's partner, Anna, who was a friend and coworker of Drea's, had passed away suddenly from a brain aneurysm right in front of Drea. By the time Sam had made it to the hospital, Anna was already gone.

Drea had stayed by Sam's side through it all. She was the steady force when Sam could barely function, and she cared for Jake until Sam was able to again. She and Jake had been close before Anna passed, but being thrust into a maternal role, or cool aunt role as Drea preferred to think of it, sealed him into her heart forever. She and Sam never talked about what Drea had witnessed the day Anna died, and Sam never knew how much it still haunted her.

"Hey, little guy," Drea said as Jake jumped forward and hugged her around the waist. She tousled his shaggy hair and noticed he wasn't struggling to reach her waist like he used to. How had he grown so much? She hadn't seen Jake in longer than she cared to remember and had been missing their TV nights, but seeing the little growth spurt, small as it was for a six-year-old, tugged at her heart.

"Thanks again for watching him," Sam said, smiling. "It's been so long since we've been here, I was afraid your doorman wouldn't recognize us."

"He remembered us," Jake said. "He even let me press the buzzer!"

"Always." The warmth in Drea's voice was sincere. She adored Jake.

"All right, be good, bud," Sam said as she knelt down and hugged her son.

"Bye, Mom." As soon as Jake was released, he ran inside

to see Pickles.

Just as Sam started to walk away, she turned back to Drea, her face turning stern. "No scary Halloween movies. I mean it."

Drea raised her hands innocently. "Of course."

A look of doubt passed through Sam's eyes, probably knowing her best friend excelled at saying what people wanted to hear but usually doing quite the opposite.

"All right, well, I'll see you in a couple of hours."

"Have fun." Drea hoped that Sam would enjoy herself tonight. She was working so hard with the new company, but Drea knew Sam needed to refresh soon or she was going to burn herself out.

Drea found Jake kneeling on one of the tall chairs around the kitchen island, petting Pickles' belly as the cat sprawled across the marble countertop, purring contentedly. Like many cats, Pickles wasn't fond of small children, but he had always been different with Jake. Jake was mature for his age, for sure, and lacked the frantic movements of many kids. An image of a demon child chasing a frightened cat passed through Drea's mind. No, Jake was chill and calm with Pickles. And Pickles, well, he was the master of chill.

"Shall we dine, my lord?"

Jake looked up as Drea grabbed the popcorn bowl from the cabinet, a mischievous smile quickly filling his face. "Aye, my lady."

"Please accompany Lord Pickles to his throne, good sir."

Jake scooped up the hefty cat and carried him to the massive brown leather sofa, where a makeshift throne built from a cat bed, one of Drea's creations, sat on one end.

When Drea finished making the popcorn, she joined the boys on the sofa, placing a goblet of apple juice in front of Jake followed by a goblet of Malbec for her. Jake already had the next *Game of Thrones* episode cued up on the large flat-screen TV.

As engrossed as she usually was with the show, Drea's

thoughts kept drifting to Cassie, especially their interaction at the printer earlier that week. She hadn't been sure why she had opened up a little to Cassie. Maybe it was the disarmingly sexy way she had whispered to her. She knew Cassie wasn't trying to be sexy, which made it all the more so. In the short time she had been around Cassie, Cassie didn't seem to have any idea how incredible her brown eyes were or how her bold lipstick made her skin look like porcelain, the kind you ached to touch. Drea noticed these things. She was nothing if not a fan of women. It was natural she would notice things about Cassie. What she wasn't prepared for was the jolt to her senses that Cassie's proximity incited. Though she had been with many women—okay, many, many women—very few made her feel anything beyond a fun encounter. But why did it have to be Cassie of all people? One of the only people she ever had her guard up against. She still wasn't sure why that was, more a gut feeling than any formal reason. Was it jealousy over Cassie's relationship with Sam? Drea wasn't normally the jealous type, but Sam was family, more so than her actual family, so maybe different rules applied in this situation.

Drea sighed and ruffled her hair, trying to shake the thoughts from her mind.

Jake stirred next to her.

"Bathroom break?" she asked.

"Okay." Jake raised the bowl from his lap. "And more popcorn."

Drea grabbed the bowl and headed for the kitchen. "A boy after my own heart."

A couple of hours later, they were on the third episode of the night, having only stopped mid-second episode to refill their goblets. Drea and Jake huddled together, the popcorn growing stale in the bowl resting between them, as they stared at the screen, entranced.

"That's who I want to be for Halloween."

Drea blinked, returning to the real world for a moment. "Jon Snow?"

Jake nodded. "Yeah!"

"How come?"

"Because he's strong and he has honor." Jake grabbed a piece of popcorn and munched on it. "And he's good-looking." He grinned.

"Sounds good to me." Drea grabbed a handful of popcorn.

"Do you think my mom would say yes?"

The slight hesitation in Jake's voice tugged at her heartstrings. "Leave it to me. I got you." She'd have to maneuver that one delicately to keep Sam from knowing what they watched together, but she figured she could be vague enough to get the costume idea across without enough detail to concern Sam. Besides, the huge grin on Jake's face was worth it.

They settled back in, and as the screeches of a dragon and eerie music started to play, Drea's hand instinctively moved toward Jake's face, covering his eyes. He spread her fingers to peek between them. Even Pickles' eyes opened from his nap, apparently sensing the lack of oxygen in the room. The dragon leaned toward Jon Snow with a mouth full of teeth that would inspire anyone to see a dentist. Drea felt her eyes widen and held her breath, hoping Jake's favorite character wasn't about to get disemboweled. Just as the dragon growled, the intercom buzzer filled the apartment. Jake and Drea both jumped, sending the bowl of popcorn flying as kernels rained down on the sofa and hardwood floor.

Drea grabbed her chest. "Je-sus Christ!"

She glanced at Jake who was also breathing heavily. "You OK?"

He nodded.

She tousled his hair, and they both looked at the TV screen to see Jon Snow petting the dragon. *Phew.* She quickly turned off the TV and turned back to Jake. "Can you clean up the popcorn while I get the door?"

Jake nodded eagerly and hopped off the sofa, getting to work as Drea headed to the door. She unlocked it, then walked back to Jake. They held each other's gaze as each placed their fist against their chest and mimed locking their lips and dropping the key, the sacred sign of Drake's Lair, what they affectionately called Drea's living room, a mishmash of their names.

Sam opened the front door, catching Drea's eye.

"Hey," Drea exclaimed. "Great timing!"

Drea needed to get out and clear her head a bit, and since she had been on Jake duty Friday, it had been a low-key weekend so far. On Sunday evening, she decided to head to Rosie's.

The crowd at Rosie's was a lot more chill than on Friday nights. A smattering of patrons sat at booths, drinking and chatting, and a few played pool. The lighting was like a typical bar rather than a nightclub. It seemed like a different place.

As much as she tried, Drea couldn't get Cassie out of her mind. She had to admit that Cassie's sincerity about her art had been appreciated. Maybe she had been wrong to put up a wall with Cassie. After all, it wasn't her fault Sam relied on her. It was just hard not being the main person Sam turned to anymore, personally or professionally.

Drea got a beer at the bar and walked up to two women at one of the pool tables. "I'll play the winner next." They looked at her, then at each other and smiled.

"Okay."

She leaned against the wall watching them play. Her eye was drawn to a booth in the corner of the bar where a head of lilac hair caught her attention. Could it be? What were the odds? The woman across the table facing her looked like the same woman Cassie had been dancing with the other night. She was attractive and they seemed to be in a lively conversation. Drea absently wondered if they were a couple.

"Sucker!" One of the women at the pool table had clearly won and was rubbing her friend's nose in it. Drea sipped her beer and sauntered over to them.

"You ready to play?" There was a slight flirtation in her voice and the woman gulped.

"Kick her ass," the friend said, but it was directed at Drea, not her friend.

"Hey," the friend frowned and turned around, "you're supposed to root for me."

"Not with that cheap shot you just pulled." She caught Drea's gaze. "Make her pay."

Drea chuckled. "Alrighty."

About halfway through their game, Drea was winning easily, and the friend of her opponent was enjoying every second of the beating. She lined up her next shot, but just as she was about to shoot, she saw Cassie approaching. She whiffed the ball, sending it ninety degrees from where she intended, knocking one of her opponent's balls in the side pocket.

"Ohhh, she felt sorry for you, cuz you're losing so badly," the friend chided.

The other woman flipped her off, but she was laughing. "Shut up. I am not."

Drea's attention was on Cassie, though, who had stopped when she saw Drea and was surveying the table.

"Hi," Cassie said cheerily. "Which are you?" She nodded at the pool table.

"Stripes." Drea held on to her pool stick and sipped her beer as she watched Cassie make a face of approval. "Do you play?"

"A little here and there." The twinkle in Cassie's eye made Drea suspect that statement.

"You wanna play next?" Drea asked.

Cassie glanced back at the booth where her companion was

sitting. "I probably shouldn't."

"Scared?" Drea couldn't help flirting sometimes. It was practically involuntary.

Cassie's eyes locked on Drea's. "Not at all."

The confidence in her words sent tingles through Drea. "Prove it."

"Careful what you ask for." Neither of them broke eye contact, and Drea enjoyed the challenge.

"Um, your turn," Drea's opponent interrupted.

Drea looked over to see her opponent and the friend were waiting on her.

"I'm going to get another round for my friend and then I'll be back . . . to win." Cassie's bright purple smirk both irked and intrigued Drea, and she couldn't help but smile.

"Yeah, we'll see about that."

A short time later, Cassie had definitely backed up her bravado. Drea considered herself pretty decent at pool, but Cassie was proving herself to be a contender. It would take more than a close game to rattle Drea, though. The two women from the previous game had settled in to watch, and Cassie's companion was leaning against the wall taking in the scene as well. Drea was used to women hanging around, but only one woman was holding her attention. She couldn't take her eyes off Cassie, and Cassie seemed to be feeling the same way.

Cassie perched herself atop the edge of the pool table, threading the pool stick behind her back, as she took aim. Drea had to give her points for flair. As Drea took in the view, she started to realize Cassie might be much more of a force than she had anticipated. There was something unassuming about her, which made it all the more surprising to see her take command. There was also something incredibly attractive about her that held Drea's attention. The lilac hair for one, shaved on one side but with a wave to it on the longer side that covered her right eye. The bold lipstick, always varying in some shade of purple, that contrasted sharply with her fair skin in a way that captivated Drea. Her features somehow managed to be full of bold, sharp angles, and soft at the same time. Drea sipped her beer and let her eyes wander. Black boots; skintight, torn black jeans; and a gray oversized sweater falling off one shoulder revealing a black tank top underneath.

The clack of pool balls slamming into each other pulled Drea's gaze up to Cassie's eyes, which were watching her. Perfectly arched eyebrows and hoops and studs traversing Cassie's earlobe created a severity in her expression as she held Drea's attention. As one eyebrow raised, a twinkle passed through those brown eyes, daring Drea. Drea never broke eye contact as she walked over to Cassie with a slight grin. Cassie never budged. As their faces came within a few inches, Drea took a moment to appreciate those eyes up close. As much as she flirted with women, the effect of Cassie's eye contact was something new. She felt it deep in her chest, but she didn't back away, not wanting to let Cassie know what she was feeling. She placed her finger on Cassie's knee, still resting atop the edge of the pool table. "Do you mind giving me a little space?"

Cassie's eyes lingered on Drea's finger, then she shrugged. "Sure. I'd hate to make you nervous." She hopped off the table and grabbed her water, taking the metal straw in those lips that had Drea's mind doing somersaults.

Drea chuckled and shook her head. She bent down and lined up her shot, then sunk a ball in the near pocket before glancing back at Cassie with a self-assured grin. "Not at all."

Drea walked around the back side of the pool table and took aim to get within one shot of Cassie, who stood just beyond where Drea aimed, the weight of her eyes on Drea. She exhaled slowly, steadying herself. It had been a long time since any woman had thrown her, and she wasn't going to let that change now. She took her shot, the cue ball driving straight into the ball she intended, and watched as it hit just left of the hole. *Fuck.*

She leaned against the wall as Cassie sank her final ball, then hit the eight ball in to end the game.

Cassie's companion clapped and high-fived Cassie as Drea walked over to them with a smile, ready to accept defeat.

"Drea, this is my friend Janay." Cassie nodded at the woman Drea had seen her with earlier.

Drea shook Janay's hand. "Nice to meet you, Janay."

"You as well."

Drea extended her hand to Cassie. "Good game."

Cassie took it with a satisfied grin that faltered for a brief moment before returning to its previous wattage.

"I didn't realize you were a ringer," Drea teased.

Cassie laughed. "We all have our special talents." She punctuated the remark with a wink that made Drea's temperature rise.

Before Drea could give a witty reply, Heather, the woman she had left with the previous Friday, entered Rosie's and waved at her. Drea inwardly groaned, preparing to dissuade any lingering feelings or disillusions Heather might be carrying. She plastered a smile on her face, causing Cassie and Janay to look at who had taken Drea's attention.

Cassie grabbed her jacket off the chair beside her. "We better head out. See you around, Drea." Before Drea could respond, Cassie had linked her arm through Janay's and was dragging her to the door. Drea watched them go, a brief shadow of sadness lingering in her chest before she grabbed her beer and took a sip, shrugged it off, and headed for the bar.

Chapter 4

Cassie got it. That . . . thing that Drea did. That thing that made women—gay, straight, or otherwise—chase after her like lovesick puppies. She got it now.

As much fun as she had pummeling Drea at pool, the flutter she felt when Drea conceded defeat and took her hand had kept her awake most of the night. The way time stopped and everyone disappeared when Drea made her feel like the only woman in the room, not to mention the sexy drawl that—*damn*—had an effect. But after letting herself feel these things, she realized she was only being human. Drea was attractive. She could be attracted to her without acting on it. It wasn't like she was, well, Drea.

She was probably just feeling the void in her personal life. It had been nearly a year since her last relationship. But despite that, she required a lot more than Drea could offer. And Cassie doubted she was even a second thought to Drea. After all, it didn't take long for that woman who came into the bar as they were leaving to steal Drea's attention. So, coworkers it would be. No problem. Maybe now at least, Drea would start being nicer to her.

Suffering a case of the Mondays, Cassie walked into the break area to fill her coffee, needing a surge to make it through the rest of the morning. Drea sat in the cushy, purple chair by the windows, the breeze from the river wafting inside and gently rustling a stray strand of her hair as Tom, the lead wordsmith at the firm, chatted about his weekend. Cassie tried to ignore the flutter in her chest as she watched Drea laugh at something Tom said.

Mentally shaking herself, she walked to the counter to make a cup of coffee, looking down at the barge and tugboat on the river below. Chuckling to herself that such a tiny vessel could be needed to help out a massive barge, she watched, mesmerized, at the waves emanating from the barge's bow and the ripples left long past its wake. Though it looked very different from Boston, Cassie was thankful that when she and her sister left New England, at least they moved somewhere near the water. It always seemed to steady her. The beep from the coffee maker grabbed her attention as she realized she was smiling like an idiot at the river.

She grabbed her cup and added a hefty spoonful of sugar with a splash of 2 percent milk, stirring the luscious chocolate-brown concoction, noticing for the first time the silence around her. Sipping her sugary drink, she turned, meeting Drea's eyes. It took effort not to choke when she saw the sexy grin and curious look in Drea's deep blue eyes. Tom was nowhere to be found.

"Hi," she said cheerily, hoping Drea couldn't sense the effect she had on her. Though she must know. She had that effect on every woman.

Drea's smile spread a little wider, and the glimmer in her eyes sent a lightning bolt through Cassie's body. "Hi."

Cassie sipped her coffee, centering herself. She was not one of the many girls to fall for Drea. Drea was a player, plain and simple. Cassie had substance. She required more than a one-night stand. No. Drea was a coworker, and that was all she would ever be. "You're much happier than I thought you'd be after such a brutal loss last night."

Drea laughed. Damn it, she had a sexy laugh too. Of course she did. Though it was the first time Cassie had heard it directed at her. She found it far less irritating that way.

"Well, after a few hours of licking my wounds, my shattered pride somehow managed to restore itself." Drea's smile didn't falter and Cassie had to admit, it felt good having it directed at her rather than feeling the usual standoffishness of their interactions at work.

Cassie could feel the air growing thick between them. Were they flirting? It had been a while since she had flirted with anyone. Though this was probably the safest venue since Drea seemed to flirt with nearly everyone. "That's good to hear."

"I'm actually not that competitive despite my Italian roots. Sam, on the other hand . . ." Drea nodded toward Sam's desk. "Very competitive."

"That tracks." Cassie took another sip, reveling in the taste again as Drea returned her attention to her tablet.

"Whatcha workin' on?"

Drea turned her tablet so Cassie could see the screen. "Just the final touches on the Daily Bread stuff."

Cassie stepped closer to see the design. Two images filled the screen: the new logo for Daily Bread, a large steaming cup of coffee with a baguette and some pastries in the forefront, and beside it an image of an elegant three-tiered cake. "I didn't know they had cake on the menu," Cassie said.

Drea grinned. "Yeah, Jody's expanding into cakes for events and asked for some menu designs."

"Looks good." Cassie's eyes wandered to flecks of color in a thumbnail image peeking out behind the logo. "And that?"

Something passed through Drea's eyes for a brief moment, her face growing serious as she clicked on the icon to open the image.

A mighty tugboat charged forward on the water, pulling a monstrous barge from dark gray clouds and rough waves toward a spot of sun peeking through light clouds in the distance. Cassie was struck by the emotion flooding the imagery.

"It's beautiful," Cassie said. She watched as Drea stared at the image, her expression so different from the laughing Drea just moments ago.

Drea shrugged as her normal smile returned. "It was just something I made a while ago."

Cassie nodded, not sure what to make of this side of Drea.

"So, do you always hustle on Sundays, or was I merely in the wrong place at the wrong time?" Drea joked. The twinkle had returned to her eyes, along with the playful banter in her voice.

Though Cassie enjoyed this new side of Drea, she couldn't help but feel like a chance to share something important had been missed. She considered digging deeper, wanting to uncover this new layer, but decided it was safer to play along. She arched a brow. "Only one way to find out."

"Drea, ready when you are." They turned to see Erin standing a few feet away.

"I'll be right there," Drea said. She turned to Cassie. "To be continued."

Cassie raised her mug to Drea as she followed Erin back to her desk, both sad and relieved they had been interrupted.

Drea sat on her balcony, letting the warm breeze tickle her toes atop the railing as she inhaled the earthy smell of the river below. She watched the river in the distance, the water ebbing and flowing. The gentle cadence always soothed her, and as she thought of the many important moments in her life, she realized the river had always provided solace to get through them. There were the big moments with Sam, working through life's trials and tribulations on their bench at Riverview Park with the help of a strong daiquiri.

But Sam never knew about the times Drea came out to that bench alone, to work through things she couldn't bring herself to tell Sam. Somehow, being on that bench at their spot made Drea feel the strength of Sam's friendship, which helped her process things on her own.

But as close as they were, there was a part of her she had never shared with her best friend. Sam's friendship had surprised Drea from the moment they first met in middle school. The level of loyalty and admiration Sam expressed for her made her almost believe whatever it was that Sam saw in her. And after a lifetime of being a disappointment to those who were supposed to matter, she needed Sam's belief in her.

Drea would never allow herself to be a disappointment to Sam. She couldn't bear seeing the look of promise in Sam's eyes fade to sadness. So, she became the Drea Sam needed to see. Sure, it was who she was, a part of her at least. But bitter experience had taught her that no one should know everything about her—not even Sam.

She had learned to become that version of herself for others as well. Keeping her struggles and darkness to herself. But sometimes it was a very lonely place. She found ways to cope and move through it. Not healthy ways for sure, but ways nonetheless. And no one knew. Not anyone who mattered at least. She made sure of that. The revolving door of women meant she never truly had to open up to anyone.

The closest she'd come lately was when Cassie saw her painting. Drea had been tempted to share its importance with Cassie, who seemed as if she'd understand. She shook her head. No, she'd found what worked for her. No long-term relationships meant no judgment. She'd had enough of that for a lifetime.

A honking horn from a nearby street shook her out of her thoughts. She lifted the glass of whiskey from her lap and took a sip, letting the liquid burn, then warm its way down her throat. Cassie's face flashed in her mind. This week had her head spinning. Whatever had shifted at the pool table seemed to have shifted for both of them. She liked this new side of Cassie. All week they had teetered on the edge of flirtation, Cassie giving as good as she got. It was light and fun, but with just enough edge to feel like a challenge. And Drea rarely backed down from a challenge. She found herself looking forward to work more than usual, excited for the next duel.

Apparently, Cassie was pretty cool after all. She wasn't like the other women Drea typically interacted with. They always had an angle. And Drea was pretty good at satisfying them. Okay, very good. But Cassie didn't seem interested in Drea like that, at least not as far as she could tell. She didn't seem to notice that she had an effect on Drea either, thankfully. And that had died down over the week as banter became more of their thing rather than a prelude to something else. Maybe they'd end up being friends.

Drea shook her head. How quickly things change. It had only been a few weeks since she wanted nothing to do with Cassie at all. And now. Now she was a little sad tomorrow was Friday because she was going to miss the banter over the weekend.

Even the slightest feeling of wanting someone to be around shook her deep down. People viewed Drea as the funny, good-time girl who took nothing seriously. Drea had purposely crafted that perception so no one ever got close enough to see the darkness she struggled with. She knew she was broken inside, so she created this outward life, leaving the rest for only her to see.

A tugboat passed by on the river, and Drea followed its progress. She had promised herself long ago never to invite someone into the dark part of her life. The banter with Cassie would stay where it was, at a distance.

Drea rolled her shoulders to release the tension and went inside, filling her glass again, before heading to her bedroom. Pickles followed dutifully. She selected an EDM playlist on her phone and sat down in front of a blank canvas. As the bass pumped from the speakers, Drea closed her eyes, letting the beat of the music sync with the beat of her heart until both hammered through her chest. Flashes of color and composition swirled in her mind as the buzz from her drink let creativity crystallize. She opened her eyes, grabbed a paintbrush, and entered the one safe space where she was truly herself.

"Yeah, well, maybe if you spent more time practicing your pool skills rather than your *other* skills at the club, you'd win occasionally," Cassie jabbed. She leaned against the counter in the break area, staring at Drea over the rim of her coffee cup.

Drea knew there were other people in the break area, but she was only interested in watching Cassie. Fire flickered in Cassie's eyes, and Drea geared up for another exciting sparring match.

Someone cleared his throat, and Drea glanced around to see Tom, whose eyes were about to bulge out of his head as he looked from Cassie to Drea standing a few feet apart. "Shots fired. I'm outta here." He grabbed his coffee mug and rushed from the break area.

Drea laughed as he hightailed it away, but in an instant her attention was back on Cassie. "I don't hear many complaints about my *other* skills," Drea said, matching the challenge in Cassie's eyes.

"But, honestly, do you ever stick around long enough to hear them?" Cassie's tone was conspiratorial as she sat down, which took the edge off her words.

"Not if I can help it." She waggled her eyebrows and they both burst into laughter.

"Y'all seem to be having fun." Drea turned to see Sam standing behind her.

"Hey Sam," Cassie and Drea said simultaneously.

"Hey Cassie." Sam smiled at Cassie before meeting Drea's eyes. "Drea, can you chat for a minute?"

"Of course." Drea raised her eyebrows at Cassie as she followed Sam to her desk. "What's up, boss?" Drea said as she took a seat.

A curious expression filled Sam's face. "I wanted to touch base because this week has flown by. And one reason for that is I couldn't help but notice you and Cassie have really been getting along. There's been more laughter in the office this week than in the last couple of months. It's been . . . nice."

Drea nodded. "Yeah, she's pretty funny."

"That's interesting. I haven't had the chance to see that." Sam's voice held a tinge of sadness.

Drea shrugged. "Well, you've always been her boss, right? So, it's probably just that."

"And yet it's never stopped you." Sam smiled at her.

"I respect you, but we were friends first. Since birth basically . . . or at least tween years, same diff."

Sam gave her a knowing look. "Well, I'm glad everyone's getting along. I enjoy things being light. And how are things with Erin?"

Drea sensed there was more to the Cassie subject but welcomed the change in topic. "They're good." She ran a hand through her hair thinking through her time with Erin. "It took a couple of weeks, but she caught on fast and we've worked out a rhythm." Drea felt a sense of pride bubbling up in her chest. She had worked with interns before, but this time felt different. She had been more of a mentor and helped Erin find her strengths, whereas before she had spent most of her time plotting the next prank. "I know you didn't doubt me for a second." Her words dripped with sarcasm.

Sam chuckled. "Not one." They passed a knowing look to each other, because of over two decades of friendship. "Anyway," Sam continued, "the real reason I wanted to chat with you is to see if you'd be up for Charlie's tonight. It's been too long."

Drea held in a sigh of relief. For some reason, she'd been worried Sam was going to tell her to stop flirting with Cassie. She didn't want to unpack why the idea of that request made it hard to breathe. Relieved, Drea practically jumped out of her seat at the change of subject. "Yes!"

"Cheers." Drea clinked her margarita glass against Sam's as they both licked the salt off the rim and took a sip. Charlie's was their place. The gay dive bar had been like a home to Drea and Sam for years. It sported the typical bar accoutrements, pool tables and dart boards, but the clientele was a little more colorful than the typical New Orleans bar, which was saying something. Drea looked around, enjoying the mix of people, a table of guys in varying stages of drag catching her eye. She took in the elaborate brows, huge eyelashes, severe cheekbones, and luxurious curves. Drag queens played with the hyperfeminization of women in a way that had always spoken to Drea. It was an art form she respected.

Drea returned her attention to Sam and took another sip of her drink. They used to come here every Friday to relax, catch up, and commiserate, but since Sam met Ash and launched the company, they barely saw each other monthly outside of work.

Sam closed her eyes. "Damn, I forgot how good these are."

"Me too." Drea took another sip. "I've missed you, bud."

Sam grimaced. "I know, me too. I'm sorry. It's just been so crazy with the launch and Ash and everything. Thanks for not giving up on me."

Drea shook her head. "Never."

"I'm glad you and Cassie seem to be hitting it off. I was a little worried there for a minute."

Drea noticed the strain in Sam's voice and frowned.

Something about Sam's tone put her on guard. "Worried? Why?"

Sam took a moment, seeming to search for the right words. "It just seemed like you weren't clicking, which was weird because you're both awesome people."

Drea shrugged, a little ashamed by her initial walls with Cassie. "I guess it took a minute to figure out the dynamic."

She tensed, waiting for more, but Sam just nodded. If Sam sensed there was more that Drea wasn't sharing, she hid it well. The waitress came to the table with chips and salsa that they hadn't ordered. "It's great to see you both back here." She smiled at Sam, then placed her hand on Drea's and winked as she turned to leave.

Drea watched her go. When she turned back, Sam was shaking her head. "Some things never change."

Drea put her hands up in the air and shrugged, before grabbing a chip.

Sam rolled her eyes, then grabbed the chip from Drea and bit into it.

"Hey, *boss*."

"Uh-uh, I'm not your boss here. We're off the clock." She dipped another chip into the salsa and crunched away.

"How are things with Ash?" It had taken a while for Drea to come around to Ash. It was a bit of a sticky situation given their high school history. But since Sam had found a way to forgive Ash for being part of the bullying crew that had tormented her back then, Drea did too. People grow and change, and for Ash it was growth for the good. And now that Drea had seen how happy Sam and Ash were together, she was supportive of their relationship.

Sam's face lit up. "It's really good. It almost scares me because I keep thinking it can't stay this good, ya know?"

"Why not?" Drea grabbed another chip, but when she saw the expression on Sam's face change, she knew the answer.

Sam shook her head and forced a smile. She took a sip of

her drink, then grabbed her napkin and dabbed at the corner of her eye. "It's stupid, I know."

"Hey." Drea took Sam's hand. "It's going to be okay."

Sam's eyes held worry. "And what if it's not?"

"Then we'll get through it together." She squeezed Sam's hand. "Like we always do."

Sam smiled at her and squeezed back. "Thank you. For the 'we.'" She grabbed her margarita and took a long sip.

Drea waited as a sense of calm came back to Sam.

Sam met Drea's eyes and continued. "Anyway, enough of that. I asked Jake what he wants to be for Halloween, and he said you'd explain it to me."

"Mmhmm." Drea nodded and grabbed her drink to buy some time. How exactly to explain a Jon Snow costume without admitting to binging *Game of Thrones* with a six-year-old? She grabbed a couple of chips and started munching while giving Sam her warmest smile.

Chapter 5

Cassie sighed as she glanced across the office on Monday. Drea, flawless in another T-shirt and jeans combo with those boots that did things to Cassie, lounged across the printer, reaching for another paper jam.

When Drea looked up and caught her staring, she dropped a slow wink and a half-smirk. Cassie rolled her eyes but couldn't stop from laughing as she looked away. Laughing and struggling. The more bothered she was, the happier Drea seemed. Which made her even more bothered. She had never been the type to crush hard on anyone or let her feelings cloud her judgment, at least not where relationships were concerned. Yet she barely knew Drea and couldn't get her out of her mind. Drea was beautiful, yes, but what Cassie felt went way beyond looks. Drea was a force. A sexy, charming, complicated, funny force with a southern drawl that echoed in Cassie's mind late at night when she couldn't fall asleep.

She had enjoyed the new dynamic with Drea over the past week, but the more Drea challenged her and made her laugh, the more the attraction grew. At this point, she was thinking maybe it was easier when Drea barely acknowledged her. She at least understood and was in control of her emotions then. Drea seemed blissfully unaware, probably like she was with every woman who yearned for her. Yearn? Oh god, is that what she was doing?

The cell phone buzzing on Cassie's desk ripped her away from her thoughts. How long had she been staring at her computer anyway? She glanced around quickly to make sure others, especially Drea, hadn't noticed her departure from having a grip. Everyone seemed to be busy with their own stuff, thankfully. When she picked up her phone and saw who the text was from, she smiled as a warmth spread through her.

Hey Cas, can I stay at your place tonight?

Cassie texted her sister Molly back without hesitation. *Of course!*

Thanks.

She took a moment with the information as something in her gut told her things weren't okay. She texted back. *Everything okay?*

Yeah, we can talk later tonight.

Then she knew. Things were not okay. Her heart sank as thoughts of what it could be raced through her mind. She glanced at the time on her phone. Just after four o'clock.

I'll be home just after five.

I'll see you there.

Hey Mol?

Yeah?

I love you.

I love you too, Cas.

Cassie stared at the text for a few moments. The chatter in the office became distant, as if through a cloud, muffling everything. Drea and her intense flirting suddenly disappeared as fear for Molly filled Cassie's chest. Ringing started in her ears and she had to blink back the beginnings of tears as memories flashed of the last crisis she and Molly had endured together many years ago.

At five exactly, Cassie jumped up from her desk, hardly waving goodbye to anyone. She barely registered Drea's confused expression as she ran out of the office and jumped in her car. She negotiated the rush-hour traffic in Mid-City, barely stopping at stop signs and blowing through yellow lights to make it home in record time. Her hands shook slightly as she unlocked the front door to her duplex, knowing that things would forever be different on the other side. They always had been in these situations.

Digit, her cat, wasn't at the door meowing incessantly for his dinner, rubbing against her legs to greet her like usual. She peered inside and saw him on the sofa in Molly's lap.

Cassie walked slowly toward the sofa, pushing past the hesitation in her step. When Molly raised her gaze from Digit, the look on her face sent a chill through Cassie. It was a look she had seen once before.

Molly tried to force a grin, but it didn't form fully on her lips. "Eva and I broke up." She looked down quickly to hide the tears welling in her eyes.

Cassie hugged Molly as she broke into sobs. Tears pricked at Cassie's eyes, mostly for her sister but also for herself, waves of emotion nearly overwhelming her at the shock of Molly's words.

Eva and Molly had been together for nearly twenty years, and Eva was a friend, almost another sister to Cassie. She had always been sure Molly and Eva would be together forever, that they all would. It just didn't compute. But right now Molly needed her.

Cassie held her until Molly eventually calmed a little, Digit staying on her lap the whole time. Cassie sat next to Molly and put her hand on her back. "I'm so sorry, Mol. What do you need? What can I do?"

Molly stared at Digit as she stroked his black-and-white fur for a few moments. "Do you mind if I stay here for a little while …until I figure out the next step?" Molly looked up, her stunned and baffled expression almost too much for Cassie to take.

"Of course. You can always stay here. For as long as you need." They sat in silence for a moment as Digit's purring filled the room. "Can I make you something to eat?"

Molly forced another weak smile and shook her head. "No, I think I'll just take a shower."

"Okay, I'll make up the guest bed for you."

While Molly showered, Cassie put fresh sheets on the bed. She didn't know what to say to her sister. Eva and Molly were solid, or so Cassie had thought. If they couldn't make it work, no one could. Cassie wanted to know what happened, but also knew this wasn't the night to ask those questions.

Her chest ached at the thought of losing Eva. She knew it wasn't anything compared to what Molly was going through, but it felt a little as if she had been broken up with too. This had to be temporary. Just a disagreement or something. Molly and Eva could work it out. You don't give up after nearly two decades together, right?

Cassie heard the water turn off. A few minutes later, Molly came into the room, her long, auburn hair a few shades darker from the shower.

"Are you hungry? I can make some pasta." Cassie tried to inject false cheer into her voice as she tried again to offer something that might soothe her sister. Molly shook her head and sat on the side of the bed. "Thanks, Cas. I think I'm just going to go to bed. It's been a long day."

Cassie nodded. "Okay. Get some rest."

Digit ran in from the living room and jumped up next to Molly, making Cassie chuckle. "Apparently, Digit will be sleeping with you tonight."

"I'm cool with that." Molly gave her a tired smile and

scratched under the cat's chin.

Cassie walked over to Molly and hugged her tight. "Good night, Mol. I love you."

"I love you too, kiddo."

When Cassie woke, it took a moment before the reality of the previous night hit her. It had taken her forever to fall asleep, her thoughts racing about Molly and Eva. She actually appreciated the brief moment of nothingness before her world was shaken by memories of how everything had changed for her sister. And for her.

She took a shower and was surprised to see Molly in the kitchen when she went to make breakfast.

Molly was already dressed and looking beautiful—like a boss—except for the redness around her eyes. Pain gripped Cassie's chest, knowing Molly had probably been up all night crying.

Molly looked up and smiled. "I made breakfast." She handed Cassie a plate of pancakes.

Cassie took the plate and hesitated a moment. She knew Molly must be heartbroken, but Molly was always the one who took care of her. She wasn't quite sure what to do in this situation.

"Mol, do you want to talk about it?"

Molly stopped cleaning the island and took a deep breath. "I'll be okay, Cas."

They held each other's gaze for a moment before Molly turned and rinsed off the cleaning rag. "I've got to get to work." She grabbed her purse and slung it over her arm, but paused when she saw Cassie standing there, still holding her plate.

She frowned, walked over to Cassie, and kissed her cheek. "I'll see you tonight."

And then she was gone.

Cassie glanced around. Her house seemed a lot emptier without Molly in it. She sat down at her small kitchen table, petting Digit as he rubbed against her legs. "Hey, buddy. Were you a good boy to Molly last night?"

Digit purred in response.

Cassie ate a few bites of the pancake, but mostly just pushed her food around. It was hard having an appetite when her sister was in so much pain. As much as she wanted to hope this was a temporary thing between Molly and Eva, something in her gut told her it was bigger. And if Molly and Eva weren't together anymore, it would just be her and Molly now.

Tears pricked the corners of her eyes as distant memories of the last time she lost the family she knew threatened to surface. Panic started to grip her, so she grabbed her wrist and took a few deep breaths. After a few moments, her body began to calm. She took an extra beat to let Digit rub against her leg, the press of his body further stabilizing her. After a final inhale and slow exhale, she washed her plate in the sink and headed to work.

The ease and joy Drea had felt in the office the previous week was gone. She had no idea what had changed, but Cassie was like a different person. Their banter was nonexistent. She had tried joking with Cassie earlier in the week, but it was like watching a comedian bomb on stage as nothing was landing. Cassie would crack the faintest of smiles and return to work. The chill permeated the office and Drea felt helpless to fix it.

The others were starting to notice something was off, too, though not to the same extent as Drea. Cassie was professional, but the challenge in her eyes, the twinkle, all of it was gone. She seemed stressed and not like herself.

If Cassie had been dating someone, Drea would have guessed she'd been dumped. But she didn't think Cassie had been seeing anyone unless she had been wrong about Janay just being Cassie's friend. But what did Drea really know about Cassie anyway?

Drea packed up to go home and stopped by Cassie's desk. "Hey, any chance I'll see you at Rosie's this weekend?"

Cassie raised her eyes from the computer screen, but all Drea saw there was sadness. She shook her head. "Not this weekend, I'm afraid."

"You sure? I could line up some unsuspecting women for you to hustle." *Come on, Cassie, give me something.*

As the corners of Cassie's mouth turned up ever so slightly, Drea could feel the heaviness weighing on her.

Drea longed to see Cassie's real smile again, but didn't know how to make it happen. "Well, have a good weekend," she said, sliding her bag over her shoulder.

"Thanks, Drea. You too." Cassie focused back on her work before Drea had even walked away.

Drea wondered if she'd done something wrong, if she'd somehow hurt Cassie's feelings. Whatever had changed, Drea wished she could see the fire in Cassie's eyes again. She blew out a breath and walked out into the warm October air, hoping the weekend would be enough to bring back the Cassie she knew.

Chapter 6

Cassie entered the large ballroom and scanned the people, all focused on different tasks and moving at a frenzied pace. A cloud of stress hung in the air. Cassie knew how important this event was to Molly. In the week since Molly had moved in, she'd been up late every night stressing over seating charts, table arrangements, and budgets. And as the days went by, Cassie's hope that Molly and Eva's breakup would come to a happy resolution began to dwindle.

She walked up to a woman in her early twenties. "Hi, is Molly here?"

The woman glanced quickly around the room. "Oh, she went to the bathroom, but that was a little while ago." Her brow furrowed with the realization.

"OK, thanks." Cassie headed out to the main hallway and found the women's bathroom. When she opened the door, she glanced at the four stall doors inside. The door closest to the far wall was closed.

She looked to the floor and saw Molly's black high heels as she registered a small sniffle from inside.

"Molly?" she asked gently as she walked across to the sinks.

"Cassie?" Molly's voice was weak. There was a pause as the

toilet paper roll turned and Molly blew her nose. The toilet flushed, and Molly opened the door.

When Cassie saw Molly's red eyes, she felt like she had been punched in the gut. "Mol, what's going on?" She tried to infuse as much kindness into her voice as possible. She had never seen Molly like this and didn't quite know how to handle it.

Molly let out a long sigh. "I don't know if I can do this, Cas."

Cassie stared at her for a moment. "What do you mean?"

Molly opened her mouth to speak just as the bathroom door swung open. The woman who had told Cassie to check the bathroom stood there. She glanced at Cassie, then at Molly, as a look of understanding crossed her features.

"Oh, I'm sorry. Excuse me," she uttered before rushing out of the bathroom.

Molly walked over to the sink and stared at her reflection. "God, I look horrible."

Cassie turned toward her sister, taking in her puffy eyes and red nose. She wet a paper towel and handed it to her to wipe away the mascara starting to run.

"What can't you do, Mol?"

Molly met Cassie's eyes through the reflection in the mirror. She stopped wiping her mascara and lifted her palms in the air. "This. All of this. Planning a wedding for a couple when I can barely breathe." Her voice cracked and she closed her eyes for a moment, gathering herself.

Cassie placed her hand on Molly's shoulder, hoping it would help her feel somewhat supported.

When Molly opened her eyes, Cassie saw the tears ready to fall. "I want to tell them to go. Run. While they still can, before it's too late." Molly shook her head. "How am I supposed to celebrate something I don't believe in anymore?"

Cassie's heart sank in her chest. She had no answer for this. Molly had always been the anchor in times of crisis. She always had words of wisdom. Now she was faltering and Cassie had no idea how to be the one to right the ship. She suddenly felt guilty for all the years Molly must have felt overwhelmed, stressed, and lost, and yet only showed strength and resilience to her. Molly bore that weight when she had just lost everything too. Anger boiled up in Cassie, at her own ignorance for not realizing how much Molly had shielded her from over the years. Now Molly needed her. She could be the strong one for her. She would be.

Cassie wrapped her arms around Molly and hugged her tight. Molly hesitated for a moment, then sank into the hug and sobbed. After a few long moments when Molly's sobs quieted, Cassie whispered, "I've got this. Tell me what you need and I'll take care of the wedding."

Molly pulled away from the hug, a look of concern in her eyes. "Cassie, I can't ask you to do that." She wiped the tears from her cheeks.

"You didn't ask. I offered."

Molly bit her lip, mulling it over.

"Mol, you have always been there for me. Please, let me be here for you."

Molly's lip quivered as tears filled her eyes once more. She exhaled and her shoulders slumped as if an enormous weight had finally been lifted. "Cassie." Her voice cracked with emotion. "Thank you."

"What are you going to make?" Drea asked, pointing the carving tool at Jake.

"Goose!" Jake giggled. Ash's brown terrier mix, Goose, ran into the kitchen at the sound of his name, sniffing Jake's leg and sitting at his feet in case something tasty might fall off the kitchen table.

Sam finished scraping the insides of Jake's pumpkin with a metal spoon. "Okay, pull all the guts out, bud."

Jake's eyes grew wide as he plunged his hands up to his elbows into his pumpkin. He oohed and aahed as he pulled slimy strings of pumpkin innards and seeds out, fanning his fingers like a spooky ghost at Drea before pieces fell onto the newspaper-covered table.

Drea pulled some out of her own pumpkin, draping it from her ears and across her upper lip like a mustache before feigning a British accent. "I do say, you're rather spooky."

"That's a choice," Sam said as she sipped her Malbec.

Jake put some up his nose and pretended to sneeze so it shot out onto the table, which sent him and Drea into a fit of laughter.

Drea caught Sam rolling her eyes, but she couldn't hide her grin.

They set to carving, Sam helping Jake with his design, cutting where he told her, as Drea worked on her own.

"What are you making, Aunt D?" Jake asked.

"It's a surprise," Drea said with a flourish of her hand.

Jake giggled and grabbed some candy corn from the bowl on the table.

"Hit me," Drea said and opened her mouth as Jake lobbed one in the air. She missed the first one, much to Goose's delight, who inhaled it as soon as it hit the floor, but she caught the second one with finesse.

"Drea, can you help with the ears?" Sam's brow furrowed as she gestured at Jake's pumpkin. Drea hopped up and carved a couple of realistic dog ears to make the homage to Goose come alive.

She sat back down and figured now was as good a time as any to share the news she had been sitting on. "Hey, there is something I wanted to tell you both." Sam and Jake both stopped what they were doing and looked at Drea. The expectant looks on their faces made her news even harder to share. "For some reason, my parents moved up their annual gala by a week, so it's on Halloween this year."

"Oh no," Sam said.

"What?" Jake asked.

"Drea has to go to her parents' gala, so she won't be able to go trick-or-treating with us." Sam softened her voice when she spoke to Jake, but it didn't make the news any easier to take.

"No," Jake said in the saddest voice Drea had ever heard. "You always go with us. You can't miss it."

Drea got up and knelt next to Jake, meeting his eyes. "I'm sorry, bud. I would rather be with you one million times more than going to the gala, but I have to go." The frown on Jake's face was hard to take, but the sadness in his eyes made Drea want to cry. Jake and Sam were more family to her than she had ever known, but her parents expected her to be there. And as much as she wanted to say no, they were still technically her family, by name if not much else. She wished she didn't care what they thought, that she could just bail and take their disappointment and anger. "Listen, I will still come by Halloween night and help get you ready in your incredible costume. You're going to look amazing, okay?"

Jake nodded.

"Come here. Give me a hug." Drea hugged him and wished that things didn't always have to change so fast. She tousled his hair, trying to lighten the mood before sitting down.

She looked to Sam, who mouthed *It's okay*. Drea knew Sam understood how touchy the relationship was with her parents.

Drea added some finishing touches to her pumpkin, then said, "Ready to see the surprise?"

Jake perked up a little, unable to hide his never-ending curiosity.

"Here it is!" Drea turned the pumpkin so Sam and Jake could see it.

It took a moment as they both stared; then Jake said, "It's Pickles!"

"And . . ." Drea said.

"A cowboy?" Jake said.

"Howdy Doody?" Sam guessed.

"Who's Howie Doody?" Jake asked.

Drea felt insulted. "No. It's Jake ... as a jack-o'-lantern face with a cowboy hat."

"Oh," Jake and Sam said in unison, still tilting their heads trying to see it.

"Anyway," Drea dragged out the word and grabbed some candy.

"Well, Pickles looks good." Sam smiled.

Drea threw a piece of candy corn at her, making Jake laugh.

"Hey y'all," Ash said as she entered the kitchen. "How's the carving going?"

"Hey babe." Sam got up to greet Ash.

"Not bad, though some people have no imagination," Drea said and nodded toward Sam. Drea pointed to her pumpkin. "Who do you see?"

"Um, Pickles? And ..." Ash grimaced and turned to Sam for a hint, but Sam just shook her head to give up.

Drea placed her closed fist over her heart. "Ouch, y'all. Just ouch."

Jake handed Drea some candy corn to heal her pain.

"Thanks, bud."

Jake bowed his head in solidarity.

"All right, bud, time for your bath," Sam said.

Ash rubbed Sam's shoulder. "I got it."

Jake flashed Drea a mischievous grin as he snuck a few pieces of candy corn before following Ash to the bathroom. Drea returned a conspiratorial wink. She'd never rat him out and he knew it.

"I'm worried about Cassie. She hasn't been herself lately," Sam said as she folded up the newspaper containing all of the pumpkin guts.

Drea's heart skipped a beat at the mention of Cassie, and all her worries came flooding back. She nodded. "Yeah, I've noticed that. I think the whole office has."

"I don't want to pry. I want to be professional, but I also want her to know she's supported, whatever it is, you know?"

Drea sipped her wine, not knowing what to say. She had been grappling with the same questions since Cassie had shifted so dramatically over a week ago.

"She hasn't said anything to you, has she?"

Drea met Sam's eyes. "To me?"

"It just seemed like you two were growing closer."

"No." She shook her head. The thrill she felt at Sam noticing how close she and Cassie were was overshadowed by the sadness that they no longer appeared to be close at all. "No, she hasn't said anything to me." Saying the words out loud sent a pain to her chest that caught her by surprise.

Fall had always been one of Cassie's favorite times of the year. Though she was exhausted from all of the event-planning hours she'd been putting in on top of her usual workload, she had helped Molly enough over the years to have some idea of what to do and it was getting easier the more she got the hang of it. Every fall, she and Molly went on a hayride to get a pumpkin and despite this year being tougher than usual, Molly had agreed to come along.

It was a tradition their mom had started when they were too young to even remember it. After they lost their parents, Cassie and Molly had made a point to always be together and continue the tradition. In some small way, it helped them both feel connected to the original version of their family, the family they had before everything changed.

The first year they had gone on the hayride was only six months after their parents passed. It was heart-wrenching. The people sitting beside them atop the prickly hay bales had tried to inch away from them and focus only on the passing pumpkins as if there weren't two girls in their midst with tears streaming down their faces.

A piece of hay stabbed Cassie's leg as the wagon lurched forward, ripping her from her memories. She readjusted and turned to look at her sister. Though they had shared many joyful hayrides since that one so long ago, the new pain was written across Molly's features as she stared, unseeing, at the green fields dotted with orange pumpkins. The sadness drove a jolt of pain deep into Cassie's chest. It hurt beyond description to see her sister so down. She'd tried unsuccessfully to get Molly to open up about what had happened, to try to convince her to give it another chance. But Molly shut her down each time, refusing to even utter Eva's name aloud.

Cassie knew breakups were painful and required time to progress through the stages of sadness, denial, hurt, anger, and grief before someone could come out on the other side, hopefully changed for the better. In time.

But Cassie knew that Eva was more than just a partner to Molly. Eva had been the rock Molly needed when they lost their parents. Cassie was eleven when their parents were killed in a car accident. Molly was ten years older, and even though she had always been mature for her age, taking on full custody of her younger sister was a lot. Molly became a mixture of big sister and parental unit in one night. It was dizzying, dealing with the loss and grief over their parents, which was complex enough in itself, and somehow trying to create a new version of their family. Eva had stayed by Molly's side, buoying her on the tough days, and they all did their best to find a way forward.

Eva was inextricably linked to the greatest loss Cassie and Molly had ever experienced, and Cassie's biggest fear, as she looked at the emptiness in her sister's expression, was that a piece of Molly might be lost forever. That little spark that had been so bright when her big sister was just a kid dimmed slightly when she took over the role of parent and guardian of Cassie, but was kept alive by the love Eva wrapped her in.

No, this was all wrong. It had to be a misunderstanding. If anyone could work through this, Molly and Eva could. Cassie would not let things go down like this. She needed answers and she was going to get them.

Cassie wasn't sure how this was going to go, but she couldn't just keep watching Molly suffer and not do anything about it. She needed answers, an explanation, something, for how Eva could treat Molly like this.

She scanned the cars outside the pastel-blue creole cottage Molly and Eva had called home. She didn't see any nearby vehicles to indicate Eva was in a photo session. Molly and Eva had turned the back room of the house into a studio where Eva could photograph clients to save money on rental space.

Cassie rang the doorbell, and when the door swung open, the look on Eva's face disintegrated into one of weariness with the realization that this moment was finally here. Her posture slumped as if the weight of the impending conversation was already a little too much to bear.

Eva tried to force a small smile. "Hey, Cas. Come in," she said with a wave of her hand.

Cassie entered cautiously, the sadness emanating from Eva momentarily striking Cassie with great empathy. Gone was her confident quest to find the truth and maybe even put Eva in her place.

Cassie scanned the front room, the main living space, taking in the blank spaces where Molly's stuff had been. Anger rose in her chest at how quickly and easily Eva seemed to erase nearly twenty years of a life together with Molly. She was about to turn to Eva and give her a piece of her mind when something caught her eye from the white shelf of the built-in. She walked toward it and picked up the black frame with two photos crammed side by side into a space big enough for one. The image on the left showed a young Eva and Molly; they must have been around twenty—before Molly and Cassie had lost their parents. They were sitting on the hood of Molly's VW bug, clad in grunge flannels and beanies, with their arms draped over each other's shoulders and heads resting against one another, full of smiles and clearly in love.

The image on the right was from Molly's first wedding reception client, the same year Eva had decided to pursue her photography passion as a career. Eva stood with her camera draped over her shoulder, smiling at the camera with her arm wrapped around Molly, who was placing a kiss on the side of her head. Cassie remembered the love and support they had demonstrated that year, helping each other to fully realize their true selves and lives' missions, and how incredible it had been to watch.

It all came through in that one photo. The love, commitment, understanding, loyalty—it was all there in their eyes. Grief gripped Cassie's chest. Tears threatened and her lip quivered as she turned to face Eva, who stood several feet away, watching her, the glisten of unshed tears in her eyes. The love was clearly still there. What Cassie couldn't understand was why they were apart. She raised a hand toward Eva, a plea. "I don't understand."

Eva gave a soft, sad smile. "Want some tea?"

Cassie's eyes returned to the frame in her hands before muttering, "Sure."

Eva joined Cassie on the sofa and handed her a white porcelain teacup with a strand of faint pink roses painted along the rim. The heat of the tea warmed Cassie's hands, either still cold from the slight chill outside or the emptiness permeating her body at the thought that this relationship could be over. The bohemian mix of warmth and texture in the furniture and design elements in the room mixed nicely with Eva's black-and-white photographs of their favorite New Orleans places hanging on the walls. These were all things Cassie had come to recognize as Molly and Eva's things, right down to the teacup. It had been her mother's, and the sight of it created a hard knot of emotion in her throat. It all combined into an eerie sense of familiarity and finality that something significant had changed. Molly was still there, they all were, but more the ghosts of their former selves.

The conversation she had planned to have, even the answers, seemed futile. She could feel the shift. But the years they had all shared, everything they'd been through together, pushed her forward, needing some explanation or understanding of what had led to this.

While she had thought a little bit about what she'd say, words failed her now, not coming close to encapsulating her feelings in the face of such a huge loss. All she could utter was the truth. "I don't get it. What happened?"

Eva let out a small chuckle. "I've asked myself that same question so many times over the past few years."

Few years? Cassie felt her face scrunch up as she tried to compute those two words. She didn't think the breakup had been a rash decision, though she still didn't know for sure, so maybe it was, but she definitely wasn't expecting that timeframe. Eva and Molly had seemed so happy. She tried to rack her brain over the times they'd all been together over just the past year, searching for any indication that either had been unhappy. There was nothing. How had she missed it? The two people she knew almost as well as herself. The realization hit hard in her chest.

"I don't think anything I say will satisfy what you're needing to hear. It certainly doesn't satisfy me. We just changed."

Cassie stared at Eva, probably not disguising that it was the stupidest reason she'd ever heard.

"I mean, we've been together forever and we've changed a lot in that time. But we'd always grown together. And this . . . well, this time we grew apart. And it wasn't something either of us could control or fix." She gave Cassie a pointed look. "Trust me, Cas, we tried. We just . . . we want different things now. And the more we tried to ignore that, the louder it got."

Cassie shook her head. "What different things? You've always supported each other."

"It's not about supporting each other. I can't ask Molly to devote her life to something she doesn't even want. And she can't ask me to stop wanting something that's important to me."

"What do you want?"

"I want a family."

"We're your family."

"I know. I'm sorry." Eva blew out a breath. "I meant I want to have kids."

Cassie sat back, the blow and confusion physically moving her. She had never once heard Eva talk about having kids, though Molly and Eva were both in that period of their lives when they needed to make those kinds of decisions.

She sat with the new information for a long moment, her brain working hard to find a way around it, to still keep them together. And she couldn't.

Cassie knew how Molly felt about having kids. They had talked about it not long after they lost their parents and again maybe around ten years ago when Molly would have been twenty-nine, Cassie's age now. Maybe she had been feeling the pressure of needing to make that decision for herself. Neither of them had that urge or desire. Having had an abusive alcoholic father didn't leave them with too many fond memories of childhood, and they both had fears about passing on some pieces of that. That maybe some parts of that were in them too. As loving and warm as their mom had been, it didn't assuage those fears.

The sadness of the moment filled Cassie, knowing it really was over for Molly and Eva. Tears pricked at the corners of her eyes as an even deeper sorrow gripped her. She looked up at Eva. "But what about us?"

Eva nodded as her face crumpled and tears ran down her cheeks. She leaned forward and wrapped her arms around Cassie. The strength of the embrace comforted Cassie, but it wasn't enough to overpower the feeling that maybe it would be the last time. It was a goodbye hug.

Eva eventually let go. "I love you, Cas. And I'll always be here for you, wherever we are."

Cassie nodded, tears still wet on her own cheeks. "I love you too." Though the words were true, an emptiness filled her chest, knowing this chapter was over. There would never be a Molly and Eva again. They would never all be together again. Nearly twenty years of a sister and friend were coming to an end and it hurt more than any breakup Cassie had ever experienced.

Chapter 7

Drea watched Cassie during the Monday morning meeting, still worried about whatever was bothering her. She had hoped it was just something temporary, but after a couple of weeks it was only getting worse. Everyone else noticed it too but was trying to respect personal boundaries and not pry. Drea, on the other hand, was ready to pry. She battled a need to know that threatened to consume her.

Cassie still kept up with everything at work; she was Cassie after all. But the energy and cheer that usually radiated from her was gone. Even Drea's jokes elicited only a weak smile.

Sam said the best course of action was to soldier on, give space to Cassie to come out of it on her own. She treated Cassie the same as ever, only expressing her concern to Drea. Cassie was still showing up and getting her job done, so there wasn't much she could say beyond being concerned.

But Drea wasn't Sam. She had seen this vibrant, joyful woman wither away, and it was too much to watch. She was going to get to the bottom of it. Today.

After the meeting, Drea walked over and sat on the edge of Cassie's desk, demanding her full attention. Cassie sat back in her chair and looked up.

"I wanted to show you the new brewery concept."

Cassie's normally beautiful brown eyes looked tired, and most of the glimmer had vanished. It tugged at something deep in Drea to see such a change up close. She knew she couldn't ignore whatever was causing Cassie to shut down.

Drea went over the design and strategy for the brewery on her tablet. Instead of interjecting with a plethora of ideas and suggestions, which Drea had to admit, she kind of missed because they usually did improve the design, Cassie merely agreed with everything Drea said.

Flustered by Cassie's refusal to respond, Drea finally said, "And I've decided to add a scantily clad woman with fireworks shooting out of her bra to the cocktail party design."

"Sounds great," Cassie muttered, already turning back to her computer.

Drea couldn't take it anymore. Where was the spunky girl from a few weeks ago? It was like talking to a caricature of a human. Drea had to go in for the big guns.

"I'll be at Rosie's tonight, if you feel like getting your ass handed to you in pool." Drea smiled her sly grin that worked on pretty much everyone.

Cassie's lips barely moved as she looked down at her desk. "I can't tonight."

No snarky retort. No challenge in her words. No Cassie. *What the fuck?*

Cassie changed the subject, pointing at the screen. "I think the design is great. Run with it. I need to finish scheduling meetings for next week." She turned back to her computer, effectively cutting Drea off.

Drea stared at Cassie for a moment, anger rising in her chest at the sudden dismissal. Fine, then. She didn't have to do this now. "All right. I'll leave you to it then." She got up and stalked back to her desk. Cassie wasn't going to give in, but Drea was more determined than ever to know what was going on. If Cassie wouldn't talk to her in front of the others, she'd get her alone.

It was nearing the end of the day when Cassie finally went to the bathroom and Drea wasn't busy with Erin needing anything. Drea waited a few moments so it wasn't obvious she was following Cassie.

When she walked into the dark blue bathroom, the moodiness of the color scheme was fitting for whatever seemed to be going on with Cassie. She saw Cassie holding onto the edges of the pedestal sink, motionless. Cassie's pale face and hunched posture tugged at Drea's heart and she wanted nothing more than to do something, anything to help.

Cassie looked into the mirror to see who had entered and quickly turned on the water to wash her hands.

Drea walked up beside her. "What's going on, Cassie? Please talk to me."

She saw Cassie's jaw clench, but Cassie wouldn't look at her. "What do you mean?"

"I mean I don't even recognize you anymore. The energetic and cheery Cassie, the workhorse, the one-woman show seems to have left the building—for weeks now."

"I'm still here." Cassie's voice faltered, and she took a moment before continuing. "I work all of my hours each day." Her tone was flat and she avoided Drea's eyes.

Drea turned off the water and saw Cassie's body slump at the loss of a distraction.

"You might be here physically, but nothing else. What happened? You're like a ghost right now. Everyone sees it, but they are too afraid to say anything."

Cassie looked at her then. There was so much pain in her eyes that Drea almost regretted asking.

"It's my sister." She barely got the words out before her voice broke and she started to cry.

Drea put her hand on Cassie's shoulder, gripping it to steady her. "Breathe."

Cassie gripped her own wrist and took a few breaths.

"Molly and her partner broke up, and she's falling apart. They've been together nearly twenty years. Eva is like another sister to me. And Molly? I've never seen her like this. I'm trying to help with her business, but it's too much and I don't know how to make it better." Cassie's words came quicker as she started to cry again.

Drea kept her voice calm, hoping it would somehow permeate Cassie. "What business?"

Cassie wiped the tears from her cheeks. "She's an event planner, but right now the weddings are killing her. So I'm trying to help. I go there after work, but there's always more that needs to be done and she is getting worse." Cassie shook her head. "I'm barely sleeping after working all day, then doing the wedding planning all night. And then I come home to try to keep Molly sane and I just . . ."

Drea interrupted. "What do you need?"

"What?" Cassie looked up at her with wet eyes.

"What do you need?"

"I need help with the weddings. Molly's trying, but she's not at full force, and there's too much for me to keep up with. I feel like I'm failing her. And I can't fail my sister." Cassie's voice faltered on the last word.

"All right. I can help," Drea said, willing to do almost anything to stop the misery pouring from Cassie. "I'll go with you after work."

Cassie squinted at her words. "You? You want to help me plan weddings?"

Drea crossed her arms and shrugged though the irony wasn't lost on her. It must be some cosmic joke for her of all people to help plan a wedding. "You need help and I want the old Cassie back. There's no one to give me shit anymore. Who am I supposed to beat at pool if you're not around?" She grinned at Cassie.

Cassie stared at her for a moment. "You're serious?"

"Yes." Drea dragged out the word for emphasis. "Not that I agree with the idea of weddings. Those poor saps are delusional."

Cassie frowned and gave a slow nod. "Right."

Drea walked to the door before turning back. "See you at five." She flashed a sly grin and noted the faint glimmer of light creeping back into Cassie's eyes. Relief flooded through Drea. She felt bad for Cassie's sister, but part of her was glad to find out Cassie's sadness hadn't stemmed from anything Drea had done. She'd ponder why that was so important to her another time.

As Cassie packed up her stuff at five, Drea walked by and out the main door of the office. Cassie wasn't sure if Drea had forgotten her offer to help or maybe she had changed her mind, but she felt too defeated to ask for help again. She took a deep breath and headed for the door. When she descended the stairs and pushed through the exterior door into the calm light before sunset, she saw Drea leaning against Cassie's car with her arms crossed. Under different circumstances, seeing a woman as beautiful as Drea leaning against her car would have led to butterflies in her stomach or at least a brief happy dance. But these weren't different circumstances, and Cassie could only acknowledge the fact of the situation. For some reason, Drea was being kind to her during a tough time. Nothing more.

"All right, where are we headed?" Drea asked as Cassie approached her.

Maybe it was the stress of her life or the doubt that Drea would actually follow through with her offer to help, but Cassie hadn't fully acknowledged that Drea would be heading out with her after work. And it definitely hadn't occurred to her that Drea would be riding with her.

Cassie's eyes dropped from Drea's mesmerizing blue eyes to her clunky old sedan. It was mostly champagne in color, despite some chipping paint, and it wasn't much to look at, but it ran well, and that's what mattered most to Cassie. But standing there, feeling Drea's eyes on her, she felt a tinge of embarrassment that she didn't drive something nicer. She didn't know much about Drea's background, but she figured anyone who drove a convertible Mercedes probably wasn't a poster child for financial struggle. She winced. That was judgmental. She had no idea about Drea's upbringing. She shouldn't assume anything.

Cassie realized Drea was still watching her. "Um, hang on one sec." She walked over to the driver's side to unlock the car and quickly grabbed copies of *NOLA Magazine*, a spare brush, and matte purple lip gloss off the passenger seat. She popped the trunk and tossed everything in.

Drea raised a brow. "Doing some extra reading?"

"I like to keep up with local happenings." She nodded down at the magazine. "That's how I learned about The Well, and Beau and Lorna's story."

Drea nodded faintly.

Cassie got into the driver's seat and leaned over to open the passenger door for Drea.

When Drea got in and buckled up, the close proximity made Cassie's heart beat a little faster. She wasn't sure why this felt so much more intimate than being the same distance from Drea in the office. It just did.

She looked at Drea, trying to hide any hint of the effect she was having. "We are headed to the wedding venue. The florist should be on her way, and I have to make the place settings and table runners." She bit her lip. "How crafty are you?"

Drea held her gaze for a moment and Cassie tried to ignore

the heat that crept up her neck, hoping that the shade of her skin wasn't undercutting her air of confidence. If it was possible for Drea's eyes to get any sexier in that moment, they did. Cassie swallowed. Hard.

"I'm pretty good with my hands." The grin Drea unleashed could have inspired a nation to follow her wherever she led them. Half tempted to laugh, Cassie rolled her eyes and started the car. Drea's cockiness was sometimes irritating and always amusing.

A small smile formed on her lips as she gripped the steering wheel. Bantering with Drea felt like a little piece of her had come back. She checked over her shoulder and shifted easily through the gears as they maneuvered toward downtown.

"Stick, huh?" Drea raised a brow at Cassie. "Guess I'm not the only one who's good with my hands."

Cassie shot Drea a look and sped on.

When they arrived at the venue, Drea followed Cassie up a high-rise to a fancy ballroom, complete with a wooden dance floor with fleur de lis inlay and floor-to-ceiling windows. She watched as Cassie conversed with the people buzzing around the room. It was like watching a conductor of an orchestra, each element moving seamlessly to make an intricate whole. The confidence Cassie emanated stirred something in Drea.

A woman carrying flower arrangements walked in and headed over to Cassie. Drea decided to take a look at the view while Cassie was busy, welcoming the moment to shake off whatever the feeling was deep in her belly.

She walked over to the windows overlooking the river. It was similar to her apartment's view, except a lot more expansive. She watched the barges gliding slowly along the water in the distance and took a breath, for the first time all day it seemed.

"Hey."

The sound of Cassie's voice made Drea turn. "Hey yourself." Cassie's eyes looked harried, but she seemed to be doing her best to press on.

"You ready for some place settings?" A small grin appeared on Cassie's lips, and the sight sent a shot of calm through Drea.

"Let's do it."

Cassie picked up a gray napkin. "Okay, each of these need to have the couple's initials painted on them. Since you're the artist among us, that's your job."

Drea nodded. "I think I can handle that. And what will you be doing?"

Cassie grabbed some dried leaves from the table. "The skill for a non-artist. Folding the napkins you paint and adding these fun decorations." She twirled a leaf by its stem.

"Lucky me," Drea said.

They worked silently at the table together for over an hour. When the setting sun cast an orange glow across the white tablecloth, Drea paused and looked up, noting the autumnal feel around the room.

She glanced at Cassie who was still working diligently across the table from her. As if feeling Drea's eyes on her, Cassie raised her head and held Drea's gaze. The orange light ignited flecks of fire in her brown eyes. Time seemed to stop for a moment as Drea felt her heart pounding in her chest, but then Cassie's eyes darted away.

Cassie stood up quickly. "I need some water. Do you need anything?"

Drea shook her head and watched as Cassie rushed out of the ballroom, hoping that her helping wasn't causing more harm than good.

She looked down at the stencils of the happy couple's initials and, for the first time in a very long time, wondered if she might be missing something important in her life.

Chapter 8

"Hey, got the stuff," Drea called as she entered Sam's house and hung her leather jacket by the door.

"We're in the bathroom," Sam called back.

Drea ducked under three ghosts made from tissues and cotton balls that hung near the front door, a craft project with Jake for sure. A two-foot-tall green-faced witch replete with a black dress and pointy hat stared at her from the hallway. She took a moment to appreciate the level of detail, though the eyes seemed to follow her as she moved, ratcheting up the creepy factor. When she reached the bathroom, she found Sam crouched on the tile floor putting costume makeup on Jake's face. She smiled at the attempt. "Aw, are we making a mini Titan here?"

Sam paused and gave Drea a look that revealed the amount of stress she was under. Drea immediately regretted that her sarcasm had hit her best friend on what was apparently an emotional day. She squatted and put her arm around Sam's shoulder, squeezing gently. "Here, let me help."

Drea took in Jake's black shirt underneath a cape made from a blue bedsheet tied around his neck. Black pants and a pair of brown rain boots cinched the look, along with a very light and equally misguided makeup attempt. Drea met Jake's eyes, always the solid little man who would not make his mom feel bad even if his soul was being crushed by the lack of authenticity in his Halloween costume's debut role. They shared a silent agreement.

"Hey Sam, got any nectar for the gods?" She looked up at Sam who was standing beside them, the bags under her eyes more prominent than usual. Sam had been pushing herself since before the company launched, but if she didn't start taking some time off for herself, Drea decided she was going to say something. Nothing was worth burnout. She had seen Sam at her lowest and would do whatever it took to keep her from that again.

"Yeah, be right back," Sam said absentmindedly.

When she had left, Drea grimaced at Jake. "Jesus, bud, what did she do to you?"

Jake looked down at the ill-advised mishmash defacing his body and shrugged his tiny shoulders. "She tried." The boy was a saint. A six-year-old who could see past his own wants to recognize that his mom was hanging on by a thread. *Were there Nobel Peace Prizes for kids? There should be.*

Drea cocked an eyebrow at him and placed her hand on his shoulder. "Don't worry. We can do better. Aunt D's got you."

Jake's dismay quickly gave way to a huge grin.

She started pulling the pieces she had brought out of a huge canvas tote adorned in purple, green, and gold, the Mardi Gras colors that were pretty much the official colors of the city. Then she untied the knot around Jake's neck and tossed the sheet to the floor. "I've got something much better than that."

She grabbed a pair of leather belts out of the tote, helped Jake put an arm through each, and fashioned them to intersect across his torso. She should have gotten here earlier, and her heart broke at the thought that Sam had tried to do it herself because she was afraid Drea wasn't going to show. Had she been that absent lately? She had underestimated how long it would take to find all of the costume elements, but she resolved to do better. The last thing she wanted was to add to Sam's stress. Jake's body vibrated with excitement as the costume started to come together.

"Take those off." Drea pointed to the rain boots.

Jake wriggled each one loose and flung them out the door, a dull thud sounding as they met the wall.

Drea bit back a laugh and handed him a pair of UGGs that she had embellished with faux fur.

Jake's eyes widened as he accepted the gift with reverence. "Whoa."

"And one final piece."

Jake looked up from pulling on his new boots as his mouth dropped open. He and Drea rose in unison as she placed a massive faux fur cape over his shoulders. Jake's eyes grew large as he looked from one shoulder to the other at the intricate detail and rubbed his hand along the soft fur. "Oh my gosh, oh my gosh, oh my gosh." He lunged forward with a squeal and wrapped his arms around Drea's waist.

"Ha, you're welcome, bud. Okay, ready for the final transformation?"

Jake nodded, his eyes still huge with excitement.

She led him over to the toilet and lowered the lid so she could sit down and work on his face paint. Her broad, dark lines quickly erased Sam's faint attempts at facial hair, which resembled that of a prepubescent boy. Jake giggled as she made fast, small lines for texture.

By the time Sam reappeared with two glasses of Malbec and an apple juice for Jake, Jake had been transformed into a very ornate and authentic Jon Snow.

"My . . . that's, uh, that's robust. My son seems to have aged twenty years in only a few minutes." Sam sipped from her wine as she leaned against the doorjamb. Drea could hear the shock in Sam's voice, which at least meant her efforts looked believable.

When Drea finally finished, she sat back to take Jake in, in all of his glory. "Take a look." She pointed at the mirror above the sink.

Jake's mouth dropped open when he saw his reflection, before turning from side to side to check himself out, a huge smile appearing on his lips. Sam's mouth was open as well, though it seemed to be more with concern than joy. Drea grabbed her phone from her back pocket and quickly snapped a photo to remember Sam's horror and Jake's glee, in unison.

"Thanks, Aunt D." Jake beamed and opened his arms to hug her.

She stopped him with one hand on his shoulder. "Watch the makeup, I mean, face paint. You won't look too fierce smeared." She leaned in and hugged him while avoiding disrupting the artistic genius on his face. "And you're welcome, my lord." She gave a flourish of her hand and a slight bow of her head.

"Thank you, my lady," he retorted with great importance, defined even further with a bow of his own.

"You guys here?" Ash called in the distance.

"Hey, babe, we're just finishing up," Sam called. Drea grabbed her wine from the bathroom counter as they headed to the living room. Sam leaned over and whispered into her ear, "I clearly, even in my wildest dreams of what you two watch together, truly underestimated. I definitely need to step up boundaries."

Drea smiled. "You'll have to clear it with Jon Snow first." The wink she gave Sam punctuated the sentence perfectly.

"Oh my gosh, you look incredible," Ash exclaimed when she saw Jake. "Drea, that is seriously impressive."

"Thanks, Ash." Drea smiled as Jake did a circle to show Ash the whole costume.

"There is one thing missing though." Ash reached into a tall brown bag by her feet and pulled out a sword.

Jake jumped and clapped at the same time before grabbing the sword for a full inspection.

Ash looked at Sam, and Drea saw something exchange between them.

"Ash, would you help Jake with the sword and find his candy bag while I talk to Drea?"

"Of course. Come on, Jake." Ash squeezed Sam's shoulder as she passed.

Drea sat on the plush, gray sofa—it always felt like sinking into a hug—and watched Sam as she slid onto the cushion beside her.

Sam finally noticed that she was still holding Jake's apple juice and set it on the coffee table. She sipped her wine, but it didn't seem to ease the stress radiating from her body since Drea arrived. "What time does the gala start?" she asked.

"Seven o'clock. I would much rather be trick-or-treating with y'all instead."

"You gonna be okay?"

Drea took a deep breath and blew it out. "It will be the usual—boring and soul-crushing—but yeah, I'll be fine." She sipped her wine. "Can we talk about you now? What's going on?"

Sam's brow furrowed. "What do you mean?"

"I mean, you seem off and stressed. What is it?"

Sam stared at the blank TV screen for a moment before turning back to Drea. "Do you think I'm a bad boss?"

"What? Of course not. Why would you even think that?"

"The change in Cassie . . . it made me realize how hard everyone has been pushing to make this company succeed. I knew I was working hard, but I don't think I fully understood how hard Cassie has been working until it took a toll on her." Sam rubbed her forehead. "I feel like such an asshole."

Drea put her hand on Sam's knee. As much as she wanted to tell Sam what was going on with Cassie, it wasn't her news to share. "Hey, you're not an asshole. Everyone is working hard because they believe in you and want you to succeed. It's a team."

She took another sip of wine and rested the glass on top of her leg. "Besides, if you fail, we all fail. And I do not want to have to go back to my last job." She made a horrified expression. "It su-u-ucked."

Sam smiled. "Thanks, Drea. I want to do something special for everyone as a thank you for all of their hard work. Will you be around for Thanksgiving?"

Drea raised a palm to the sky. "Where else would I be?"

"Mom, look!" Jake ran into the room holding a white plastic bag that was half as tall as him with a jack-o'-lantern face on it. He skidded to a stop in front of the sofa and held his arms out to show off his full ensemble, sword and all.

"Wow, you look great!" Sam said. "You ready to get some candy?"

"Yeah!" The words were barely out of Jake's mouth before he ran to the front door.

Ash joined them and grabbed Sam's jacket off the hook by the door. She helped Sam put it on before grabbing her own, and Drea smiled to herself at the sweetness of it.

"Hey, bud," Drea said as she put on her jacket, "grab me some chocolate-covered wafers and gumdrops, deal?"

"Deal." They high-fived to seal it, but Jake's face suddenly turned sad. "I'm going to miss you."

Drea bent down and hugged him, trying not to reveal the ache in her chest from his words. "Not as much as I'll miss you."

Sam opened the front door and patted her shoulder. "Hang in there tonight. I'll see you tomorrow." Drea nodded and started to walk to her car as kids clad in their Halloween best filled the sidewalk. "And Drea." She turned back to Sam. "Thank you."

Drea got into her car and watched Ash, Sam, and Jake walk down the street together, holding hands. Streetlamps filled the crisp night sky with a warm glow, but it did nothing to soften the pain in Drea's chest. Jake and Sam had always been family to her, but she'd never felt more like an outsider than right now.

Except, of course, with her own blood family.

She let out a sigh. "Okay. Hell, here I come."

Cassie sat next to Molly on the sofa, ready for a chill Halloween movie night.

"Thank god for peanut butter cups." Molly groaned as she bit into one.

Cassie smiled at her, seeing a little of her sister peeking through the sadness that had taken over Molly the past few weeks. "Just leave a few in case any trick-or-treaters come by."

"Do you get many here?" Molly asked.

Cassie shrugged. "A few usually." She petted Digit, who was curled up between them. "Can you pass me the chocolate malt balls?" Molly reached into the plastic pumpkin bowl and handed her a fun-size package. They settled in and watched the Charlie Brown movie, which was as scary as they got on Halloween. They'd had enough trauma in real life that they didn't seek it in movie form. It had been a long time since she and Molly had spent an actual Halloween together since Molly was usually busy doing events on Halloween night. It was nice being with her sister again.

As the movie credits rolled on the screen, Cassie decided to come clean with Molly. "Hey Mol." Molly turned to her, and the lack of sadness in her eyes made Cassie doubt whether this was the best time to tell her. "I wanted to tell you that I, um . . . I went to see Eva."

Molly sighed. "Cas, why would you do that?"

"Because I hated seeing you so sad, and I didn't understand what happened. I thought if you both just talked, you could figure it out." Cassie could feel herself being defensive, which was not what she was aiming for, but she felt dumb for going behind Molly's back.

Molly moved the bangs out of her eyes, taking a moment with the information. She met Cassie's eyes, and Cassie could see their mom in her face. Everyone always said how much Molly and Cassie looked alike, but Molly had always looked more like their mom, which stung a little. They both had a gentleness in their eyes that Cassie had never embodied. "Do you think we didn't try talking? That we just got bored and gave up?"

"I don't know what I thought, except that you weren't talking to each other, and you weren't talking to me about it. I just wanted to make it better."

"All we've been doing is trying." Molly shook her head. "It shouldn't be this hard."

"Don't you even want to know what she said?" Cassie asked.

Molly sighed but didn't answer, so Cassie forged ahead.

"She said she wants kids," Cassie said, curious to hear Molly's response. It had been a while since they'd discussed their views on the topic. If Eva and Molly were ending over it, Cassie wanted to know how Molly felt.

Molly nodded and looked away for a moment before speaking. "And I don't."

A distant thought quickly built up inside Cassie, forcing her to ask. "It isn't because of me, is it?"

"What? What do you mean?" At least the shock in Molly's voice was comforting, implying that it might not be the reason.

"You basically raised me after Mom and Dad died. Is that why you don't want to have kids? Did that experience ruin it for you? Did I ruin it for you?" Cassie heard her own voice trembling, only realizing in this moment that this had been a deep-rooted fear for her. She hated feeling so vulnerable, unsure if the next words out of Molly's mouth might rip her heart out, the way only a sibling's could.

"Hey." Molly wrapped her in a hug. "Of course not. Me helping to raise you and me having kids don't even exist on the same planet in my mind. You didn't ruin anything. I love you and the family we've built. It will be smaller now, just you and me, but you're all I've ever needed, Cas." She squeezed Cassie tighter for a moment to emphasize the words. "And you know why I don't want to have kids. The thought of ever passing on even a piece of what we went through. I would die before I would do that to another person."

Cassie tried hard not to entertain memories of their childhood, focusing instead on the situation with Eva. "I wanted to believe it was just a rough patch with Eva. That you two could fix it. If anyone can, you and Eva can." Cassie could hear the childish pleading in her voice and felt embarrassed by it. "But when she mentioned kids, I realized how naïve I was being."

Molly gave her a sad smile. "I know how much Eva means to you. We will always love each other, but sometimes love just isn't enough."

Hearing Molly, the romantic one, the committed one, the epitome of a solid relationship for so many years, say that was crushing. The final realization that Molly and Eva were really done brought a lump to Cassie's throat, and she swallowed it down hard.

"Cas, I know it hurts. But I need you to trust me. This is what is right for me, for all of us—to move on."

As much as she wanted to be strong for Molly, and herself, she wasn't sure how exactly to close the door on the family she had known since she was eleven. She had thought Eva and Molly would be together forever. That Eva would be her sister forever. And now—she blinked back the tears welling in her eyes, not wanting to make it harder for Molly. Now, they would have to start over, again.

It took Drea ten minutes to find a parking spot, and she fought an internal battle in every one of them not to turn around and go home. Her parents' annual gala was supposedly for charity, but it had always seemed to her like more of a power play. To anyone else, the two-story mansion in Uptown lit to the brim against the dark night sky with the perfectly manicured lawn and palm trees framing the grand entryway probably seemed like a dream house. But to Drea, it had always been sterile and cold. More for show than for living in.

Normally it was a black-tie event, but because it was being held on Halloween for the first time, her parents had decided on the theme of a masquerade ball. She had quite a collection of masks, having lived in New Orleans most of her life, and she was more than happy to be masked all night and hopefully never have to interact with anyone, her parents in particular.

She followed a couple up the walkway, the sounds of classical music escaping into the night as the front door opened.

The butler held the door for the couple, then bowed his head at Drea with recognition. "Madam."

"Good evening, George."

She scanned the people inside, not seeing anyone she would have to greet, and made a beeline to the most important spot in the main room. The bartender met her eyes after handing two glasses of champagne to the women next to her. "Whiskey," she said. He nodded.

When he handed her the glass, Drea turned and took in the room. A string quartet's tunes filled the room as a number of people danced on the ballroom floor and others chatted along the border. She sipped her drink, wishing it would transport her out of here, having wasted enough of her life being the dutiful daughter at boring events like this.

"Drea, dear." She turned at the sound of her mother's voice, dropping the mask from her face and taking in her mother and father, dressed to the nines as usual. Her mother wore a sequined, figure-flattering light blue gown and her father, as always, wore a crisp tux. The only part that had changed over the years was the increasing amount of gray hair and wrinkles. Too bad their harsh judgment hadn't diminished along with their skin elasticity.

She nodded at them both. "Doctor, doctor."

Her mother rolled her eyes at the played-out joke, which brought a flutter of joy to Drea. She sipped her drink to hide her grin.

"How are you?" her mother asked, leaning in to hug her without managing to actually hug, protecting her makeup. There was no hint of any true emotion beyond annoyance.

"I'm here." She couldn't feign enthusiasm for any more of these events. Showing up was her limit. "And you?"

"Oh, we're fine. Glad you could join us." Her mother glanced down at Drea's black dress and frowned. "Same as last year I see."

"Well, I don't have a lot of black-tie events warranting a dedicated wardrobe." She took a long sip of whiskey at the cold expression on her mother's face.

"Let's be civil," her father warned.

Drea forced a polite smile that made her want to throw up. "Always."

One of the family's longtime friends waved at Drea's parents, and they started in that direction before her mother turned. "Please behave, Drea." The disdain in her voice mixed with the disappointment in her eyes had been Drea's constant companion.

Drea raised her glass to them, then finished it off. She returned her attention to the bartender and held her glass up to signal another. If she had to be here physically, she might as well escape mentally. She had wasted so many years at her parents' bullshit events. For charity. For image. For status. Drea couldn't care less about those last two. And that was the crux of the problem. Though her parents both had noble professions as doctors, they got lost in the grandstanding, always needing to throw the best party, invite the wealthiest guests. Drea never fit in. She cared about authenticity and art, about expression. And her parents rejected everything that was authentic to her. Her career choice, her hobbies, and definitely her lifestyle. She had gotten used to the disappointment she inspired in them, though it had been lonely for more years than she cared to remember, but now, deep down, it felt right. Not fitting in. Not pleasing them. They weren't her people. Family was much deeper than shared biology.

The bartender handed Drea her drink and she took a sip, letting the burn chase away her thoughts. At least alcohol made these events slightly more tolerable. A woman in a merlot sleeveless dress accentuating all the right spots and lipstick to match stood at the end of the bar. She held a mask in front of her eyes and smiled at Drea. Drea took another sip, then turned more fully to the masked woman, holding her gaze for a long moment, before a slow smile spread across her lips. *Even better.*

Drea woke up with a gasp. She glanced around the dark room, realized she was in her bed, and tried to slow her breathing. She turned to see the woman from the gala asleep next to her. Without disturbing her, she slid out of bed and tiptoed down to the kitchen, grabbing a glass and the bottle of whiskey from the cupboard, before heading out onto the balcony.

The chilly, late-night air hung around her and she glanced up at the full moon illuminating the river below. She poured herself a glass and sipped, closing her eyes, waiting for the burn to steady her pulse. Even a night with a beautiful woman hadn't quelled the demons. They never did. Drea tried to steady herself after the nightmare that always seemed to surface when she was overly tired or stressed. Apparently, even a carefree romp with a stranger didn't make up for the stress of a night back with the fam. Drea groaned to herself.

As always, the nightmares revolved around her late friend,

Anna. It had been several years since Sam's partner had died suddenly in front of her. That first year after losing Anna, Drea frequently had nightmares reliving that tragedy. And while the nightmares lessened in frequency over time, the intensity never diminished.

The recurring nightmare was always the same. Anna was normal, happy, full of life, then suddenly dropped to the floor, her life gone in an instant. Drea's role in this scenario always had her trying to change history, to get to Anna before she died, but the nightmare never changed. Anna disappeared before her eyes and there was nothing she could do to save her. Drea never told Sam or anyone about the nightmares. Sam lived her own hell the first few years, and then finally found happiness with Ash. Drea would never do anything to encourage her to relive Anna's death. Though Sam never actually saw what Drea had been unfortunate enough to witness, both Sam and Drea knew Anna hadn't suffered. But reliving that horror over and over was something Drea wouldn't wish on anyone.

As Drea's heart rate slowed, an image of Cassie smiling popped into her mind. She was glad that helping Cassie with the event planning after work was slowly starting to bring back the smiling Cassie she knew. It had only been a few evenings together, but the light seemed to have returned to Cassie's eyes and she was more upbeat at work.

The more time Drea spent with Cassie, the more she wanted to know about her, which was not a common thought for her. She still wasn't sure what to make of that. So, as usual, she avoided it. Drea rubbed her face as if that might make her thoughts disappear. When that didn't work, she turned to something more effective. She swallowed the rest of the whiskey, took a deep breath and one last look at the water dancing under the moonlight, and headed back to her guest.

Chapter 9

Cassie hadn't slept much after her conversation with Molly the previous night. She was trying to help Molly get through this, but everything she did seemed to be wrong. It was times like this she missed her mom the most. She would've known exactly what to do to make Molly feel better. She always did.

Her parents had been gone eighteen years and in many ways it still felt like yesterday.

The smell of bacon caught Cassie's attention and lured her to the kitchen. "It smells good in here," she said, seeing Molly at the stove and Digit on the island keeping her company.

Molly turned with a pan of bacon in her hands, then slid a couple of pieces onto a plate of scrambled eggs. "Hey, I wanted to apologize for last night." She slid the plate and a mug of coffee over to Cassie and put the pan back on the stove.

"You didn't have to do that, but I do appreciate it." Cassie smiled. She usually grabbed a yogurt for breakfast, but the smell of bacon made her realize how hungry she was. "Join me?" She nodded toward the kitchen table.

"Sure." Molly grabbed the other plate and her coffee and followed her to the table.

"Besides, I should be the one apologizing. I shouldn't have

gone to Eva's. I just didn't know what else to do." She took a bite of bacon, the salty goodness reminding her of weekends when her mom used to make a huge breakfast for the family. "God, this is so good."

Molly chuckled. "I'm glad you like it. And you helping with the weddings means everything to me. I couldn't get through this without you." She shook her head as tears welled in her eyes. "I want you to know how grateful I am for everything."

"That's what sisters do," Cassie said, getting up and hugging Molly. Digit interrupted their moment with meows as he rubbed against Molly's leg.

Cassie sat back down to eat while Molly wiped the tears from her eyes. "Digit is a very attentive support cat."

"Oh, I know. He hasn't slept with me once since you got here." Cassie ate a forkful of eggs, tamping down the mild sense of loneliness from Digit's absence at night. But she knew Molly needed him more right now.

Molly frowned. "I'm sorry. I didn't mean to uproot your life."

Cassie waved her off. "Please. I've enjoyed having you here. Though, of course, I wish it were under different circumstances. And Drea's been helping with the wedding details."

A twinkle entered Molly's brown eyes. "Drea?"

Cassie shook her head. "Nope, not like that. She's just my coworker. I don't think she even likes me."

"She must like you enough to help you." There was still a hint of hope in Molly's voice.

Cassie paused for a moment to think. Why *was* Drea so invested in helping her? "I think she pities me or something. Anyway, it doesn't matter."

Thankfully, Molly left the comment alone and sipped her coffee.

Over the past few weeks, Cassie had mostly dealt with the final touches for a couple of already-planned weddings. Besides a few craft sessions, which Drea had helped with, Cassie's main role was coordinating all the moving pieces to make sure the weddings went off without a hitch.

Molly had been focusing on several parties and upcoming holiday events, and Cassie had no idea how Molly had managed to keep track of so many details and clients without any help. Thankfully, they were both good at organizing things. Cassie understood why Molly needed to step away from the weddings while she dealt with her own heartache. Beyond the stress and demands of the clients, the whole wedding experience was romance on steroids. If Cassie had recently ended a relationship she'd spent her whole adult life in, she wouldn't have been able to sit through all those promises of forever either.

This coming weekend's wedding was one Cassie had been working on the past few weeks. She was excited to see it all come together since she had had more of a hand in planning this one than any of the others. The young couple, in their mid-twenties, had met abroad during college and realized they were both from Louisiana. Luckily, the families were kind and supportive, not pushy or demanding like the first two clients Cassie had helped. They also didn't have a lot of money, so Cassie had tried to find ways to make the bride's vision a reality without breaking the bank.

"Everything's okay with the Pearson-Lamay wedding?" Molly asked, as if reading Cassie's mind.

Cassie smiled, thinking about Drea helping her make table settings and painting the couple's initials on the cloth napkins, so in her element. "I think I've got it all under control."

"Shit!" Cassie said as she got off the phone with the florist, her anxiety rising.

Drea looked up from where she was kneeling on the ground painting a sign for the soon-to-be-married couple to go over the barn where the reception would be held. "What is it?"

The view of Drea holding a paintbrush in a form-fitting black Henley nearly jarred the sense of panic from Cassie. Nearly. "The cold snap this week froze the dahlias that were the centerpiece of the flower arrangements."

Drea grimaced. "Do you know any other florists?"

"No." Cassie sighed, trying hard to push the fear of failure from her mind and focus on a solution. "I need to call Molly. I'll be right back."

After Cassie called Molly and they both made several calls to other florists in the area, Molly found one with just enough dahlias for the wedding.

With the crisis behind her, Cassie headed back to Drea, finding her putting the final touches on the sign. "Hey, that looks so good," Cassie said, peering over Drea's shoulder. "Has anyone ever told you you might have a future with this art stuff?"

Drea sat back on her heels, taking in her work, then looked up at Cassie. "Now that you mention it, maybe once or twice." The grin on her face made Cassie forget the wedding. "Did you figure out the flower issue?"

"Yes! Crisis averted. Thankfully, Molly knows a lot of people in this town." Cassie checked her watch. "The guests should start arriving in two hours. Want some help putting that up?"

Drea grabbed the sign and headed for the barn. She was already climbing a ladder by the time Cassie caught up. "Let me know if this looks straight," Drea said over her shoulder.

Cassie waited until Drea had the sign in position. "A little left and down."

Drea shifted the sign slightly. "How 'bout now?"

Cassie tilted her head from side to side. "I think that's it."

Drea glanced down at her. "Can you hold it and I'll screw it in?"

Cassie looked around and grabbed a step ladder nearby. She set it up next to Drea's ladder and climbed up to where she could reach the bottom of the sign.

Drea grabbed the drill off the top of her ladder and reached up to secure three screws across the top of the sign. Cassie looked up, coming face-to-face with Drea's taut stomach peeking out from under her shirt. She quickly averted her eyes, then snuck another peek ... or two. Apparently Drea was as sexy underneath her clothes as with them on. Though that wasn't really news, merely the first time Cassie had seen it, and the view didn't disappoint. She blinked hard, trying to shake the image from her mind. She was not going to be just another girl drooling over Drea. NOLA was full of them already.

The drill went silent. "Think I got it," Drea said, starting to climb down the ladder.

"Mmhmm." Cassie gave her a thumbs-up without looking and climbed down a couple of steps before hopping to the ground.

Drea stood at one of the tall tables surrounding the dance floor and waited for Cassie. Laura and Nick, the bride and groom, had invited Drea and Cassie to stay for the reception as a thank you for all of the extra tasks they had done to make the wedding and reception come together. So after everything was set up and the guests had started arriving, Drea had gone home to change.

A gathering by the door caught Drea's attention. The crowd of family thinned out a little to reveal Laura and her mom hugging Cassie. Cassie spotted Drea and headed in her direction. The light pink V-neck dress with three-quarter-length sleeves wasn't fancy, but on Cassie it stopped the room. Or more to the point, Drea's heartbeat.

"Hey," Cassie said, beaming.

"Hey." Drea glanced at Cassie's dress again. "You look nice."

Cassie looked down at her dress. "It's all I had. It's a little plain, but oh well."

"No, it's good. You look good." What was happening? When did she start channeling the flirtation skills of a five-year-old?

Cassie's eyes traveled down Drea's body and Drea felt the heat of it. "You look . . . good too."

Drea suppressed a shiver at Cassie's visible appreciation. "Can I get you a drink?" Drea nodded toward the bar.

"Sure, an iced tea." Cassie rested her forearms on the table.

"Long Island?"

Cassie started to reply but saw the smirk on Drea's face and smiled.

As Drea headed back to the table with the drinks, the bluegrass band played a catchy tune and a bunch of people began to dance. She handed the drink to Cassie.

"Thank you." Cassie took a sip, then grabbed a sugar packet from the glass dispenser in the middle of the table, and emptied it into her glass. She took another sip and nodded at the taste.

The process struck Drea as pretty adorable. She sipped her whiskey and tried not to focus on the thought of Cassie as adorable, or hot, or anything else swirling in her mind.

"I never asked you. How was your Halloween?" Cassie asked.

Drea moved her head from side to side, remembering the events of Thursday night. Her mind quickly bypassed the memories of the ball and went instead to the adventure afterward. While she had never been one to sleep and tell, her inner voice warned not to say anything to Cassie, which was new. "It had its moments. How about yours?"

"Oh, it was nice. Just a low-key night at home. Did you go trick-or-treating?" Cassie smiled and Drea wasn't sure if she was being serious.

"Nah, I had a family thing." She took a hefty swig of whiskey and watched the people dancing.

"Are you close with them?"

She felt her jaw clench involuntarily in response to the

question. She wasn't ready to talk about her parents with Cassie. With anyone. She met Cassie's eyes and shook her head.

"What about you?" She realized she didn't know if Cassie had family here other than her sister. "Are you from here?" She watched something sad pass through Cassie's expression, gone almost as quickly as it appeared, and sipped her drink, more curious now.

"I'm from Boston originally." Cassie swept the lilac hair out of her eye.

"Ah, that would explain it." Drea grinned.

"Explain what?"

"Cah. Pahk the cah."

Cassie laughed, almost spitting out a mouthful of iced tea. "I'm not that bad."

Drea laughed. "Yeah, you're not. But," she held her thumb and index finger an inch apart, "a little."

Cassie rolled her eyes. "I've lived here long enough that some of the southern words have slipped in. I've been known to fling a y'all or two."

"Impressive," Drea teased.

"And what about you, Miss Sexy Southern Drawl?"

Drea held Cassie's gaze, noticing her eyes widen for a brief moment as she seemed to realize what she had just said. "You think my drawl is sexy?" She couldn't hide her grin or the pleasure Cassie's comment inspired.

Cassie shook her head and took a big gulp of iced tea, seeming uncomfortable with how the conversation had turned. "You must know that everyone . . . you know . . . everyone . . ." Her words died on her tongue and her shoulders slumped as if she was in an impossible situation.

Drea didn't care about everyone. She cared about Cassie. And she desperately wanted her to finish that sentence, but she could see Cassie felt stuck, so she gave her an out.

"Do you want to check the meteh on the cah?"

Cassie shook her head again, but this time it was accompanied with soft laughter. "Whatever."

The music slowed and the dance floor cleared out as Laura's dad took her hand and they started to dance. Drea suddenly felt annoyed by weddings and all of the expectations they brought. She glanced at Cassie who was watching Laura dance with her dad with an expression Drea couldn't place. She finished her whiskey and leaned toward Cassie. "Sure you don't want something stronger?"

Cassie turned to Drea and her brown eyes seemed lost for a moment before she blinked, noticing Drea. "What?"

"Do you want something stronger?" Drea nodded at her iced tea.

"Oh, no thanks." Cassie focused on the dance floor again.

Drea walked to the bar and, as she waited in line, thought back to the times she'd seen Cassie at Rosie's. She had never seen Cassie drink anything other than water or iced tea before, and felt like a jerk for not realizing sooner. She got Cassie another iced tea and headed back to the table where Laura and Nick were chatting with her.

"Hey, Drea." Laura beamed as Drea handed Cassie the tea. "I was telling Cassie what a wonderful team you two are. All the things you did to get us what we wanted within our budget: the sign and the table decorations." Laura shook her head. "You two are incredible. Thank you for everything." She gave them each a hug and started to head off to talk to the next table but called over her shoulder. "You should dance. Have some fun! You earned it."

Cassie held up the iced tea Drea had placed in front of her. "Thanks for this."

"You're welcome." Drea couldn't help but notice the blush on Cassie's cheeks.

There was a long pause. Drea focused on the music, but couldn't miss the slight tension in the air.

"What do you think about that?" Cassie finally asked.

"What Laura said?" Drea asked.

Cassie nodded.

She wasn't sure which part of Laura's comments Cassie was referring to, but judging by the slight blush still on Cassie's cheeks, she figured it was the initial comment. "I'd agree. We aren't too bad at this wedding stuff."

Cassie nodded and bit her lip.

Drea sipped her whiskey, waiting her out.

"I really appreciate everything you've done. This wasn't your obligation, at all. But you've done more than I could ever ask. So, I just wanted to thank you." Sincerity filled Cassie's eyes.

"Does that mean the weddings are done?" Drea felt confused by the finality in Cassie's words.

Cassie hesitated. "No, there's one more left, but I feel like you've already done so much. It doesn't feel right asking more of you."

"Good thing you didn't ask then." Drea grinned and clinked glasses with Cassie.

They stood in silence, watching the people around them, a hint of expectation still in the air. Damn it, Laura. She probably hadn't meant anything by the dancing comment. She probably saw them as coworkers, which they were, so why should this be awkward. *Fuck it.* Drea turned to Cassie. "Want to?"

Cassie looked confused. "To what?"

Drea held out her hand and grinned. "Dance."

Cassie held her gaze for a moment, seeming to weigh the question thoroughly. Just when Drea thought she was going to say no, she replied. "Sure."

She placed her hand in Drea's, the warmth comforting Drea, and they walked out to the dance floor as the band started an upbeat tune. They stopped and faced each other, then looked around at the other couples dancing hand in hand around them. Not exactly Drea's first choice in music or type of dancing, but she doubted the band would switch to electronica in the next minute.

She held out her right palm for Cassie to take. "Here goes nothing."

Cassie took her hand with a grin. "Indeed."

Drea stepped closer and placed her hand on Cassie's waist and as they gazed into each other's eyes, her breath caught. She had danced with many women before, but even when it was flirtatious and fun, she had never had a physiological reaction to any of them. Ever. She had built some pretty solid walls around her heart, and she had always been able to separate the two. To avoid any further confusing thoughts or feelings, she swung Cassie out and they began to hop, skip, and glide along the dance floor amid the other dancers.

She was surprised how easily they moved together. Sure, she didn't often dance hand in hand with a woman. Grinding was the more typical movement at Rosie's, but even then sometimes things clicked and sometimes they didn't. There was a give and take, a negotiation on the dance floor, and she and Cassie seemed to flow naturally. As the final notes rang out, Cassie spun into Drea and Drea dipped her. Cassie beamed in her arms, and it was one of the most beautiful sights Drea had ever seen. She didn't want the moment to end, wanting Cassie to stay in this flash of joy for as long as possible after all she had been through over the past month. But the music had stopped, so Drea raised Cassie until she was back on her feet and their faces were mere inches apart. The smile slowly faded from Cassie's lips as they held each other's gaze, breathing in each other's ragged breath. Drea had made avoidance an art form, but this time she stood there, letting the sparks hit her. After a long moment, a nervous chuckle escaped Cassie's lips and they both took a step back.

"Water," Cassie's voice croaked. "Let's get some water." She turned on her heel and hightailed it to the table, leaving Drea to follow, confused at how she felt both grateful and sad the moment had ended.

Chapter 10

"Again! From the top." Janay's voice echoed through the gymnasium.

Cassie wiped the sweat from her forehead and clapped to cheer the girls on. "You got this!" she yelled. With all of the wedding planning, it had been weeks since she had seen her best friend and she missed showing up for the girls as well, so she had decided to stop by for the Wednesday practice.

The girls wiped the sweat from their faces and took their positions. The music started to blast from the speakers. Angel, one of the oldest girls on the team, yelled out the count, "Three, two, one." The gym came alive with the stomps and claps of thirty girls. Cassie nodded with the beat. Five lines of six girls formed, and as the front one moved forward, hitting their moves, and knelt, the next took over until the last line hit the floor. Carly and Moira, the best gymnasts on the team, ran to opposite ends of the floor while the rest of the team formed an X, radiating out from the center of the gym. As the stomps led to a crescendo, Carly and Moira each did three flips from either side of the gym, landing in splits in the center of the floor in front of the team.

Cassie jumped up and cheered, awed by how well they had

performed. Janay clapped loudly as she approached the team. "That is it! That's what I want. Bring it in." The girls, Janay, and Cassie gathered around with their hands in a pile and Angel led them in their team chant.

They raised their hands upward in unison. "Together!"

"Get some water. Nice job, ladies." Janay and Cassie slapped hands with the girls as they grabbed water bottles and gym bags and headed home.

"Oh my god, Janay," Cassie said as she and Janay walked to the bleachers to grab their water bottles and sit down. "They look incredible." She hadn't seen the whole routine before and she was impressed. "That was epic."

Janay took a seat and a long gulp of water. "Thank you. They've been working hard. That's the first time they nailed it." She beamed at Cassie. "I'm glad you got to see it."

"Is that what they'll perform at the Thanksgiving Day Parade?"

Janay nodded. "Speaking of Thanksgiving, you and Molly are coming, right? Mama J said she's about to come hunt you down it's been so long."

Cassie laughed. "Of course we're coming." The thought of Janay's mom, who everyone affectionately called Mama J, warmed Cassie, but then her smile faltered. "Eva won't be joining."

Janay nodded again. "I figured as much. How's Molly doing?"

"She's . . ." Cassie thought through the past month, trying to be hopeful. "She's better than she was, but I think it's going to take a while."

Janay drank some water. "And how are you?"

Cassie passed her a weak smile. "I think it's going to take a while."

Janay bumped her shoulder into Cassie's. "Well, y'all always have us. Don't forget that."

Cassie leaned her head on Janay's shoulder, thankful for the steadying force Janay had always been in her life. Janay returned the gesture.

"How's the wedding planning going?"

Cassie lifted her head. "It's actually been pretty cool. Almost makes me believe in love."

Janay arched a brow.

"Almost." Cassie sipped her water. "Drea's been helping me." Cassie's words were hesitant and she waited, curious for Janay's reaction. They both knew Drea's reputation, and Cassie didn't want Janay to read more into it than what was obviously just a friend helping a friend. She had replayed their dance in her mind more than a few times over the past few days, stuck on the sparks she felt in such intimate proximity to Drea. And how dumb she felt for giggling nervously at the end, wondering what might have happened in that moment if she hadn't acted like a kindergartener. But it was futile. They were coworkers and it was Drea. Despite what she might have felt in her body, she couldn't imagine Drea feeling the same. Drea didn't do relationships so, sparks or not, they were friends and that's where it would stay.

"Miss Drea, huh? Well, excuse me."

"I told her she didn't have to help with this last one, but she insisted." Cassie shrugged.

"Interesting." A slow smile spread across Janay's face. "I guess she wouldn't have anything to do with you *almost* believing in love, hmm?"

Cassie scoffed. "Absolutely not." She shook her head and hoped the blush she felt creeping up her neck didn't betray her.

Janay arched another brow, supremely confident. "Mmmhmmm."

The next morning, Cassie sat at the conference table along with Drea and Erin as Sam presented the new logo and cake menu to Jody for her bakery, Daily Bread. There had been a lot of back and forth over the past few weeks between Drea and Jody as Jody kept changing details on the menu design. Today was the unveiling, and Cassie hoped Jody would be happy with the result.

Cassie had communicated with Jody a number of times before Drea took over on the design details. From what she could tell, Jody seemed like an upbeat, positive person. The kind who had endless energy and probably didn't sit still for long. But other than caring a lot that the product came out right, she also seemed kind.

In the years at her previous firm and in the handful of client meetings at her current position, Cassie had developed a knack for sensing what the client was feeling. She had learned it from Sam, who had saved a number of campaigns at their previous firm by understanding the clients and their needs. As she watched Jody now, she noticed a hesitation in her, but she wasn't sure if it was about the presentation or something else.

The new logo was a slam dunk, but when Sam presented the new cake menu, a war of emotions crossed Jody's features. They waited in silence as Jody took in all of the details before Sam finally spoke up. "So, what do you think?"

Jody seemed to awaken at Sam's words. "Sorry, I'm just taking it all in. It looks fantastic." She turned to Drea. "Drea, you really are an incredible artist."

Drea smiled at the compliment.

"But . . ." Sam said the words everyone was thinking.

"Sorry, I think I'm overthinking it. I'm just wondering—if you were customers, would you find it helpful? I'm worried I missed the mark in my requests."

"Well, I am your customer, so I don't have to pretend." Sam smiled. "And absolutely. You have great illustrations of the kinds of cakes you can make, and the different sections make it easy to find cakes for smaller events and birthdays versus the wedding cake section. And your prices are clear." As Sam spoke, Jody's face relaxed. Sam to the rescue yet again. Cassie realized that she had been holding her breath with the tension in the room and took a much-needed deep breath.

Jody's entire demeanor relaxed with the reassurance that the menu hit all the right points. Once Jody decided she was ready to move forward with the design, Sam covered the details for rolling out the logo and menu, then offered to walk Jody out.

Cassie caught up to Drea, who was chatting with Erin about what to get as a celebratory lunch. The campaign presentation was the last official assignment of Erin's rotation with Drea. Next, she'd work with Tom to learn how to write effective ad copy. "Hey, you got a second?" Cassie asked.

Erin excused herself to pick up some po' boys and Drea sat on the edge of her desk. "Sure, what's up?" No matter how much time they spent together, Cassie could not get over those striking blue eyes. They hadn't talked one-on-one since their dance, only a few nods in acknowledgment and polite hellos around the office, which had helped Cassie dismiss any lingering thoughts that the dance had changed anything for Drea. Clearly, it was just another Saturday night for her. And Cassie was trying hard to feel the same.

"Planning for the last wedding is upon us. I'm headed to the venue after work to check it out and meet the couple. Would you like to join me?"

The look that Cassie had coined Drea's sexy listening expression gave way to an even sexier smile. "Ye-e-es."

She hoped Drea didn't notice the heat traveling up her neck or any sign of the butterflies that drawl inspired. Okay, maybe she needed to try a little harder to mirror Drea's indifference about the other night.

"Where is it?" Drea asked.

"In the French Quarter."

Drea nodded. "Okay, I'll follow you since I don't live too far from there."

The tinge of disappointment that Drea wouldn't be riding with her caught Cassie by surprise and she quickly tamped it down, replacing it with the most upbeat tone she could muster. "Sounds good."

Drea parked behind Cassie's sedan outside the two-story creole cottage in the French Quarter. Drea appreciated speed, but Cassie had lit out of the office so fast, she had barely kept up with her. The sun had just set, casting a romantic glow on the people walking through Jackson Square. A horse-drawn carriage sat on the edge of the street as the sounds of jazz music floated through the air along with the sweet smell of beignets from nearby Café Du Monde. Drea could see the appeal of the venue as the most romantic parts of NOLA all seemed to be right here.

She met Cassie on the sidewalk, the light making her look even more beautiful than usual. *Damn it.* She shook the thought from her mind and smiled. "Hey, Mario Andretti. Ready to go in?"

Cassie laughed and the softness of it echoed through the sky. They walked up the cobblestone path to the main door. White lights wrapped around the palm trees and the live oak in the front yard. The lights on the front of the white cottage cast an inviting glow, and Drea could feel the warmth of the place.

A brown-haired woman in her twenties stood in the entryway as Cassie and Drea walked inside. "Cassie?" she asked.

"Yes, are you Nellie?"

"Yes."

Cassie reached out and shook the woman's hand, then turned toward Drea. "This is Drea. We'll both be helping with your wedding."

Nellie smiled. "Wonderful. It's great to meet you both. Let me show you where we'll be."

They followed Nellie outside to a brick courtyard. A fountain stood at one end with a brick wall behind it covered in ivy. Shuttered windows from the second story of the cottage opened up to the courtyard. The neighboring buildings formed the east and west walls. One had windows casting a warm glow onto the courtyard, but the other side was a plain wall.

"Hey, honey. Sorry I'm late." They all turned as a tall, blonde woman walked up to Nellie and leaned down to kiss her.

"We were just getting started." Nellie placed her arm behind her partner's back and gestured to Cassie. "Katherine, this is Cassie."

Katherine leaned forward and shook Cassie's hand. "Nice to meet you."

"And this is Drea," Nellie said.

Katherine's eyebrows rose. "Drea, nice to see you again." The sentiment caught Drea by surprise, but as she shook Katherine's hand, recognition hit her and she smiled.

"You too."

Nellie seemed confused. "You know each other?"

"Oh, Drea and I knew each other years ago." Katherine put her arm around Nellie. "Did you show them the wall?"

"Not yet."

Katherine gestured toward the blank wall. "I'm not sure if anything can be done about this wall, but it seems really stark compared to the warmth of the rest of the courtyard. We wanted to see if you had any ideas." They both looked from Cassie to Drea, hope filling their eyes.

"We could add some palm trees or lights," Cassie suggested.

Katherine and Nellie exchanged an unconvinced glance.

Drea looked around the courtyard and at the wall in question, as mural ideas started to percolate. "I could paint something if you'd like. Have it as a feature on that wall."

Katherine's eyes lit up. "That's right. I forgot what an amazing artist you are."

Drea could feel Cassie's eyes on her. It wasn't uncommon for Drea to run into women she'd slept with, but unless Sam was around, she didn't usually have someone with her making it that much more awkward. Someone whose opinion she cared about. The thought stopped her. Did she care about Cassie's opinion of her?

"Do you have anything in mind?" Nellie asked, ripping Drea from her thoughts.

Drea needed more information to tailor an idea that might be meaningful to the couple. "How did you two meet?" she asked.

Katherine and Nellie turned to each other and smiled. "You tell it," Katherine said.

"OK," Nellie said, affection permeating her voice. "It was on one of those dinner cruises on the river. My family was visiting, so I thought it would be a fun way for them to see part of the city. There was this beautiful woman at the next table," Nellie tilted her head at Katherine and chuckled, "who was on a date."

"A horrible date," Katherine added.

Nellie grimaced. "A horrible first date. My family couldn't help but notice, and we were all feeling bad for Katherine as the night went on. At one point Katherine got up and went outside, so I went to see if she was okay." Nellie shrugged. "And that was it."

Katherine nodded. "That was it." She grinned at Nellie who beamed back at her.

Drea glanced at Cassie who wore a polite smile that didn't seem to reach her eyes, but Drea found the story charming and ideas for the painting rushed through her mind. "If you trust me, I can paint something to honor that night."

Katherine and Nellie searched each other's eyes, then turned to Drea. "Okay," they said in unison, laughing at each other's enthusiasm.

The couple showed Drea and Cassie the ballroom where the reception would be held, going over details about the number of guests, the colors and flowers, food, and table arrangements. Drea marveled at Cassie's professionalism, but worried over the distance in her polite responses. Not noticeable to the couple, but certainly noticeable to Drea.

"There is one other thing," Nellie said hesitantly. "The baker we had hoped to use for the wedding cake called me earlier this week. A kitchen fire destroyed their oven, and they won't be able to get the damage repaired and a new oven in for about a month so we need to find a new baker."

Drea immediately thought of Jody. Working on her cake menu had made her yearn to try Jody's creations. She turned to Cassie, wondering if they were sharing the same thought.

"I think I might know someone who can help," Cassie said. "I'll look into it and let you know."

"Really? Oh, that would be wonderful." The stress on Nellie's face gave way to relief. "We don't need anything fancy. We're paying for the wedding ourselves and this venue is taking most of our budget, so we were just going to do a three-tiered chocolate cake."

Cassie nodded. "Okay, no problem."

"So, the wedding is the Saturday after Thanksgiving?" Drea asked.

"Yes, we figured our family would visit for the holiday and we could kill two birds with one stone." Katherine grimaced at the expression. "So to speak."

Drea nodded. That gave her just over three weeks to paint something that would hopefully make them happy. That would be tight with all of the other things she and Cassie would need to work on together.

"Perfect," Cassie said. "Well, we'll be in touch with details. Thanks for trusting your wedding to us. It's going to be amazing." The smile on Cassie's face seemed more genuine than before.

Drea followed Cassie out to their cars. The night had turned dark except for the glow of the streetlamps by the cars and around the square. She didn't know if Cassie was upset she knew Katherine, but it wasn't like Cassie seemed interested in her anyway. She had barely spoken to her all week after the dance until she touched base about this wedding. The dance had been on Drea's mind, but she figured she'd see how Cassie acted at work to determine if it was an issue or just a fluke . . . a few moments of connection between two people. Not something to be concerned about or spend days thinking about, like she had.

Cassie turned to her when they reached the sidewalk. "So, you already know Katherine?"

Drea shrugged. "I wouldn't say I know her. Our paths crossed once. A while ago."

Cassie nodded, but there seemed to be more hanging in the air between them. Drea prepared to give an explanation, not excited at the prospect of how it might make Cassie view her. But just as quickly the little bit of tension disappeared. "OK, good night," Cassie said.

Before Drea could respond, Cassie got in her car and drove off, leaving Drea wondering what had just happened.

Chapter 11

Cassie parked along the residential street, not far from the office, and she and Molly followed the smell of freshly baked pastries to Daily Bread, situated in an inviting cottage amid a bunch of houses. A few patrons, clad in warm coats to ward off the slight chill in the air and unwilling to sit inside on such a beautiful Sunday afternoon, enjoyed pastries and coffee at the wrought-iron patio tables along the sidewalk. Cassie walked through the open front doors and saw Jody at the front counter.

"Hey, Cassie!" Jody said with her usual warm smile as Cassie approached the counter.

"Hi, Jody," Cassie returned the warm greeting and gestured toward Molly beside her. "This is my sister, Molly."

Jody raised her eyes to Molly and seemed awestruck for a moment.

Molly reached out her hand in the brief silence. "It's great to meet you. Thanks so much for doing this for us."

The handshake seemed to bring Jody back to the moment at hand as the smile returned to her face. "My pleasure. Why don't y'all take a seat at that round table," she said, pointing to a white wooden table in the middle of the bakery. "And I'll be right back with some flavors for you to try."

Cassie had called Jody right after finding out that Katherine and Nellie had lost their baker to see if she could fill in and Jody had graciously accepted. Cassie had relayed the basic chocolate cake request, but when she mentioned it was a budget issue, Jody insisted on giving them the wedding cake of their dreams at a deep discount that would make it affordable. Jody invited the couple to do a tasting the following Sunday, but since they both had to work, they asked Cassie if she could stand in for them. And since Cassie had no idea how to do a cake tasting, she had asked Molly to come with her.

Jody brought out a large silver tray that seemed to overwhelm her small frame, but her lean, muscular arms stayed solid under the weight. The tray held a bunch of white ceramic plates adorned with delicious-looking slices of cake. Cassie had to stop herself from clapping at the sheer joy rising inside her as Jody laid the tray in front of them. She knew Molly's job was stressful and laden with details, but getting to taste wedding cake for a client seemed like a pretty awesome perk.

"We can do pretty much anything the brides want, but I thought I'd let you try a few classic options along with NOLA-inspired flavors and a few signature flavors I've been working on." Jody pointed at the different plates as she continued. "The classic options are chocolate with a vanilla buttercream and chocolate ganache, vanilla with vanilla buttercream filling and frosting, and lemon chiffon with a lemon zest buttercream frosting." She glanced at Molly. "We can also do a vanilla and chocolate swirl cake. And we can also do fondant on any of the flavors if that's preferable."

Molly smiled and nodded at her, and Cassie couldn't help but notice a slight blush on Jody's cheeks.

Jody pointed to the next cluster of plates. "These are the NOLA-inspired flavors. Almond cake with pineapple filling and almond buttercream frosting. Our bananas Foster has banana-infused cake with hints of rum and cinnamon and a caramel and banana filling."

As much as Cassie loved the presentation, she was more than ready for the tasting part to start.

Jody continued. "It's finished with caramel frosting, chocolate drip, and actual bananas Foster along the top edge. And this is our chocolate praline. Chocolate cake, praline filling, finished with chocolate ganache and praline crumble. We can also do layered king cakes or king cake-inspired cupcakes."

Cassie exchanged an impressed look with Molly. This might be her first tasting, but so far she couldn't imagine anything better than the flavors Jody had just described. Until she continued.

"And these are our signature flavors. Just some ideas I've been playing around with. The chocolate and wine is chocolate cake with cocoa crumble and a Malbec-infused curd finished with a French meringue, cocoa crumble, and cacao powder. Chicory decadence is chocolate cake with chicory coffee buttercream finished with chocolate ganache, dark-chocolate-covered espresso beans, and coffee mousse. Lastly, for the season, Maple Street is maple pumpkin cake with praline filling finished with maple chocolate ganache and maple syrup brittle." She stepped back and clasped her hands in front of her navy-blue apron waiting for Cassie and Molly's reactions.

"Am I drooling? I feel like I'm drooling," Cassie said, wiping at her mouth, and Jody and Molly laughed.

Even Molly seemed relaxed and excited about the cakes. "Jody, this might be the most incredible spread I've ever seen at a tasting. You didn't have to go to all of this trouble for us. And I can't believe you did all of this in just one week."

Jody seemed a little more relaxed now. "I know you said the couple wasn't wanting anything too fancy, but I don't know, it's their wedding. It should be special. And," Jody looked down at the tray of cake, "my hope is that you like the cake enough to become a repeat customer." She raised her eyes to meet Molly's with a shy but genuine smile.

Cassie watched the exchange with curiosity before Molly spoke. "Well, if these taste half as good as they sound, you don't need to worry about that."

Jody nodded. "Great, well, enjoy, take your time, and let me know if you have any questions or need anything." And with that, she headed back to help the young woman behind the counter who was waiting on the growing line of customers.

"Which one do you want to try first?" Molly asked.

"I don't know, which one are you going for?" Cassie replied.

They both reached for the chocolate and wine at the same time and laughed. "You first," Cassie said, gesturing for Molly to take it as Cassie reached for the chocolate praline.

Thirty minutes later, Cassie was beyond full, happy, and on a sugar high. "So, are we decided?"

Molly nodded, a satisfied smile on her face. It was the most relaxed Cassie had seen her since she moved in.

"Alrighty. Let me video chat with Nellie and Katherine to see if they like the plan." Cassie rang the couple and showed them the table full of cake slices. What was left of them anyway. While she was explaining the flavor profiles, Molly walked over to the counter and started talking with Jody.

Once the couple agreed on flavors and the presentation, Cassie ended the call and watched the exchange between Molly and Jody. Jody, as Cassie had sensed, was clearly smitten with Molly. She had a permanent blush on her cheeks and occasionally tucked her hair behind her ear with a shy grin. And, as Cassie expected, Molly was clueless. Molly was pretty adept at social interactions. It made her excellent at what she did for a living, which primarily revolved around pleasing clients. But Molly had always been unaware of the effect she had on others. And being in a relationship for nearly twenty years made her more oblivious. Cassie couldn't blame Jody for being a little starstruck around Molly. She was striking, after all. She had the same auburn hair as Cassie, though few knew that since Cassie's hair was almost always dyed a different color. They also shared the same fair complexion. But Molly, ten years older and a little taller and thinner, had always possessed an elegance and grace that lit up the room around her. The most attractive thing about Molly, however, was her blissful ignorance of her beauty and charm. She was giving and kind and thought the best of people. Something Cassie wished she was better at.

Molly and Jody joined Cassie at the table. "So, what's the verdict?" Molly asked.

"They trust our judgment." She turned to Jody. "It's going to be a three-tiered cake with each signature flavor as one layer. Chocolate and wine will be on the bottom, then chicory decadence in the middle, and Maple Street on top. They're expecting a hundred people, so that should be perfect."

Jody nodded. "Sounds great."

Molly placed her hand on Jody's arm. "Jody, we can't thank you enough. I'm glad you decided to follow your passion and expand into wedding cakes." Between the touch and Molly's words, Cassie didn't think Jody's smile could get any bigger.

As they walked back to the car, Cassie's curiosity got the better of her. "What were you talking to Jody about?"

"Oh, just about how incredible her flavors are and how she got started making cakes." Molly brushed her bangs out of her eyes and shivered in her thin, knee-length cream coat.

"How did she get started? She never told me that part of her story when we were working on her designs."

"She made a cake for her wedding."

Cassie stopped walking. "Jody's married?"

Molly stopped and frowned. "Not anymore." The sadness in Molly's voice seemed to stretch much deeper than Jody.

Cassie stood there, not knowing what to do. Molly had been like her old self during the cake tasting and Cassie didn't want that to slip away.

"What are you doing? Come on, it's freezing." Molly rubbed

her hands together to warm them, and Cassie joined her as they walked briskly to the car.

Cassie cranked on the heat since the temperature had dropped while they were in the bakery. The weather this fall seemed more like her days in New England than the typically hot and sticky weather in New Orleans, but thankfully the car warmed up quickly. She glanced at Molly as she put the car in gear. The worry line that had been a fixture between her eyes the past few weeks had disappeared. It was nice to see Molly relaxed and happy again, even if only for a short while.

Drea rolled out the blank canvas along the hardwood floor in her bedroom and placed one of the wood frames she had built on top. She knelt over the canvas, starting a cut with her knife before tearing it the rest of the way. As she folded the canvas over one of the edges of the frame, she grabbed her staple gun and secured the canvas to the wood, then continued working around the perimeter of the frame. When the stapling was done and she had turned it over to make sure the canvas was stretched tight, Pickles joined her. He hated the sound of the staple gun and always waited until that part was over to inspect.

Drea sat back on her heels and petted him as he rubbed against her. "Sorry, bud, there's two more to go."

After the three panels were stretched, primed, and dried, Drea stood with a glass of whiskey, staring at the canvases leaning against her wall. She thought back to Nellie's story about how she and Katherine had met and began to sketch a design across the three panels.

A while later, after she had completed her sketch, she grabbed her paint and set the first panel on the easel. Pickles watched her from his usual spot on the bed, supervising. After a few minutes, Drea entered the zone, her brushstrokes free and easy as her natural ability steered the ship and her mind wandered to Cassie. She had been standoffish at work ever since Thursday night at the wedding venue. At first, Drea thought maybe it had to do with Molly, but then she remembered Cassie asking how she knew Katherine and how things had felt off when Cassie left.

Drea grabbed a different brush and color, building on the base she had created. Was Cassie worried that there was something between Katherine and Drea? Was she jealous? Drea's hand stilled at the thought. Women being into her wasn't foreign territory, but other than the playful banter, Cassie had never done anything to indicate she might be interested in her as anything other than a coworker. Sure, Drea had occasionally had thoughts about Cassie, but only because she was cute—well, attractive. Cute and attractive. And Drea noticed most women in that way. It didn't mean anything. At least that's what Drea kept telling herself, unwilling or unable to comprehend why something about Cassie stayed with her, lingering in her mind long after their time together. She didn't want to entertain such thoughts, that any woman might have an effect on her. That was dangerous territory she had spent her life avoiding.

Plus, Cassie was probably too busy with the wedding and work to even entertain such thoughts. It was probably just due to stress from Molly and all of the extra work Cassie had been dealing with. Though Cassie admitting Drea's drawl was sexy and how uncomfortable Cassie got after realizing her slip made Drea chuckle. She returned her focus to her painting, pushing back the part of her that enjoyed the idea of Cassie being into her. Ridiculous. They were friends. Nothing more.

Friends. Drea sat with the word, rolling it around in her mind. Is that what they were? She did enjoy her time with Cassie, and since there could never be anything more than that between them—it would go against the rules she had set for herself, rules she wasn't willing to change for anyone—maybe friends was perfect.

Feeling more certain that everything was fine, Drea took a sip of whiskey and continued painting into the early hours of the morning.

Cassie glanced at Drea's desk. Again. Ever since Drea's vague explanation of how she knew Katherine, Cassie had retreated from the natural back-and-forth that she and Drea had developed.

She had convinced herself it was about the wedding, using the past six days to envision every scenario possible where the wedding planner, having slept with one of the brides, would cause disaster. But when she quit spinning out doomsday scenarios, she recalled no animosity in Katherine's voice when speaking to Drea and the way that Katherine and Nellie looked at each other. There was no threat to the wedding. The threat was the pang of jealousy she felt deep in her chest when she thought about Drea hooking up with Katherine.

She wished she didn't care. And the fact that some part of her did scared the hell out of her. But with only one and a half weeks left until the wedding, she needed to touch base with Drea.

Drea was working on her laptop, her feet crossed on top of her desk. But something about Drea seemed off.

Cassie took a deep breath and walked over, but Drea didn't seem to notice. "Hey," Cassie said.

Drea looked up, the bags under her eyes apparent. "Hey yourself."

Cassie nodded to the break area. "Can I talk to you for a minute?"

"Sure," Drea said, putting her laptop on her desk and following Cassie.

When they had some privacy, Cassie continued. "I wanted to touch base with you about the plan for the remaining wedding tasks to make sure we've got everything covered and are on the same page."

"Okay," Drea said as her gaze wandered out the window.

Sensing hesitation in Drea's response, Cassie jumped in. "Look, if you're too busy or whatever, I can do this. I don't want you to feel obligated or anything."

Drea met Cassie's eyes. "I don't feel obligated. I'm happy to help."

Cassie searched Drea's face but only found sincerity. "Okay, thank you. Do you have time we could talk tonight?"

Drea leaned back against the counter. Cassie's brain tried to comprehend how such a basic outfit, a black button-down with a few buttons open at the top and jeans, could be so effortlessly sexy. But that was Drea. "How about Rosie's?"

Cassie forced her mind to focus on the words and not the visual in front of her. "Rosie's?"

"Yeah. Seven?"

"Perfect. See you then." She headed back to her desk, feeling Drea's eyes on her.

When Cassie found Drea in a booth at Rosie's a few hours later, she was sipping a margarita and seemed more relaxed than earlier. Cassie took off her jacket and noticed the iced tea in front of her. She glanced at Drea. "For me?"

Drea nodded and raised her glass in the air. "Cheers."

Cassie raised hers and peered around the club as she took a sip. The Wednesday evening crowd was more chill than on the weekend, but a fair number of people still filled the space.

She filled Drea in on the cake tasting and all of the amazing flavors Jody had made for them. "I've been dreaming about those cakes ever since Sunday." Cassie swooned at the memory and Drea laughed. "What kind of cake would you want for your wedding?" Cassie asked.

For the first time since Cassie had known her Drea seemed at a loss.

"What?" Cassie asked.

Drea shrugged. "I have never once thought about that question in my entire life."

"Oh, not a big cake person?"

"Not a wedding person." Drea took a sip of her drink, but held Cassie's gaze.

"Ah." Cassie had no idea how to respond, feeling like she had gotten them both into a deeper conversation than she had intended, so she sipped her iced tea to buy time.

"I suppose you are."

Cassie laughed. "My views on weddings and marriage are . . . complicated. But I would marry those cakes." She arched her eyebrow and Drea burst into laughter.

Cassie pulled out her notepad full of wedding details, and they discussed the timeline until the wedding and the remaining duties needing to be covered. As Cassie plowed on, Drea's energy seemed to drift.

Cassie stopped what she was saying. "Are you okay?"

Drea had been staring at her drink, twirling it slowly on the table, but the question got her attention. "Yeah, sorry. I didn't get much sleep last night."

Another pang of jealousy hit Cassie as she imagined what, exactly, had kept Drea up all night. *Damn it*. Cassie had no interest in hearing details about whoever Drea had been with the night before. She looked down at her notepad to see what else needed to be decided on. "OK. What did you decide about the painting? Are you still up for that or do we need to think of another plan?"

"I sketched it out and have a lot of the first panel done."

"First panel?" Cassie perked up, intrigued.

"Yeah, I decided to do a three-panel feature to cover the majority of the wall." Drea's tone was casual, matter-of-fact, and

Cassie wondered if she even knew how impressive or sexy that statement was.

"Really?" Cassie was surprised by how much effort Drea was putting in to help make the wedding a success. She had been helpful since she started helping Cassie. Hugely helpful in fact. But this seemed to be on another level. Cassie put her elbow on the table, resting her chin in her hand, and smiled. "Can I see it?"

Drea locked eyes with her, and Cassie wondered if she had overstepped. But before she could backpedal, Drea nodded.

"This is it." Drea said as she held the door open for Cassie. Usually when she held the door open for a woman, they both knew what was going to happen. This was the first time in a long time Drea had had a woman over, other than Sam, for other reasons.

Cassie glanced around the apartment. "Very nice."

"Thanks," Drea said, increasingly aware that her normal guests usually could care less about her apartment.

As they passed by the kitchen on the way to the painting, Pickles jumped up on the island and meowed.

"Who is this?" Cassie asked in a lilting tone Drea hadn't heard before and immediately headed over to pet him. Drea watched as Pickles shamelessly threw himself at a total stranger and was rewarded with lots of pets and nuzzles from Cassie in return.

"Well, it used to be my cat, Pickles. But after that display, I feel like the third wheel here." She joined them at the island and scratched under his chin. "Traitor."

Pickles lay down between them so they both could dutifully pet him.

"Wow." Drea shook her head. "You think you know someone. The adoption fee is $50."

Cassie laughed. "He probably can tell that I'm a cat person. My cat is the same way. He pretty much abandoned me when Molly moved in."

"I didn't know you had a cat," Drea said, petting Pickles again.

Cassie smiled, the warmth of it adding a twinkle to her eye. "Yeah, his name is Digit."

"Digit? How'd you come up with that name?"

"He's polydactyl."

"Poly what?"

Cassie laughed. "Polydactyl. It means he has extra toes, so Digit seemed fitting."

The idea of extra toes made Drea curious. "Does it bother him?"

"No. He has six toes on both of his front paws. You should see him play ball." The boastful tone in Cassie's voice made Drea laugh. "How did Pickles acquire his name?"

"That was all Jake." At the questioning look on Cassie's face, Drea added, "Sam's son."

"Aw, Jake's such a sweetie. I've only met him once when Ash brought him to see Sam at work, but he seems pretty incredible."

Drea smiled at the thought of him. "He is." Silence filled the room other than Pickles' purring. "Anyway, you want to see the painting?"

"Yes!" Cassie, with Pickles in tow, followed Drea through the living room and up the two steps to the bedroom.

Drea gestured toward the panels. "Here it is." For the first time in a long time, no, maybe ever, Drea felt nervous at a woman's response in her bedroom. Showing Cassie her unfinished work seemed a lot more intimate than sharing her other talents.

Cassie's eyes widened as she walked closer to the panels. Drea watched her taking in the details of the river and the lights reflecting on the water. After a moment, Cassie turned to Drea. "Drea, this is incredible. They're going to love it."

The awe in Cassie's voice warmed Drea, and she breathed for what seemed like the first time in a while. "I hope so. It took me most of last night and this morning to get that much done, but I'll be able to finish the rest of the panels in time for the wedding."

Cassie's smile faltered, and she turned to stare at the painting. Drea walked over and joined her, trying to see the painting the way Cassie might see it. Cassie turned to her. "Drea, thank you for doing this."

The emotion in Cassie's voice tugged at her. She searched Cassie's brown eyes before her gaze fell to the bold-colored lips that always caught her attention, lingering there, imagining what they might feel like. The air turned thick around them and though Drea had been in this position with many women before, something felt different about this time, with this woman. None of her usual words or moves were of any use now. She could only stand there. She met Cassie's eyes again, darker now as they watched her. She wanted to reach out and close the distance, but something inside held her back. It felt much more vulnerable than any time before.

Cassie turned back to the painting, ending the moment between them. "I should get going. Thank you for sharing this with me."

"Of course," Drea said. Part of her felt sad to see Cassie go, but another part felt relieved, as if she had been saved from something dangerous.

Cassie reached down to pet Pickles, then headed to the door. She smiled as Drea opened the door. "Good night, Drea."

"Good night." Drea shut the door behind Cassie and leaned her back against it, taking a deep breath to steady herself. Pickles stared at her from a few feet away and meowed. "Don't even, mister."

Chapter 12

Drea rang the doorbell of the shotgun duplex, taking in the vibrant exterior colors typical of New Orleans houses, a detail of the city that always made her feel at home. It figured Cassie lived in a place bursting with rich colors, purple and yellow in this case. It matched her personality. *And her hair,* Drea thought, grinning.

Cassie opened the door with a big smile. "Hi." She looked comfortable in a fuzzy sage sweater hanging off one shoulder. It reminded Drea of the outfit she wore the day they played pool at Rosie's.

"Hey." Drea felt a little out of her element, which was odd for her. Something about moving her work relationship with Cassie to more of an out-of-the-office friendship seemed risky and new to Drea. Especially after the other night at her place.

She stepped inside as Cassie shut the door behind her. She took a couple of steps before stopping at the sight. The entire front room was covered in fall leaves, pumpkins, and all kinds of craft supplies. It was like a craft store had vomited all over the living room.

Cassie gestured at the mess. "Welcome to my workshop."

Drea raised her eyebrows as she scanned the room. "Please

tell me this comes with wine."

Cassie laughed. "That can be arranged."

Drea knelt by the metal arch lying on the hardwood floor and riffled through some of the leaf choices. She picked up one of the miniature pumpkins and tossed it to herself as she assessed the situation.

"Here you go." Cassie handed her a glass of red wine.

"Thank you." Drea took a sip, grateful for the comfort it always brought her.

"So, you sure you're up for this? There's still time to run." Cassie shot her a challenging look.

"I can handle it if you can," Drea shot back.

They held each other's gaze for a moment, a spark of electricity in the air, before Cassie seemed to back down, shifting her attention to the floor. "I was thinking you could work on the altar while I start the table centerpieces." Cassie placed a hand on her hip. "How are you with a glue gun?"

Drea held her palm up at Cassie. "I got this."

Cassie arched an eyebrow but said nothing. She grabbed the glue gun off the desk behind her and handed it to Drea.

Drea took the pumpkin in her other hand and spun it on the floor like a top. Out of nowhere, a black, furry blur appeared at the pumpkin, hit it left then right, and chased it out of the room. Drea barely had time to jerk her hand out of the way.

"What the hell was that?"

Cassie stared in the direction where the blur had run off. "That was Digit." As if on cue, a black-and-white cat walked into the room looking bored with the pumpkin in its mouth. "He's developed a bit of an affinity for the pumpkins."

Digit walked over to Drea, dropped the pumpkin by her hand, and made a trill sound. Drea's jaw dropped. "He fetches?"

"Yeeeaaahhh. I think he thinks he's a dog or something."

Drea rolled the pumpkin across the floor and Digit scrambled after it, then brought it back to her with another trill.

"Wow."

"You don't have to keep doing that. He'll go all night. Molly can play with him when she gets home."

"Oh, I was wondering if I might meet her tonight."

"No, she's doing a fall party tonight before the holiday craziness starts." Cassie swept the hair off her forehead as it started to cover her eye.

Drea picked a few different types of leaves out of the large plastic bag in front of her. "Do you have a preference for how I do this?"

Cassie shook her head. "No, I trust you. You're the artist after all." She put some music on and they worked without speaking for a while as a mixture of EDM, pop, and R&B played.

When Édith Piaf started to sing, Drea caught Cassie's eye. "Interesting choice. Wouldn't have pegged you for a Piaf fan."

Cassie shrugged as color appeared on her cheeks. "I like a lot of things." She started to tie a bow in the twine she had just wrapped around a mason jar, then stopped. "What kind of music do you like?"

Drea sipped her wine. "Country. All day, all night."

Cassie's brow furrowed. "Really?"

Drea grinned. "No."

Cassie laughed, and Drea turned back to her work, pleased by the sound.

A little while later, Drea stood up, brushing the crafting detritus from her jeans, and raised the altar adorned in leaves for Cassie to see. "What do you think?"

Cassie's eyes lit up. "That looks incredible."

"Good." Drea leaned it against the wall and took in the various pieces around Cassie. Mason jars, a ball of twine, wood slices, floral accessories, and pumpkins. "What can I help with?"

Cassie paused at tying another bow and glanced at the chaos around her. "If you want to put a stalk of dried wheat in each of the mason jars with bows on them, I'll finish these last few jars and then I just need to glue them to the wood slices."

"Got it." Drea knelt a few feet from Cassie and started separating the mounds of wheat into the different jars. She stopped at the sound of Cassie sucking air through her teeth, and glanced over to see Cassie shaking her hand in the air for a moment with the glue gun in the other hand. Cassie blew on her hand for a second, then grabbed a pumpkin and placed it on the wood slice in front of her. Drea returned her attention to the wheat in her hand and put a few stalks in different jars, lost in the meditative state of the repeated steps until Cassie yelled. "Mother fu . . ."

Drea looked up to see Cassie sucking on the side of her finger, the glue gun still in the other hand. She stood up, walked over to Cassie, and knelt beside her. "Hand me the gun," she said with an outstretched hand.

Cassie turned to her, still trying to assuage the pain in her finger.

Drea motioned Cassie to give it to her. "Come on."

Cassie reluctantly handed it over.

"Let me see." Drea nodded at Cassie's finger.

Cassie tilted her hand toward Drea, who took it and held it closer to her eyes to see the damage. She suppressed a shiver at Cassie's nearness, at the warmth coming from her skin.

"You'll be okay." She let go of Cassie's hand and Cassie slowly took it back. Drea picked up the pumpkin in front of her, put glue on the wood slice, and held the pumpkin on the glue for a few seconds. She nodded at the jars that Cassie had just finished. "Hand me one of those."

They continued working like that sitting side by side for a few centerpieces, Cassie handing pieces to Drea as the music added a mellow soundtrack to the rhythm of their flow. Drea kept busy with the decorations, trying not to focus on how close she and Cassie were sitting, but when the music paused between songs, an awkward silence filled the room.

Cassie must have felt it too because she started talking to fill the gap. "I guess this is not how you envisioned your fall going. A non-wedding person elbows deep in wedding planning."

Drea bent over to glue another jar down. "It *is* pretty close to my idea of hell freezing over."

"So, why? Why are you doing all of this?" There was no judgment in Cassie's voice, only curiosity.

Drea sat back. She had asked herself that question many times, but the most obvious and true answer was all she was prepared to share. "Because you needed help."

Cassie held her gaze, her furrowed brow relaxing. Everything around them seemed to fall away. Drea swallowed, waiting for the fate of the moment to reveal itself.

Cassie opened her mouth as if to ask another question, but as the next song picked up, the moment ended. She grabbed one of the centerpieces, stood up, and walked over to the corner of the room. "I'll put the finished ones over here."

Something made Drea want to continue the connection, rather than return to joking and chitchat like usual. "Are you and Molly close?"

"Yeah. She's ten years older, so she was always more like a mom to me than a sister, but then …" Cassie paused as she looked at the decorations in her hand, but seemed to be elsewhere.

"But then?" Drea offered gently.

Cassie raised her eyes, hesitation gripping her. She grabbed her wrist and took a breath before continuing. "My parents died when I was eleven. Molly had always taken care of me growing up, but she basically raised me from that point on. So, yeah, we're close." She forced a weak smile.

"I'm sorry." Seeing the pain in Cassie's eyes made Drea wish she hadn't pushed the topic.

"Thanks." She shrugged. "It's been a while."

One thing Drea knew for sure was there was no timeline on grief. She tried to think of a different topic that would take away whatever pain Cassie was feeling. "So, did you say you were a wedding person? Or no, you want to marry a bunch of cakes." She flashed Cassie a mischievous grin.

Cassie chuckled and stooped to pick up another completed centerpiece. "Molly is the wedding person." She frowned. "Well, usually." A smile appeared as she continued, "She's always been a hopeless romantic, but she did practice what she preached with Eva, her ex." She shook her head. "God, I'm still not used to that word. They were together for nearly twenty years, and they were the one example I've had of a stable relationship. That love really did exist, ya know?"

Drea thought of the examples in her own life. A stable relationship and love? For her, those didn't always go hand in hand. Her parents had a stable relationship, but she had never witnessed much love between them. No, Sam and Anna had been her one example. Memories of their wedding, then the devastation following Anna's death swirled in her mind. She grabbed her glass of wine and took a long sip so Cassie wouldn't see the tears welling in her eyes, the pause giving her time to blink back the emotion.

"But no, I'm not a wedding person," Cassie continued. "I'm hopeful that I will meet some amazing woman one day who blows me away and who I can count on, but I don't need some elaborate day to prove to others that I've met my person. I just need her."

As Drea listened to Cassie's words, something resonated deep inside her. She had never put words to why she didn't want a wedding, at least not out loud. There was the element of a big celebration, and after all of the annual galas she had been subjected to, never having a public celebration again was more than fine with her. But, if she was being honest, it wasn't about the wedding. It was the fact that she knew it would never happen for her. There was no person out there for her. And for most of her life, that had been okay.

Cassie beamed at Molly as Sam stepped to the front of the room, thrilled that her sister finally got to see where she worked and meet Sam. The office turned makeshift dining room overflowed with staff, their families, and a select few clients.

"Thank you all for coming," Sam began. "The past few months have been a whirlwind. An incredible, somewhat stressful," a few chuckles rang through the room, "amazing dream come true. And I have all of you to thank for that. You are all family to me. So, enjoy the food, the company, and the rest of the week off. You deserve it." She raised her glass. "Happy Thanksgiving, everyone!"

Clapping and some *whoots* filled the room before everyone started to mingle again.

Cassie turned to Molly, her plus-one for the evening. "Come on, I want to introduce you to Sam." They headed toward Sam, who was chatting with the Rushes.

"Hi everyone, I'd like to introduce my sister, Molly. Molly, this is Sam, and two of our most important clients, Beau and Lorna Rush. They own The Well."

Molly shook Beau and Lorna's hands. "Oh, wow, it's wonderful to meet you both. I've been hearing rave reviews about The Well."

"You'll have to come try it out soon then," Lorna said with a welcoming smile.

"Molly, it's so great to meet you." Sam hugged her. "Your sister is an absolute lifesaver. I don't know what I would have done without her the past few months."

"I feel the same way." The warm smile never faltered from Molly's lips, but Cassie placed her hand on her back and gave her a gentle rub of encouragement.

If Sam noticed the shift in Molly's tone, she didn't let it

change the mood of the conversation. "I'm happy you're here," she said, patting Molly's hand.

"I can definitely see the resemblance between the two of you. Sisters for sure," Beau said. "Thank god I don't take after my brother." He pretended to adjust an invisible tie and puffed out his chest. "I got all the looks in the family." He winked at Lorna and she swatted at him.

"Just ignore him. It works for me," Lorna said, then laughed as Beau feigned sadness.

They all laughed, and Cassie took advantage of the pause in the conversation to notice the line forming over by the food, waving at Ash who was helping Jake with a plate of food. She looked at Sam who was smiling warmly at Ash and Jake.

"You all help yourselves to some food before it gets cold," Sam said. "I'm going to go check on my family."

Cassie and Molly followed the others to the long table along the wall, full of Thanksgiving food. Cassie's mouth watered as she took in the turkey and all of the traditional side dishes. As she filled her plate with a little bit of everything, she noticed the sparseness on Molly's plate.

She grabbed a helping of stuffing. "Hey Mol, take some. It's your favorite."

When Molly turned, the sadness in her eyes tugged at Cassie's heart. She wasn't sure if it was Eva or the holidays in general, probably all of the above. Ever since they had lost their parents, holidays had lost a lot of the warmth and meaning. Their mom had always made the holidays special, baking their favorite types of desserts and picking out a tree to decorate together, as if making those times warm and cheery could counteract the rest of the time which was pretty rough. Molly and Cassie, along with Eva, had tried to keep things going after the pain of the first couple of years had passed, but it was a hodgepodge at best, typically ordering out for Thanksgiving and focusing on being together rather than continuing any traditions. Because Molly planned so many holiday events for her job, Cassie was never sure if the lack of effort for their own holidays was because she needed a break from that or if it was the absence of their mom.

A commotion at the end of the table grabbed Cassie's attention. Jody had arrived and onlookers surrounded her as she placed pies and a delicious-looking cake on the table.

As people headed to the dining table, Cassie walked over to check out the dessert options. "Hey, Jody. I didn't realize you were going to be catering dessert tonight."

Jody paused slicing a pie. "Oh, it was the least I could do. You all have been so great to me. And Sam wanted you all to get a break and not have to plan the dinner to celebrate yourselves." She chuckled.

Cassie turned and saw Sam sitting at the table with Ash and Jake, cutting Jake's turkey for him. Her heart warmed at the sight. If Sam hadn't already won her heart as the best boss she ever had, seeing how caring she was as a mom would have done it. "Yeah, we're all pretty lucky to have Sam."

Jody nodded enthusiastically. "We are."

"I'm normally a pie person for Thanksgiving, but this cake looks incredible. What is it?" Cassie asked.

"It's pecan . . ." Jody's words stilled as Molly joined them. "Hi, Molly."

"Hi, Jody, this looks incredible," Molly said, looking like she might drool on the dessert.

"Thanks, I was telling Cassie this is my pecan pie cake. Layers of caramel cake and pecan pie filling on a shortbread crust, topped with caramel buttercream frosting and chocolate drip."

"Oh my god," Cassie and Molly said in unison.

Jody laughed. "You two like the same types of cake?"

"I think anyone who is breathing would like that cake," Cassie said. She met Molly's eyes. "We're both fans of chocolate, but I'm more the chocolate on chocolate with a side of chocolate type and Molly, well, you like fruit and chocolate still, right?"

Molly smiled and it reached her eyes this time. "Yeah, I'm a sucker for raspberries and chocolate."

"A great combination," Jody agreed.

"Would you like to join us?" Cassie asked.

Jody's shoulders relaxed a little. "I'd love to. Can you save me a seat while I finish slicing this?"

"Absolutely. I'd offer to help, but I do not want to wreck your creation," Cassie said.

They headed over to the folding tables set up in a line to make a long dining table. The nice off-white tablecloth, place settings, and fall-themed decorations ratcheted up the style factor. There were a few empty seats next to Tom, Drea, and Erin, so Cassie and Molly grabbed seats across from each other and Cassie used her water to save the spot next to her for Jody.

Drea glanced up at Cassie and smiled, and Cassie felt the sexiness of it deep in her bones. She looked over at the cake to distract herself. Why couldn't she lust after it? That was a relationship with some potential at least.

Ever since the night at Drea's apartment and this past weekend working on the table decorations together, the connection Cassie felt between them was getting harder to ignore. If it had been anyone else, she would've asked them out by now. But Drea was a non-option. There was no future with someone like Drea, so Cassie was left to war between her thoughts and her emotions. And she wasn't sure which one was winning.

"You must be Molly. I've heard a lot about you." The sound of Drea's voice pulled Cassie's attention back to the table.

"Oh, I'm sorry. I should have introduced you," Cassie said. "Molly, this is Drea." She watched as Molly and Drea held each other's gaze for a moment, and Cassie's stomach dropped.

"Drea. You're the one who's been helping Cassie and me out?" Molly asked.

"I am." Drea's voice was confident and sultry, not unlike her body.

Molly tucked a strand of hair behind her ear and took a sip of her wine. Cassie finally saw what Drea had never shown her initially, that superpower that had women line up for her. She felt a wave of nausea at the thought of Drea hooking up with her sister—a feeling and a thought she could go the rest of her life without having again. This was the first time she and Molly had ever been single at the same time except for when Cassie was pretty much a fetus. By the time she had come out in high school, Molly was already with Eva. She had never considered someone she liked showing an interest in her sister. And, of course, Drea would. Molly was classically beautiful. But more than that, she had a grace about her. As Cassie watched the two of them talking, she realized Drea had the same grace, but Molly's had an innocence to it, whereas Drea's had an edge. A hot, sexy edge, but still an edge.

"Is this for me?"

Cassie almost jumped at Jody's voice. "What?"

Jody gave her a curious look and pointed at the table. "Is this spot for me?"

"Oh! Yes. Please, have a seat." She moved her water so Jody could put her plate down, then grabbed a roll and put some butter on it as she stole glances at Drea and Molly.

"Could you pass the butter?" Jody asked.

"Mmhmm." Cassie passed the butter plate over, then took a large bite of her roll, chewing and watching a nightmare she never knew existed transpire in front of her.

Molly laughed at something Drea said and tucked another strand of long, auburn hair behind her ear.

Erin asked Drea something and Molly took the break in conversation to turn her focus to the rest of the table. She caught Cassie's eye, then furrowed her brow with a curious expression.

Cassie looked down at her plate, pretending to cut her

turkey so she could calm herself from all of the thoughts racing through her head.

The only thing worse than something happening between her and Drea would be something happening between Molly and Drea. How would she come to work each day and face a woman she knew had slept with her sister? It wasn't like Eva. That was a relationship and love, at one point at least. She felt a pain in her chest at the reminder of the loss. This would be a hookup. Just sex. Another wave of nausea hit.

"Cas, you all right?" Molly asked.

Cassie looked up and felt heat rising under her sweater. "I'm hot." She glanced around the room. "Is it hot in here?"

"It's actually a little chilly," Molly replied.

"I can see whether the temperature can be raised," Jody said. Cassie looked at her in disbelief and saw that she was looking at Molly. "If you're cold."

"That's so kind," Molly said as a smile replaced the look of concern on her face. "Thank you, but I'm fine." She passed a questioning look at Cassie.

Cassie gave the slightest shake of her head and focused on her plate again. Everything seemed upside down. Molly was the steady one, the stable one, the committed one. She and Eva were supposed to stay together forever. And now she was trying to keep Molly going, and Eva was gone, and everyone and their mom wanted to be with her sister. Why couldn't things go back to the way they were? She held her wrist and took a deep breath, then blew it out slowly. She did it once more and felt her heart rate slow and her muscles relax. Everything was fine. She was fine. It would all be okay. She raised her eyes, but the concerned expression meeting her was Drea's, not Molly's.

Drea watched the blush on Cassie's cheeks deepen as she stared into her lap and took a couple of breaths. She glanced at Molly to see her watching Cassie with concern as well.

She guessed it had only been a matter of time. While Drea didn't know much about weddings, thankfully avoiding the wave of weddings that a woman her age typically would have been asked to attend by now, except for Sam's, of course, she did know they had a reputation for being stressful as hell. Terms like bridezilla didn't exist for no reason. And while she knew Cassie to be a one-woman mountain mover in the office, she figured even she wouldn't be immune to the stresses of planning a wedding. Not to mention doing it for the first time—well, as far as she knew—while being supportive for her sister who was on a downward spiral of heartbreak. When she first agreed to help Cassie with the weddings, it had been to help get her out of her sadness because it was really bumming the office out. And her, truthfully. But seeing all that each one required and how hard Cassie worked even after working in the office all day, she started to see that things might go downhill for Cassie before she made it to the end. Plus, Cassie was not crafty . . . at all, whereas Drea had always excelled at that kind of stuff. And it felt good to be needed by someone again since Sam and Jake weren't around as often as they used to be.

When Cassie raised her eyes, they met Drea's. Drea watched as something changed in her expression. Erin and Tom asked Drea a question, but while she chatted with them, she snuck a few glances at Cassie, who ate a bit more food, but still seemed off. When a break in the conversation appeared, she caught Cassie's gaze and tilted her head toward the dessert area.

Cassie gave a half smile and nodded.

"You all right?" she asked as Cassie joined her at the dessert table.

"Yeah, I'm fine. I'm not sure what was going on," Cassie said. "I do."

Cassie's pupils dilated and the color drained from her face.

Drea grabbed a plate of cake and handed it to her, thinking she might pass out. "Here. Eat this."

Cassie stared at it for a moment. "What are you trying to say?"

"I think you're overwhelmed."

Cassie's eyes narrowed as if trying to decipher the words.

"With the wedding. You've been working nonstop for months and at a completely new job that's been pretty trial by fire so far. You need a break."

"Oh." Cassie's body relaxed a little and she took a bite of the cake, closing her eyes and savoring it. The move was a bit sensual and Drea tried to curb the thoughts and sensations that it incited in her. She cleared her throat and shifted to lean against the table.

Cassie opened her eyes and seemed to falter for a moment as her eyes scanned Drea's new position. She scratched her neck and glanced at her plate for a second before continuing, "I can't take a break. The wedding's in less than four days."

"What else still needs to be done?"

"God, so many things." She bit her lip and looked at the floor as if trying to mentally calculate it all. "But," there was a glimmer of hope in her eyes, "almost none of it can be done until we get into the venue on Saturday. I just need help getting all of the centerpieces and the altar," she pointed at Drea, "and your painting there. How is that coming by the way?"

"It's done. I can meet you Friday and take the altar and a bunch of the centerpieces in my car. I'll bring them and the painting on Saturday. But . . ." She felt a mischievous grin form on her lips.

"Uh-oh. But what?"

"Only if you'll meet me first for a little fun."

Cassie eyed Drea for a long moment until a smile finally broke through. "Fine. Deal."

A wave of relief spread through Drea. "I'll pick you up at

your place on Friday at 2 p.m. then."

"Okay." Cassie took another bite of cake.

"Oh, and wear something you don't mind getting dirty." She winked, grabbed a slice of pecan pie, and headed back to the table.

"What happened back there?" Molly asked once they got in Cassie's car to head home.

Cassie started the engine and turned the heat to full blast. "What do you mean?"

Molly nodded at Cassie's wrist. "You did your thing."

"I was feeling a little overwhelmed. Probably just the wedding stuff."

Molly watched her for a moment. Even before their parents had died, she had possessed that mom superpower to read Cassie like a book. "What is it really?"

Cassie blew out a breath and watched the people leaving the party to head home. She met Molly's eyes. "It's Drea."

The words seemed to surprise Molly. "What about her?"

"She was, you know," she gestured at Molly, "flirting with you."

Molly looked like she was trying to calculate a solution that didn't compute.

"And you were . . ." Cassie nodded to will the words to come out though the images running through her mind made her brain want to short-circuit.

"I was what?" Molly's words dripped with curiosity.

"Flirting back."

Molly's deep, melodic laughter ripped through the car, dropping Cassie's jaw until she realized how long it had been since she had heard that beautiful tune, her favorite sound in the entire world. It had been a rare beacon of normalcy through their childhood. She sat back and listened, reveling in the joy on Molly's face that had been absent for so long. Molly finally wiped the tears from her eyes as her laughter quieted.

"I'm sorry." She rubbed Cassie's shoulder. "I did not expect that at all."

"You can laugh at me all day if it keeps you laughing."

Molly returned a sincere, yet sad smile at the statement.

Cassie didn't know what to think. "Am I wrong?"

"One thousand percent. I mean, she's very beautiful, and I completely see her allure and why women would jump at the chance to be with her, in whatever capacity. But . . ." She shrugged. "Not me."

Cassie took a moment with the information as relief washed through her.

"For what it's worth, I don't know that she was flirting with me. I think that's just how Drea speaks to women."

"She doesn't speak to me that way." The admission sent a wave of sadness through her, catching her off guard.

"Are you sure?"

Cassie furrowed her brow. "Pretty positive, why?"

A mischievous grin played on Molly's lips. "Because from where I was sitting, she seemed pretty interested in you."

"She barely spoke to me at the table."

"No, when you two were getting dessert."

Now it was Cassie's turn to laugh. "No, she thought I was stressed about the wedding stuff and wanted me to take a break."

"But you said you weren't stressed about the wedding stuff."

"I wasn't."

Realization hit Molly. "You thought Drea was hitting on me and that's what got you upset?"

Cassie didn't like the way that made her look. "Upset's a strong word. Concerned. Uneasy, maybe?"

"You did your thing, Cassie."

Cassie sighed. "I've never seen someone flirt with you while you were . . ."

"Were what?"

"Single."

A flash of pain passed through Molly's eyes.

"I'm sorry."

Molly shook her head. "It's okay. Continue, please."

"Well, let alone someone I . . ." She couldn't find the right word. No, plenty of words were coming to her. She just didn't agree with them.

"Like?" Molly's suggestion came as Cassie uttered "work with," then continued. "It's not like that. At best, we're friends. In reality, I think she pities me."

"Why in the world do you think that?"

Damn it. She couldn't think of a reason other than the truth, but she hated to upset Molly or make her think she couldn't be the stable one Molly needed. "I was stressed when I started helping with the weddings, and I guess she noticed. That's why she offered to help."

"I never meant for you to be stressed helping me out." She squeezed Cassie's knee.

"It wasn't so much that as seeing you so sad and not being able to make it better." She blew out a breath. "It's been hard and I just want to be there for you the way you've been there for me."

"I couldn't ask for a better sister than you. I meant what I said earlier. You've been a lifesaver to me over the past couple of months."

"And you've always been mine."

Molly leaned over and hugged her. When she finally released her, they both wiped away tears.

"All right, enough of that," Molly said. "Let's go home."

"I couldn't agree more," Cassie replied, putting the car in gear.

Molly looked out the passenger window, but Cassie could

hear the smile in her voice, "And don't think I'm done trying to get the truth about your feelings for Miss Drea."

Cassie didn't answer as she navigated traffic. She'd have to figure it out for herself first.

Chapter 13

Cassie and Molly had barely crossed the threshold of Mama Jeffries' house when Cassie heard her call out from across the room. "Eeewww, give Mama a hug."

Cassie's heart warmed being in Janay's mom's home again, a place that had provided so much comfort and sense of family to her over the years. Mama J closed the distance between them, her flowing dress of bold and vibrant colors adding to the light and love she always exuded. As her solid, expansive embrace enveloped Cassie, Cassie's soul felt centered. Mama J's hugs were legendary, and when Cassie was struggling or missing her own mom, just the thought of them often gave her the comfort she needed to keep going.

"You too, sugar." Mama J reached out to bring Molly into the hug and held them together. When she had gotten her fill, she stood back and took them in. "I almost forgot what you two looked like, it's been so long."

Cassie ducked her head out of guilt. "I'm sorry. It's been really busy at work."

"Don't you worry about it. You're here now. That's what matters."

Cassie shrugged out of her black wool winter coat just as

Janay came in the front door with her duffel bag.

"How was the parade?" Mama J asked, as she took Cassie and Molly's coats.

"Incredible!" Cassie spoke before anyone else could. She and Molly had spent the last hour and a half in the bitter cold, and she was only starting to feel her toes again. The weather in New Orleans was usually still warm around Thanksgiving, but a series of cold snaps had it feeling like the dead of winter already. But it was all worth it to see Janay's girls nail their routine. She wrapped her arm around Janay's shoulders. "I'm so proud of you."

"Aw, thanks, girl." Janay dropped her duffel by the door and smoothed her hair back into her ponytail, the wind having done a number on it during the parade.

"Oh good, honey. Looks like all my girls are boss ladies." The sincere grin on Mama J's face reminded Cassie how much love and support this woman had brought to her life. For all the loss she and Molly had been through in their lives, Janay and her family had been the biggest blessing they could ever have asked for. "Now I hope you're hungry."

Cassie and Molly exchanged a glance as Mama J headed to the kitchen. It hadn't even been two full days since they gorged themselves at the office Thanksgiving dinner and Cassie had only started feeling like herself again, just in time for round two.

Though Thanksgiving dinner at the Jeffries' was its own being. Collard greens, corn bread, and the best mac and cheese Cassie had ever tasted, along with fried turkey and stuffing. It was a Southern take on the holiday that Cassie enjoyed even more than the dishes she had grown up with in Boston. The smells filling the house from the stuffing and cornbread were only rivaled by the sweet smell of Cassie's favorite, sweet potato pie. When Janay and Cassie met in college, Janay had invited her for Thanksgiving dinner, and when Mama J learned about their family, she extended the invitation to Molly and Eva as well. They had spent every Thanksgiving together since, and as

Janay and Cassie's friendship grew, so did the sense of family.

Cassie and Molly helped carry side dishes to the table. Renee, Janay's twin, and her boyfriend sat at one side of the table while Grandma Jeffries positioned herself near a couple of friends of the family. Cassie had never attended a holiday at Mama J's house that didn't include a few community members who were treated as family. Mama J valued community, and she had instilled that value in Janay and Renee as well. When Janay and Mama J carried the last of the plates in, they all took a seat and Mama J led them in a blessing.

Multiple conversations ebbed and flowed in and out of each other, a lively rhythm that made Cassie grateful. Even when Cassie, Molly, and Eva had their own Thanksgiving dinners before the Jeffries family came into their lives, it had been low-key and quiet. But this family was always buzzing, and the energy made Cassie feel alive.

Throughout the different conversations, Cassie caught Mama J keeping an eye on Molly. No one mentioned Eva, but they were all aware of her absence, and though she hadn't said anything, Mama J seemed to be concerned about the change in Molly—the sadness in her eyes and silence where laughter used to live. It had been eating away at Cassie since the day Molly moved in, but nothing she had done, no matter how hard she tried, seemed to make it better for more than a few fleeting moments.

"Reggie, when are you going to propose to my sister?" Janay's question ripped Cassie from her thoughts.

"Psh, come on, Janay. We're taking our time," Reggie said.

"We are or you are?" She cocked an eyebrow at him.

He shook his head at her as a bashful and slightly intimidated expression crossed his features.

She held up her left hand and tapped her ring finger. "Put a ring on it, boy."

Renee laughed. "All right, J, message received."

"We'll see, won't we," Janay pushed, but her tone was playful. It was one thing Cassie had always marveled at. Even disagreements were full of love in Janay's family. It had been new territory to Cassie when she spent her first Thanksgiving with the family, and she became nervous when the conversation turned challenging. She had been shocked when it turned into laughter in a matter of seconds. It took her a while to let that part of her past go, but Janay and her family taught her that communication didn't have to result in fights and that a family could be based on love rather than anger.

After everyone had eaten their fill and could barely move, they gathered in the living room. Soft jazz music rang out from the street. There was always music playing in the Tremé neighborhood the Jeffries called home.

Grandma Jeffries turned on the TV and changed the channel until she came to *It's a Wonderful Life*.

"Grandma, not again," Renee said. "How many times do we have to watch this movie?"

The tiny gray-haired woman sank deeper into the recliner engulfing her and waved her hand at Renee. "Shush, now."

Renee rolled her eyes and cuddled against Reggie on the sofa. They all sat in silence, either from boredom or tryptophan, and watched the movie. When the final credits rolled along the screen, Mama J got up. "Molly, honey, will you help me get the pie ready?"

"Of course," Molly said and followed her to the kitchen.

Cassie glanced at Janay beside her and Janay ruffled her hair with a wink.

After a few minutes, curiosity got the best of her, and she walked over by the kitchen doorway, staying out of sight.

"You'll be okay again," Mama J said. "I know it doesn't feel like it now, but one day, it won't hurt so much."

She heard a sniffle.

"You have been through so much in your life, Molly, and

I'm so sorry you're going through this too. But you'll make it through this, honey. I promise you will. Come here."

After a few moments of quiet, Cassie turned the corner and walked in. "Can I help y'all with the plates?"

Molly let go of the hug and wiped her eyes with a chuckle. Mama J gave her shoulder a squeeze as Cassie met Molly's eyes and gave her an encouraging smile.

Mama J turned to Cassie. "Yes you may." She handed two plates to her. "Here you go, honey. Then, come back for more." She pointed to a plate with a huge slice of sweet potato pie on it and Cassie's mouth watered. "This big slice here is yours."

With her hands full, Cassie leaned her head against Mama J's shoulder in thanks.

As they all sat together in the living room enjoying their pie, she thought about the twists and turns that had brought Molly and her to this city and to a family that had accepted and loved them more than any they had ever known. A tear welled in her eye at the beauty amid all the pain.

"Don't you turn that channel, boy." Grandma Jeffries voice cut through the silence in the room from a lull in the conversations.

Reggie grimaced and handed the remote back to Grandma Jeffries as the others laughed and teased him. The tear ran down Cassie's cheek and she brushed it away as she laughed. Family had always been a hard topic for her, even more so after her parents passed. But being here with Janay's family and seeing what a family could be, well, it made her hope something similar might be possible for her too.

Music from three different directions drifted through the air as Cassie took in the assemblage of white tents, costumes, and paint before her. "What is this place?"

"It's Art and Soul," Drea said. "One of my friends from art

school started it a few years ago to bring together art and music. It's interactive. I thought it might be a fun way to unwind a bit before tomorrow."

Cassie felt a bit guilty that Drea had mistaken her reaction to Drea flirting with Molly as her being stressed about the wedding. She was stressed about the wedding, though, so it wasn't a total lie, and she could use a fun adventure after the grind of the past few months. Between launching the marketing firm and helping with the wedding planning, this was the first week in months that she felt as if she had had any sort of a break. The fact that Drea cared enough to show her this place was both comforting and confusing. She still didn't understand why Drea had chosen to continue helping her and even hanging out with her. But something about it gave Cassie the sense that Drea was lonely and needed a friend. And maybe she did too.

"It sounds awesome, but why is it in late November and not the spring or summer?"

"Good question. My friend who started it deals with depression and seasonal affective disorder. You know, becoming more depressed during the winter because of the lack of sunshine. So, she wanted people to be able to get out and have fun one last time before winter takes over. They have standing heaters in the tents to keep people warm so the focus can be on having a good time despite the temperature."

"Wow, that's such a cool idea." She glanced back at the tents and rubbed her hands together. "All right then, where should we start?"

Drea flashed a mischievous grin and Cassie wondered if she had committed too soon. "Follow me."

They wandered past face-painting stations that took the medium to a new level. There were no little kids running around with basic shapes and whiskers slathered across their faces. No, kids and adults were completely transformed into realistic animals and avatars through a beautiful amalgamation of colors and shadows that seemed more like magic than paint.

Drea stopped in front of a blank canvas that extended from the ground to above her head. "Here we are."

The woman running the station handed them white Tyvek suits and goggles. "You're going to want to put these on."

Cassie raised her eyebrows at Drea, wondering what the hell she had gotten into. Drea gave a single nod with an expression Cassie could only interpret as *go on, try it.*

Once they were suited up, looking like a bunch of Oompa Loompas without the crazy hair, but only because hers was inside the suit, the woman handed them each a paintbrush and pointed to the open cans of neon paint on the ground.

Drea put her brush down and jogged the few feet to the canvas. She spread her legs apart and held her arms up like she was about to do a rendition of "YMCA." "Hit me," she said, before Cassie could ask what the hell she was doing.

"What?"

"Get some paint on your brush and throw it at me."

Cassie hesitated for a moment, eyeing Drea, then the paint.

"You might want to make it good too, because I'm up next." Somehow she managed to waggle her eyebrows even underneath the goggles.

That was enough to get Cassie over the hump. She dunked her brush into the neon pink paint and flung it like a baseball pitch at Drea. A wet thud sounded as paint slammed into Drea's chest and across her face and left arm.

Cassie paused, wide-eyed, teetering on the edge of exhilaration and the feeling of having done something bad. But damn, it felt good to be bad.

Drea grinned, her white teeth shining through pink paint. "That all you got?"

The challenge in her voice and the dare in her eyes hit the competitive part of Cassie and she went all in, slinging color after color, even two brushes at once. When she finally reached a point of completion, her breath ragged and heart racing, Drea stepped away from the canvas and they surveyed the scene.

Bright pinks, blues, greens, and yellows filled nearly every inch of the canvas except for the negative space where Drea had stood. The androgynous human left behind with splayed limbs exuded power, strength, and something else. Cassie stared at the arms raised defiantly to the sky. Joy.

Drea turned to her, and up close Cassie realized how drenched she was in paint. It started as a small laugh that took on a church giggles kind of fervor. Drea posed with her hands on her hips as Cassie tried to stop, but it turned into a hiccup, causing her to laugh harder.

When she finally caught her breath, Drea smiled at her. "Feel better?"

She nodded with a grin still fixed to her lips, biting back any further laughter.

Drea grabbed a fresh brush and held it up. "Good." She looked down at the brush and slowly dragged her finger along the bristles. The air stilled and a shock of heat ripped through Cassie, causing her grin to falter. Drea's eyes met hers in one of the sexiest looks Cassie had ever received, only to somehow turn even sexier as a slow smirk spread across her lips. Cassie swallowed but couldn't look away as Drea cocked an eyebrow. "Because you're next."

All heat dissipated from Cassie's body in an instant, and she gulped for an entirely different reason.

No matter how much Drea had scrubbed in the shower, she kept finding specks of paint on her body and in her hair. She scratched at a spot of green on her arm then poured herself a large mug of black chicory coffee to prepare for the long day to come.

She started to walk to her bedroom but paused to look at the river along the way as she sipped her coffee. Gray clouds threatened the horizon, but a peaceful blue stretched across the rest of the sky. She checked the weather again on her phone. Still a 15 percent chance of rain. She and Cassie had come up with a plan B in case the courtyard couldn't be used due to weather, but the courtyard was definitely the better option, so she hoped for everyone's sake that the weather cooperated.

Pickles followed her to the bedroom, hopping up the two steps to the raised floor. She stopped in front of the three panels, trying to see them as objectively as she could. "What do you think, Señor Pickles? Think they'll like it?"

He rubbed his chin against her shin and purred.

"I hope you're right."

She put her mug on the desk and started preparing the panels for the drive to the venue. As she wrapped each one in plastic to protect them from transport and potential weather, her mind wandered to the previous day.

Cassie had seemed almost like the woman she had come to know before Molly's world blew up. It had been nice to see her smile and laugh again, both of which had been pretty rare in the previous weeks. And as Drea intended, the painting experience had piqued Cassie's competitive spirit, something Drea hadn't seen since their pool game, as well as provided both of them with an avenue to release some pent-up stress.

But the thing that had stayed in her mind all night was the drive home, or rather the arrival at Cassie's place. Though there had been some banter and healthy tension between them at the event, as they sat in the car outside Cassie's place, it seemed to occur to both of them that it felt an awful lot like the end of a date. It was probably Drea's fault, which was typical. They had been out alone together before, doing stuff for the different weddings, but there was always a bigger purpose to those situations. This was the first time they had gone out just for fun.

Cassie had looked adorable if she was being honest. Maybe for the first time ever, her bright purple lipstick was the minor character amid a cornucopia of brilliant colors. Her hair even matched. It was like a palette had finally met its muse.

Drea had been in plenty of scenarios with women before and she had always risen to the occasion, finding exactly what they needed when they needed it, no questions asked. And no expectations afterward. But this was different. It always seemed to be that way where Cassie was concerned. Something had held her back. A feeling deep in her chest held her captive, paralyzed from doing anything that would come so naturally in a similar situation.

Cassie had ended the awkwardness first by opening the door, allowing Drea to take a breath of air for the first time in what felt like hours. And Drea was ready to speed the hell out of there, but Cassie reminded her about the centerpieces and altar, so they pretended to be normal as the awkwardness continued until they had loaded Drea's car. Then another quick and awkward goodbye.

It reminded her of high school, before she had honed her skills with women, and before she had written off the possibility of a future with one. She shook the thought from her mind and checked her watch. She had to get to the wedding venue. It was time for two people who did believe in love to start their future together.

Chapter 14

"All right, boss. Where do you want these?"

Cassie turned at the sound of Drea's voice. Just one day could Drea not look effortlessly beautiful? T-shirt and jeans? Sexy. Cold out and add a leather biker jacket? Sexier. Rip in the shirt because even your shirt can't take the heat? Forget about it. She tried to shake off her inner monologue and glanced down at the plastic-wrapped frames in Drea's hands. "Is that the painting?"

Drea nodded. "Yes, ma'am. As requested."

She clutched the clipboard to her chest. "Oh, I can't wait to see it. You can go ahead and hang it in the original location."

Drea saluted and headed to the courtyard.

After Cassie spoke with the chair rental people and answered a call from Jody, she joined Drea to see the grand reveal.

As soon as she stepped into the courtyard, the grandeur of the feature took her breath away. "Oh my god."

Drea finished securing the last panel to the wall and watched as Cassie approached the painting. "I hope that's a good 'oh my god.'"

Cassie pointed at each of the elements, in awe at the level of detail up close. "You got the steamboat and the bridge and, oh my gosh," she looked at Drea, "is that them?"

Drea nodded with a grin.

She couldn't believe it. She had seen a little bit of Drea's artistic talent that night at the office, and of course all of her abilities with graphic design work for different clients, but this was something else. It reminded her of Van Gogh, and the only word she could come up with was art. It was true art. Drea had created an elaborate, inviting evening river cruise scene that took her breath away. The three-story steamboat spanned the left and middle panels, with the warm glow of lights dancing on the blue water below as beautiful purples and blues filled the sky at dusk. The illuminated bridge spanned the middle and right panels, with the city's skyline in the background. But beyond the landscape, Cassie was captivated by the details, right down to the water spraying off the paddle wheel and the two women silhouetted on the bow's top level. The more she looked, the more she saw.

"Drea, I knew it would be good, but I had no idea it would be this good." She shook her head in wonder. "They're going to love this. You captured . . . everything."

Drea stood up and joined her as they looked at the painting. "I think it came out all right."

"I wish you did more of this style. I would love to see this perspective for some of our campaigns."

"I've tried. People like what they know."

She was about to argue her point, but Drea gave her a once-over. "I must say, you look decidedly less colorful today."

Cassie felt a tingle in her stomach at the weight of Drea's eyes on her. "Then my goal has been achieved. That paint did not want to go away."

Drea leaned closer and wiped at a spot by her hairline. The closeness and intimacy of the touch made her lose her train of thought. "There, you had one last hanger-on."

"Thanks." God, why did she let herself feel things when they meant nothing to someone like Drea? She felt like a schoolgirl with a silly crush, and of course the crush was aloof and devastatingly sexy. And apparently an incredible artist. And a player. That last point always ended the fantasy abruptly. Cassie surveyed the clipboard in her hands, trying to get her mind right and prioritize the next tasks to complete. There was no time to be sidetracked by thoughts of Drea. "Do you need help with the altar?"

"No, I've got it. I'm sure you've got a ton of other stuff to do." Drea glanced to the sky. "You think the weather will hold out?"

Cassie clocked the clouds in the distance for what felt like the millionth time. "I sincerely hope so. If not, we're going to have to scramble."

"We'll make it work. Off to the altar." Drea took half a step and stopped. "I meant off to get the altar."

Cassie smiled at the seriousness in her voice. "I know." She looked at the painting again. Work like this belonged in the company's campaigns. If Drea doubted her own skills, that was fine. But it didn't mean Cassie couldn't advocate for her. A half-formed idea brought a smile to her face before she turned back to the wedding tasks.

Drea finished placing the centerpiece. She had two more left to carry in when Katherine and Nellie came running over.

"Drea, we can't thank you enough," Nellie said. "The painting is epic. It's not much, but we wanted to give you something to thank you for it." Katherine held out a white envelope.

Drea put her hands up in the air as if it was a gun. "Absolutely not. That's my gift to you."

"It would make us happy if you took it," Katherine said.

"How about you put it toward your honeymoon instead?" They hesitated. "Go on and get ready; you've got a wedding in less than an hour."

"Well, thank you." Nellie gave her a hug and they scurried off to get changed.

"That was nice of you."

She turned at the sound of Cassie's voice a few feet away. A tingle of joy crept through her body at the sight of Cassie. Something about this wedding made her feel like they were a team, and for once in her life that thought didn't bother her. "It happens occasionally."

"I'd say more than occasionally."

Drea leaned toward her and whispered, "Shh, don't tell anyone."

Cassie smiled, but it didn't fully reach her eyes. She leaned against the table, probably out of exhaustion, but there was something sexy about it too.

"Everything okay?" Drea asked.

"I think so. We'll find out soon enough." Cassie looked toward the entryway and Drea followed her eyes to the guests starting to arrive.

"It will be fine," Drea said. She wanted to reach out and comfort Cassie. To wipe away her stress.

"I'll be glad when I don't have to plan any more weddings. But first, I want this to be everything they dreamed of and more."

The thought of not working on any more weddings together sent a pain through Drea's chest. There was a connection between her and Cassie that didn't fully translate to the office dynamic, and the thought of losing that inspired a wave of melancholy that took her by surprise. She forced a smile, not wanting to show the emotion to Cassie or stress her any further. "I have a feeling it will be."

Cassie nodded but didn't seem convinced. "We probably should go change. You need help with anything?"

"I'm grabbing the last centerpieces now and then I'm done."

"OK." Cassie raised her eyebrows. "See you on the other side."

Cassie eyed the decadent slice of chocolate cake taunting her from Drea's plate. "Can I try a bite of that?"

Drea slid her plate closer to Cassie. "Go for it."

"Do you want to try mine? It's coffee and chocolate."

"Can't go wrong with that," Drea said and loaded a bite onto her fork.

They both tasted their samples as they watched each other, then narrowed their eyes.

"I think I like yours better," Cassie said.

"Ditto." Drea slid her plate fully in front of Cassie and grabbed the chicory coffee slice for herself. "Problem solved."

"I like the way you think," Cassie said through another bite.

"Excuse me, ladies." Cassie turned her attention to the gray-haired man in a three-piece suit, but his focus was on Drea. "I was told you're the one responsible for that painting installation outside."

"That's right. What can I help you with?" Drea asked.

"My name's Byron Ledbetter and I run NOLA Travel and Tours. I was really taken with your painting and style. If you have some time next week, I'd love to chat about creating an installation like that for our lobby, and using it in some marketing pieces as well."

"Sure, we could chat about it. We actually work for a marketing firm." Drea gestured between herself and Cassie.

Byron nodded toward Cassie. "Wonderful. Here, take my card, and let's set something up for all three of us."

Cassie turned toward Drea after he left. "I totally manifested that for you."

"You don't say?"

"I do say."

Drea held her gaze, and if it had been anyone other than

Drea, Cassie would have said they were flirting.

"Well, I owe it all to you then." Drea said playfully as she took another bite of cake.

Cassie glanced at the centerpiece. She had lost some skin cells to the glue gun making these, but the effect was worth it as they provided an inviting sense of autumn to the reception. She allowed herself a moment of pride as she scanned the room, taking in the smiling brides, the couples on the dance floor, the upbeat music matching the jovial mood among the guests. She had done it. The brides were happy, the guests were happy, and she hadn't let Molly down. She took in a deep breath and let it out, releasing stress she hadn't realized she'd been carrying all this time.

"Would you like to dance?"

A woman with a short, styled haircut and a vest open over a white dress shirt and tie smiled down at her.

Cassie hesitated for a moment. It had been a while since a stranger had asked her to dance, but the woman had kind eyes, so she took her hand. "Sure." She glanced back at Drea, feeling a small sense of sadness to be pulled away from her and wishing it was Drea leading her to the dance floor, but Drea seemed unaffected as she raised her glass in the air in an unrequited cheer.

The love ballad seemed a mismatch for a first dance with a total stranger, but Cassie danced anyway and learned that the woman's name was Nicole and she was a friend of Katherine's. When the ballad transitioned into a dance beat, Nicole asked if she'd like to continue and since she was enjoying herself, she decided she might as well.

"Sounds like it's going to pour."

"What?" Cassie asked.

Nicole leaned closer. "I said it sounds like it's going to pour."

As she said the words, Cassie heard the thunder rumbling outside. She glanced at Drea's seat, but it was empty. "Excuse me," she said as she sprinted to the courtyard to save the painting before the rain came. She found Drea squatting next to the far right panel, unsecuring the fasteners as quickly as she could.

"What can I do?"

"Take them inside as I get them off." Drea handed her the right panel. "Here."

Cassie walked as fast as she could while being careful not to damage the painting and leaned it against the wall in the entryway. Drea had the second panel ready by the time she returned. She felt a couple of cold raindrops hit her head as she rushed it inside. *Shit.*

"Do you have an umbrella?" she asked the staff member at the front desk.

He handed her one and she sprinted to the courtyard, the raindrops coming down more steadily as she reached Drea.

Cassie held the umbrella over the painting and Drea as she undid the last fastener and they rushed inside together.

"I'll be right back," Drea said and ran back to the courtyard.

Cassie dropped the umbrella and scanned the panels, a wave of gratitude filling her when she saw that they hadn't been damaged.

A clap of thunder shook the building as the sky opened up. Drea was still out there, so Cassie ran out and found her removing the screws from the altar.

"What are you doing?" she shouted.

"I'm almost done. Don't ruin your dress out here."

"Drea, it's just an altar. Leave it here."

Drea kept trying for another minute, but it wasn't budging.

Cassie grabbed her hand. "Come on." She pulled Drea up and they ran inside and fell against the wall. They stared at each other for a moment, chests heaving as they tried to catch their breath, then burst into laughter.

Drea looked up and down at Cassie and frowned. "Your dress."

She glanced down at the hunter-green off-the-shoulder dress that was decidedly more clingy than when she started the evening. She shrugged. "It's just a dress."

Her eyes traveled down Drea's body, noticing for the first time that her white dress shirt was nearly translucent underneath the form-fitting black jacket, revealing a black bra. Sexy thoughts raced through her mind before she could shake them and when she raised her eyes to Drea's, the expression she found there seemed to know it. She was close enough to touch. The smallest of gestures would close the gap. Drea held her gaze, her chest still rising and falling as her breathing returned to normal. Cassie warred with her thoughts: the typical measured, reliable Cassie who warned her to stay away from Drea because it could never mean anything more than a good time, and the wild, unreserved Cassie who left others in her dust and chased her dreams no matter the stakes. But as she looked into Drea's eyes, she didn't see a player, only depths of emotion she would wade through for the rest of her life if given the chance. A light tremor ran through Drea's body. On instinct, Cassie raised her hand and moved a wet strand of curls off Drea's cheek.

"You're shaking," she said.

"So are you."

She hadn't even noticed. She placed her palm along Drea's cheek, but couldn't decipher the expression in those deep blue eyes. There was a calmness to Drea, but a myriad of emotions seemed to swirl within. Cassie's eyes dropped to Drea's full lips, and all thoughts ceased as she leaned closer, wanting nothing more than to feel Drea's lips on hers. All of the things that had held her back were gone. It was just her and Drea, their lips inches apart as they looked into each other's eyes.

"Here, ladies. Take these towels. You're soaked."

Cassie started at the voice behind her but held on a moment longer, not wanting it to end, whatever it was, unsure if she'd ever experience another moment like it. Finally, she lowered her hand, blinking back all the emotions racing through her, and turned to the man from the front desk, who handed her and Drea each a fluffy white towel.

Chapter 15

"I'm gonna eat this so hard." Cassie stared at her white chocolate bread pudding pancakes in their gooey, warm goodness, deciding which bite to take first.

Janay laughed. "Girl, I can feel the sugar coma just looking at that."

Cassie loaded a forkful and held it up to her. "Want a bite?"

"Nah, I'm good." Janay speared a piece of shrimp and ran it through some buttery grits while Cassie tasted the first bite of her pancakes.

She closed her eyes as cinnamon, sugar, and white chocolate bready deliciousness commingled on her taste buds, and did a happy dance in her chair. The restaurant was filled with people, and Cassie took a moment to enjoy the cacophony of conversations and laughter in the space. She had hurdled all of the wedding planning and finally had free time to herself again, and brunch was a first step in filling that time with people and experiences that rejuvenated rather than drained her.

"So, how was the wedding?" Janay asked.

Cassie smiled as she remembered the touching ceremony, the beautiful decorations, and the joy and laughter at the reception.

"It went surprisingly well. Everything worked out, thankfully."

"That's awesome. I'm proud of you." Janay sipped her mimosa but kept her eyes on Cassie. "And what about Drea?"

Something must have passed through Cassie's eyes to tip her off.

Janay's face lit up. "Did she kiss you?"

"No-o-o." She dragged out the word trying to figure out how to explain the thing that had kept her up all night.

"Girl, spill."

Cassie rested her elbows on the wood table and dropped her face into her hands for a moment. "I don't know. My mind has been spinning all night."

Janay's eyes widened. "Is it bad? Like sexy bad?" She waggled her eyebrows.

"Yes."

Janay's mouth dropped open.

"And no."

And then it closed.

"Wha-at hap-pened?" She dragged out the words for emphasis. "You're driving me nuts."

"Everything was going good. Like better-than-I-could-have-hoped-for good. And then I was dancing with this girl."

Janay's eyebrows rose as she tilted her head.

"No, not like that . . . I mean, she was attractive and nice, but no."

Janay's face scrunched up like that information didn't add up, but motioned for her to continue.

"And then it was thundering and the painting was outside."

"What painting?" Janay asked and took another sip of her mimosa.

"Oh my god, there was this blank wall in the courtyard where the ceremony was so Drea painted this incredibly beautiful three-panel piece that covered the wall but was also this amazing homage to how the brides met. You have to see it.

It's really something."

"Wow, okay, go on."

"The painting was outside, so I ran out there and helped Drea get the panels inside, but she went back for the altar and we were out there soaked, um . . ." Cassie's words faltered as she remembered how devastatingly sexy Drea had looked in her suit, staring at her as water from her rain-drenched hair ran down her cheek.

"Shit, sorry. Where was I?"

Janay shook her head with a huge grin. "You were soaked . . ."

"Right. So I grabbed her hand—because the altar wasn't coming down anytime soon and it was freezing, you know, so . . ."

Janay rolled her hand in a circle . . . to keep it moving.

"So, right, um, we ran inside and we were laughing and wet and cold and she was just, like, looking at me with this, I don't know, intensity and calm, but also emotion that I couldn't place, and I'm staring at this incredibly beautiful woman who makes the word sexy seem so woefully inept to encapsulate what she truly is. And, you know me . . ."

Janay nodded, her eyes wide as she hung on every word.

"I'm responsible and do the right thing . . . now. So, of course I couldn't act on anything."

Janay frowned.

Cassie tilted her head and continued. "But then there's this other part that, you know, doesn't always do the right thing, and Drea was cold, so I put my hand on her cheek, and . . ."

"And?"

"It was odd, like I stepped out of my body and my thoughts telling me no and all I wanted to do was . . ."

"What?" Janay's voice couldn't hide her enthusiasm.

"Kiss her. So I leaned in and . . ."

"Oh my god, you're killing me. What happened? You kissed Drea Cordeira?" Janay's eyes were wider than Cassie had ever seen them.

"And the front desk guy gave us towels."

Janay slumped back in her chair with her hands up and a *don't even* look on her face. "You're telling me that you're both soaked, staring into each other's eyes, and you leap out of your body to place your hand on her cheek and lean into her, and neither of you kiss each other?"

Cassie grimaced and nodded. Hearing it back again definitely made it sound worse.

"Like Drea, right? This is Dre-a," she pointed her finger to the sky with each syllable, "on the other side of this moment, and no one gets kissed?"

There wasn't air to even form words to respond. She put her hands up in a half shrug and continued shaking her head until something occurred to her that sank her heart. She slumped in her chair as it all added up. "She's not into me."

"She's been helping you for over a month with this wedding stuff?"

Cassie nodded.

"And you gave her an out and she chose to continue?"

Cassie nodded.

"And did she look away when you stared into her eyes?"

"No." The words were barely a whisper.

"Did she move away when you placed your hand on her cheek?"

Cassie shook her head.

"What about when you leaned into her?"

Cassie shook her head again.

"Then girl, she's into you." Janay took a bite of food as if the problem had been solved.

As much as Cassie wanted to dismiss it, Janay made some good points. When she had asked Drea why she kept helping her despite hating weddings, her answer had been sincere and surprising. But Cassie had assumed it meant she felt bad for her. Or wanted someone to banter with at work again. But last night she had felt it. There had been something between them. She hadn't been looked at like that in a long time, maybe ever. But she had acted on it. Not Drea, who always got the girl. That was the piece she couldn't explain. Why hadn't Drea made a move?

"So, what are you gonna do about it?" Janay asked.

"We work together, Janay. It's complicated. What if I'm wrong and then it's awkward at work?" She took a moment to think about how much that would suck. "This is the first job where I feel like I'm seen and my boss has my back. I can't put that in jeopardy."

"But what if you're right?"

"Drea's not the relationship type. You know that. I know that. Every queer and questioning woman in New Orleans knows that. Probably some straight ones, too. Would it be a fun time? An incredible night?" She nodded and closed her eyes at the agony of the fantasy of it, which she knew didn't come close to the reality of what being with Drea would be like. She opened her eyes to see Janay watching her with raised brows. "Yes, god yes. But that would be it. And I'd have to sit there across from her every day, just like I do now, except I'd know what every inch of her body looks like underneath those clothes and how her skin feels against mine, how devastating her kiss is, and don't get me started on those eyes."

"So, you've thought about it?" Janay grinned.

Cassie tilted her head. "A little." She jammed another bite of pancake into her mouth, but even that couldn't quench the want coursing through her veins. "You know I'm not built that way. I tried it, but I need more than a fun night." She shook her head, trying to convince herself as well. "Drea sleeps with women. I just work with her. And now that the weddings are over, that's all we'll do."

Janay shrugged. "Okay. If you say so."

"I do."

Drea sipped her coffee, trying to avoid looking in Cassie's direction, as if her work required ultimate focus for once. She tapped the screen of her tablet and added a bold purple to the design, which only reminded her of Cassie. Delete.

She was a little apprehensive about talking to Cassie after the situation Saturday night. That's what she had been calling it. The situation. She thought Cassie might act weird around her. After all, she had put herself out there and Drea had stood there like an idiot. She had to have felt rejected on some level, even though it wasn't her intention. Or maybe Cassie thought they had been interrupted and something would have happened otherwise. She would have been wrong, but at least it would have saved her from the feeling of rejection. Since Cassie definitely wasn't acting weird around her, she assumed it was option number two, but they had been at work all morning and Cassie hadn't shown the least bit of sign that she wanted to touch base about it or continue it in any way. That was the most confusing part.

She had spent most of Sunday trying to sift through her emotions to understand what had happened the night before. But it was futile. Logic wasn't at play and she normally tried to avoid it anyway, if she could. What she did know was how hard she had had to fight herself not to kiss her. She was used to sealing the deal with women and had never faltered, but faltering was all she seemed to do with Cassie. It had taken all of her strength to resist those brown eyes searching her soul. When Cassie had raised her hand and touched Drea's cheek in a move so caring and yet sensual, Drea had nearly gritted her teeth trying to shut down all the emotions it stirred. But this was one woman she couldn't pursue. She could never be the woman Cassie needed. It wasn't in her nature anymore. She wouldn't allow it to be. Plus, she wouldn't jeopardize what Sam had built by pursuing something that was destined to fail. She had no problem finding women to be with for a fun night. So she didn't need to look for one at work.

She pulled Byron's business card out of her pocket and dialed the number.

After she arranged the details and got the address, she walked over to Cassie, who was engrossed in whatever she was typing.

"Hey."

Cassie pulled her attention from the computer screen. "Hey. What's up?"

She searched for an inflection in her tone or some clue in her eyes that something had transpired between them, but found only openness. "I just got off the phone with Byron."

"Oh yeah?"

"He can meet with us on Thursday right after work if you're free. His office is off of Canal Street."

"That works for me. Thanks." And with a smile she was back to typing away.

Drea walked to the break area and poured a fresh cup of coffee. She stared out at the river wondering what had changed in two days. And how was she the only one affected by the other night?

"Great to see you both again," Byron said. Cassie waited as he shook Drea's hand, then her own. He looked dapper in another three-piece suit, herringbone this time, and Cassie surmised that it was his characteristic look, not just wedding attire. A scent of woodsy pine permeated the air, which she thought was a nice touch both as a cologne and as a nod to the season.

Byron ran his hand through his graying hair and gestured to a wall with large black-and-white photographs of the river hanging above a brown leather sofa. "This is where we'd like to put your painting."

Drea nodded and seemed to be sizing up the space.

Cassie scanned the room, taking in the matching brown leather chairs, and felt as if she had stumbled into a Pottery Barn. While it was inviting enough, the only nod to the city was the few pieces of artwork on the walls. It struck her as odd for a business focused on the sights and experiences of the city.

They followed him to his office and she breathed a sigh of relief. Jazz Fest posters adorned the walls alongside crawfish knickknacks scattered on the bookcase and desk. Whatever the lobby lacked, at least the office filled the gap.

Byron chatted with Drea about the painting for the lobby, but when he brought up incorporating it into marketing pieces, she seemed less enthused.

He turned to Cassie. "You said y'all work at a marketing firm, right? What's the name?"

"That's correct. Crescent City Marketing," Cassie said.

He glanced at the ceiling as if trying to place it in his mind. "That doesn't ring a bell."

"Samantha Parker founded the company earlier this year. She and I both worked for a number of years at McGrady Marketing."

Recognition hit. "Ah, okay. Do you think your firm could take on this workload? We'd like to do a few print ad designs and we have a feature coming up in *NOLA Magazine*, but they'd need everything by mid-January, which I know is asking a lot." He turned to Drea. "Of both of you."

"Absolutely. It is a tight turnaround, but we can make it happen," Cassie said, then turned to Drea. "How long would you need to get the artwork completed?"

"I can get it done in a week."

Something seemed off to Cassie. Drea seemed subdued, but she wasn't sure why. She had been fine when they arrived.

"Outstanding. Should we meet the same time next week to see it and discuss next steps?"

"Sounds great," Cassie said. She and Drea stood and shook hands with Byron again.

"I can't wait to see what you come up with, Drea," Byron said.

"I hope it's what you're looking for," Drea replied, but her tone didn't match the smile on her face.

"I can assure you it will exceed your expectations," Cassie said, trying not to let her concern for Drea's behavior influence her own words. Drea turned to her with a curious expression. "Drea's artistic style will turn some heads and add some lagniappe to your mission. It will definitely stand out in the best way possible."

Byron nodded enthusiastically. "Lagniappe. I like it."

Once outside, they walked along the sidewalk to Canal Street as the ding of the streetcar rang out. Night had fallen while they'd been inside and Cassie tightened her scarf to buffer the cold. As they turned the corner on Canal, Cassie paused at the sight before her. The palm trees lining the streetcar tracks down the middle of the road were wrapped in white lights. Each streetlamp had lights spiraling up its pole along with a wreath and bow at the top. Garlands and bows even adorned the front of the red and green streetcars. A large Christmas tree was all lit up on the balcony of one of the more upscale hotels lining the street. Though Christmas had lost a lot of its appeal over the years, she still could be swept away by the lights, and for that she was grateful.

She became increasingly aware of eyes on her and turned to see Drea watching her with a smile. "This never gets old, ya know?" Cassie said.

Drea took it in for a moment, but it didn't seem to please her in the same way. Something still seemed to be off.

"You okay?" Cassie asked, though she doubted Drea would

tell her what was going on.

"Yeah." Drea looked at her watch and Cassie prepared for her to call it a night. All week she had tried to put her feelings aside, but she missed the time they spent together outside of work. "You want to get something to eat?"

Surprised, but thrilled, Cassie didn't hesitate. "Sure," she said, trying not to sound too eager.

"Here you go," the waiter said as he placed their orders on the table. They'd chosen an upscale café along Canal Street, and Cassie had asked for a booth by the window so she could look at the holiday lights. Drea watched people scurrying by, probably on their way home from work or to the store for holiday shopping. She wanted to get in the holiday mood, but she was bothered by Cassie's comments to Byron about her art.

They had chatted about the weather and the decorations while they waited for their food, but Drea couldn't avoid the one question running through her mind any longer. "Why are you so supportive of my art?" she blurted.

Surprise flashed across Cassie's face. Drea felt bad for being so blunt, but she had to know.

Cassie finished chewing her catfish. "Because you're good and I don't know why you're not selling it all over the place."

Drea thought of her first few years after art school, how hopeful she had been that she would hit it big and actually be able to support herself with her art. So foolish. "I tried. People didn't take to it as much as you do."

"Well, their loss. Some people have no taste." Cassie grinned and sipped her iced tea.

"You laid it on pretty thick back there with Byron." She needed to know why Cassie had championed her work so hard. She sipped her Malbec and watched Cassie's face, waiting for a response.

A serious expression eclipsed Cassie's playful tone, a sizzle of heat behind it. "I meant every word."

The blind belief confused Drea. She knew she had skill as an artist, but she also knew that didn't amount to much in a city full of artists. She hadn't experienced someone so daringly supportive before. There was no hesitation. If she had heard Cassie's words earlier, she would have believed the conviction in her voice and wondered how soon she could see this extraordinary artist's work. But knowing it was her Cassie spoke of, something didn't compute.

"You've only seen one of my pieces. How could you be so sure of my abilities?" At Cassie's raised brow, she amended, "As an artist."

"I believe someone told me once that you were good with your hands."

The line was so cheesy Drea couldn't help but grin and roll her eyes. "I am known for that, you're right. Not only for that, of course. I have skills with other features as well."

"Interesting. Do you hold the brush in your mouth or something?"

"Something like that."

"Good to know." The reflection of holiday lights sparkled in Cassie's eyes as she tried to hide a grin by taking another bite. Drea had missed their banter. Though they had spent a lot of time together after work with all of the wedding preparations, an undercurrent of stress and exhaustion had limited the fun in their interactions. Cassie seemed relaxed again and clearly a bit playful. Drea's thoughts leapt to the hand on her cheek, and she turned to the window before Cassie could see the shift in her expression.

"Also, not true," Cassie said.

Drea knew her mind had wandered a little, but she had no idea what Cassie was referring to. "What?"

"I haven't seen only one of your pieces. I've seen two." Drea tried to think of what other piece she could be referring to, but was at a loss. "That night at work by the printer. You did that watercolor design for The Well, which you never pitched." Cassie gave a weak imitation of a stern expression.

"I—" Drea floundered, at a loss for words.

"Actually three," Cassie interrupted her. At Drea's confused expression, she continued, "The tugboat on the water."

Right, she had forgotten about that one. She hadn't shown that painting to anyone and remembered being a little shocked she had let Cassie see it. "I never intended," Drea said, before cutting herself off again. After Anna died, Drea painted it to cope with her grief. Initially, it symbolized her helping Sam through those dark times, trying to see and move toward light in the future, but they actually exchanged roles during that period, Sam never knowing how much her strength to continue on kept Drea going as well. In many ways, it reflected their entire friendship. Always being there for each other, through thick and thin. Drea's heart felt heavy as she thought about how little time she and Sam had spent together outside of work since Sam met Ash. The fact that she had shared the painting with Cassie and that she hadn't judged was yet another thing that blew her mind where Cassie was concerned.

"Sorry, you never intended what?" Cassie asked.

Drea sorted through her thoughts to remember what she was going to say. "I never intended to pitch that design."

Cassie held her gaze for a long moment, so Drea took a sip of wine as she waited. "Why is that?"

"Because I tried it at my last position. Didn't go over well. So I decided to keep my art separate from my work." She shrugged.

"But your art is your work."

"No." She shook her head. "Graphic design involves some artistic principles, but it's definitely not my art."

Cassie's shoulders slumped. "Is that why you were so weird with Byron?"

"I was weird?"

"Weirder than normal, yes."

Drea laughed.

Cassie shook her head as a blush appeared on her cheeks. "No, I mean, you're not weird at all normally. You seemed resistant to the idea of using your painting for the marketing pieces."

"Ah. Yeah, I didn't realize you noticed that."

"I notice a lot of things." The heat in Cassie's eyes was undeniable, and Drea felt they were both thinking of the other night.

Drea dropped her gaze and scooped up a spoonful of gumbo, needing a break from her thoughts. She let it warm her as the complexity of flavor hit every taste bud she had, finishing with a spicy kick.

Cassie continued. "Does it bother you that I think you're talented and want other people to see what I see?"

Drea sat back and slowly twirled her wine glass on the table. "Bother me? No. It's just not something I'm used to."

"People thinking you're talented?"

Drea grinned as her mind drifted to her other talents. Flirting was her default mode for avoiding tough conversations.

It didn't work. "I meant at art," Cassie quickly added.

Drea tilted her head to applaud the catch. "Talented wasn't the primary descriptor. Or any descriptor."

"What was?" Cassie asked with curiosity.

"Frivolous, a waste of time . . . disappointing, and so on."

"Your parents?" Cassie's voice was gentle.

"Yeah. They're both doctors and into appearances. Me going to art school . . ." She mentally flipped through the other parts of herself they had disapproved of—her style, her friends, her humor, her profession, and definitely her sexuality, or at least the way she utilized it. "Actually, they pretty much disapprove of everything I am."

"I'm sorry." The sincerity in Cassie's voice tugged at her heart.

She shrugged and sipped her wine, letting the alcohol numb the memories. She hated talking about her family. Nothing was going to change that relationship now, and it definitely was never going to improve. She just wanted to change the subject. "It is what it is. What about you? Were your parents supportive of your dreams?"

Cassie's smile disappeared as if she'd seen a ghost.

Drea felt awful for being so insensitive. "I'm sorry," she said. "You don't have to answer that."

Cassie pushed the hair off her forehead. "No, it's fine. Really. Well, my dream was to be a ballet dancer." She paused and waited for Drea's response.

Drea raised her eyebrows. Images flashed through her mind of disciplined and regimented women wearing tights and tutus with their hair up in a bun. Whereas, Cassie. Well, Cassie was pretty far from that. "Wow, I didn't expect that." Cassie never ceased to surprise her.

"Yep, I get that a lot." She laughed. "We went to a performance of *The Nutcracker* when I was six and I fell in love. I was so into it, though I didn't have the height or much at all that people associate with ballerinas. But my mom saw how much I wanted it and she took me to every practice and recital. She made sure to get out of work whenever I had a performance."

Her whole face lit up when she talked about it. Drea tried to picture a young Cassie in a tutu, but she couldn't quite envision it.

"I used to get really nervous before performances. My mom came backstage one time and saw me breathing heavy and starting to freak out. She held my hands and had me take a deep breath in and blow it out and by the third time, I was fine. The next day, she put a rubber band on my wrist and told me if I ever felt overwhelmed to hold onto it and breathe." She glanced at her wrist. "When I was in college, I replaced it with a tattoo."

"What does it say?"

Cassie pulled the sleeve of her sweater up and angled her wrist across the table so Drea could see. Drea placed her hand underneath Cassie's wrist to hold it steady. *Breathe* was written in a delicate cursive across her fair skin. So that was what Cassie had been doing at the Thanksgiving dinner and when she talked about her parents that night at her house. It made Drea sad to realize she had felt so overwhelmed in those moments. She couldn't imagine how hard it must have been for Cassie to lose her mom at such a young age, especially being that close.

"Your mom sounds pretty amazing," Drea said with a gentle smile as she released Cassie's wrist.

Cassie smiled. "She was."

Drea suddenly had a great idea. She did a quick search on her phone, then turned her attention back to Cassie, smiling.

Cassie must have seen something devious in Drea's expression because she leaned back cautiously. "What?"

Drea tried to control the excitement in her voice. "Are you free on Saturday? There's something I'd like to show you."

Chapter 16

Drea stood on the red carpet under the Orpheum Theater's marquee, trying to stay warm as she waited. This was either going to be okay, maybe even good, or a total bust. Either way, she was excited to spend more time with Cassie and hoped she hadn't overstepped. She saw Cassie's hair before the rest of her, a flash of brilliance against the gray day, though she took a moment to appreciate the rest of her as she approached in a red calf-length wool coat with large black buttons down to her knees. It was something she had noticed about Cassie over the last few months. There was a brightness to her beyond the bold lipstick and colorful hair and even the pops of color she had begun to associate as Cassie's style. She knew Cassie had been through some tough times in her past, but she led with optimism. Drea was known for her humor, for better or worse, but optimism had always eluded her.

"Are we doing what I think we're doing?" Cassie asked, and Drea couldn't tell from her tone if it was a good or bad reaction.

"That's up to you. *The Nutcracker* is playing. I haven't seen it since my parents dragged me here when I was a kid, but I thought it might be cool to see it again if you—"

"Yes!" Cassie did a little dance of joy on the sidewalk.

Drea laughed. Why was Cassie's happiness suddenly so contagious? A lightness filled Drea as Cassie bounced with barely contained excitement.

"Come on!" Cassie linked her arm in Drea's and nearly ran to the main doors.

Drea could only smile. She wasn't even bothered by the bold move.

They found their seats at the front of the balcony just right of center stage. Cassie took off her coat, and the sage cap-sleeve lace bodice underneath tipped its hat so well to lingerie that Drea's mouth went dry. A funky purple belt accentuated Cassie's waist before the dress flared at the bottom. As Cassie settled into her seat and crossed her legs, Drea caught a glimpse of brown leather boots with laces extending as far as she could see. Damn it. Sexy boots were Drea's kryptonite. She glanced around the theater trying to get her mind on anything else. Massive burgundy curtains concealed the stage below an intricately carved sign that read "Orpheum," which reminded her of the sculptures on Mardi Gras floats. The opulence struck her. Though she had hated going to stuffy places with her parents, being here with Cassie allowed her to see it in a new light. Not as a place to be seen, but as a place to appreciate art and culture. Her eyes drifted up to the ceiling where a huge dome light that could best be described as a huge boob stared back at her. She glanced around to find it surrounded by a bunch of smaller boobs. *What the . . . ?*

"What are you looking at?"

Cassie's expression was so innocent, she figured there was no way that trying to explain it would come out right. But it wasn't only her, right? Were other people seeing this? "Oh, just checking out the scenery."

"It's pretty impressive, huh? I never got to perform in as nice a theater as this, but I always loved the grandeur, even the musty smell, when I went to see shows in fancy theaters."

She hadn't noticed the musty smell because the scent of

Cassie's lavender perfume had enveloped her senses ever since they sat down.

The lights flickered a warning and Cassie's eyes lit up. "It's starting."

A few moments later, the lights went dark and the orchestra started to play as the curtains parted, revealing an intricate set design that caught Drea's eye. Ballet dancers glided across the stage and Drea sat back in her seat at an angle so she could see Cassie's reaction. Cassie leaned forward, taking in each dancer as they moved across the stage, the intensity and wonder in her eyes pleasing Drea almost as much as the corners of her mouth twisted up in a permanent smile.

Drea recognized several of the musical pieces, a soundtrack to the holidays she had almost forgotten, and while the dancing was entertaining, especially when children joined the adults, she was as taken by the elaborate sets that she had somehow missed when watching it as a child. But the best part was seeing Cassie's delight. She was mesmerized the entire night, unable to rip her attention from the stage, even moving subtly to different pieces, which made Drea smile. When the final note rang out and the curtain closed, Drea felt a pang of sadness to see it end, more for Cassie than herself. But when Cassie turned to her, there was no sadness in her eyes, only joy and longing for a time remembered.

"Thank you," she said softly. "I can't even explain how much that meant to me."

They shuffled through the crowd, finally emptying out onto the sidewalk, the early evening darker than it should be underneath a dreary sky. She didn't want to say goodbye just yet, and Cassie seemed to feel the same as they stood awkwardly together in the cold as people bustled past.

"Would you like to walk?" Drea asked.

"Okay." Cassie smiled.

They meandered a few blocks and waited as a streetcar screeched to a stop on the tracks, the distorted voice through the speaker announcing "St. Charles Avenue."

Drea turned to Cassie. "What was up with all those kids? Is it always like that?"

Cassie laughed. "No, the playbill said over one hundred local kids were involved. I thought it was cute though."

"Is that what little Cassie was like?" She tried to imagine what Cassie might have been like as a child, but only came up with a blend of a sweet and innocent kid with bright purple hair.

Cassie seemed to ponder the question. "No, little Cassie was very serious about ballet. I think these kids were just enjoying themselves."

Drea considered that for a moment, still struggling to meld the two Cassies in her mind.

"Do you need to be anywhere?" Cassie asked.

"Not that I'm aware of. Why?" Drea plunged her hands deeper into her wool pockets, the military-inspired cut of her short coat more stylish than warm.

"I was rushing earlier today and missed lunch. Would you want to grab something to eat?"

"Sure." The thought of spending more time together warmed her. She enjoyed getting to know Cassie better, especially without work or wedding planning looming over them. As her brain tried to push her on why for the millionth time, she pushed back. She just wanted to enjoy this for what it was, a nice day with a cool woman. Couldn't that be enough?

Cassie looked around them. "I don't actually know what's good in this part of town."

"I don't live too far from here. I know a good place if you don't mind walking a few more blocks." She nodded down the road. "We can cut through the square." A gust of wind blew her hair in front of her eyes and she ran her hand through it, pushing back the unruly curls.

"Lead the way."

They cut through Lafayette Square, a few daring souls braving the cold as well, as they followed the brick path past the statues before the buildings closed in on them again. Drea stopped in front of a bustling hole-in-the-wall. The modern industrial vibe of wood and metal appealed to her. She had always resonated with the mix of natural, warm tones and steel. Inside, a wall of wine bottles hinted toward the hip, upscale scene downtown, but Drea liked the food, and despite the appearances it was one of the more casual places in the area.

The hostess showed them to a small booth and Drea shrugged out of her wool coat, glad to be out of the cold.

"Have you lived downtown long?" Cassie asked as the waiter handed them menus.

"A few years. I grew up in Uptown near Sam, and she was not happy when I decided to relocate."

"Aw, I'm sure she misses you. Y'all are pretty close, huh?"

Despite the warmth in Cassie's tone and demeanor, the question struck a nerve as Drea remembered how things used to be when they were kids, then teenagers, then adults even when she moved down here. But the past year had felt like things were turning and no matter what she tried, the momentum wasn't on her side. She nodded, not knowing what to say.

"Were you born here?" Cassie asked.

"No. Baton Rouge. We moved here when I was in middle school. That's when I stormed into Sam's life." She smiled remembering how awkward and quiet Sam had been when they first met.

Cassie smiled. "I bet you were a pair."

"When did you arrive from the North?" She rotated her hand in a grand gesture.

"At the beginning of high school. Molly and Eva thought a change of scenery might be good for us."

Drea dropped her gaze to the table, the slight change in Cassie's tone making her wish she didn't always bring up troubling memories from the past.

"It's weird," Cassie continued. "I've lived here fifteen years now, but I just have my small group of people. You seem to know a lot of people, from art school and everything." Her voice trailed off.

"I think a lot of people know of me without really knowing me, ya know?" Drea smiled, though the words were truer than she wanted to admit. Maybe that's why Cassie intrigued her so much. She seemed to see into the real Drea sometimes, no matter how hard Drea tried to keep her walls up.

"Do you wish it were different?" Cassie's tone was low and the intensity in her eyes jump-started Drea's heart rate.

Every time before this, she had known the answer was no. She had seen the disappointment on the faces of many women hoping they could change her mind and help her see the light, that they'd be the one. What they didn't get was there was no *one*. This was all there was, all she could be. But she'd done a lot of things over the past weeks she never would have done in a million years. Like throwing weddings, multiple weddings, seeing the ballet, and sitting across from this woman on what many might call a second date. And as Cassie's brown eyes penetrated her walls, she couldn't help but wonder if her answer was changing.

"What can I get you ladies?" The young man in a black half-apron held his notepad at the ready, exhibiting the magical skill of every waitperson on the planet to interrupt the conversation at the most inopportune moment. Though Drea was grateful for this particular save, not having the words for what seemed like the billionth time where Cassie was concerned, her short-lived victory lost its luster as she watched Cassie's face dim with defeat. Another nonanswer, another evaded moment. She was the master of them. And though she had seen that same reaction many times before, this was the first time it truly bothered her.

They continued the dance through the rest of dinner, toeing the edge of vulnerability before retreating once again. She wanted to know Cassie, to understand her, more than anyone in a very long time. And she couldn't explain it to herself or anyone else. Why this woman? Why now? Why did she linger in Drea's mind late at night and flit in and out throughout the day? Did it matter, though? Couldn't this be enough? To enjoy her company and feel this way without risking anything, avoiding the inevitable disappointment altogether. Maybe they could forge a different path . . . all of the good and none of the bad. Was that possible?

As they finished dinner and walked outside, thunder rumbled in the distance, and she sensed a growing turmoil in Cassie. They walked halfway down the block in silence before she stopped under the light of a nearby awning. "Hey, what is it? What's going on?"

Cassie blew out a breath. "I'm so confused right now."

"Why?" She knew the answer, but she had no idea how to navigate this for the first time in her life.

Cassie closed her eyes. "God." She bit her lip and stared down the empty street for a moment. "I feel so stupid saying this, but . . . us. This thing." She gestured between them and at the air around them. "I know you're the player of all players, and I'm probably going to ruin everything by saying this, but am I crazy?"

Drea's lips parted but no words came. Her throat was dry, her heart pounded in her chest so loud she could hear it, and all she could do was stare at this woman who had eclipsed everything in her life somehow, slowly but surely. She felt things for Cassie she hadn't ever felt before, and it scared the hell out of her. A crack of lightning struck and a soft parade of raindrops began to fall.

"I thought you hated me, then pitied me, then maybe saw me as a friend," Cassie said. She put her hands on her hips and stepped back, staring at the ground as she kicked at the concrete. "And I was fine with that," she muttered at the ground. "But this," she gestured in the direction of the theater and then the restaurant, her voice tiny as she continued, "it means something to me." There was so much hope and pain in that last word. She stared at Drea, pleading eyes turning to something darker. "I mean, is this what you do? Make women fall for you and then fuck with them? Because I feel like there should be a mob of lesbians with pitchforks following you wherever you go."

Drea would have laughed if she wasn't paralyzed by heartache and fear. With all the women before, she had flirted and charmed her way to a fun night. It was mutual and they knew what they were signing up for. And if they had illusions of other things, she charmed them out of those too. But she felt helpless with Cassie, all of her charm useless and empty when it actually mattered, with someone who mattered.

The rain fell harder, sheets of white dropping from the awning behind Cassie like snow. "Drea, what are you doing?" The anger had left her eyes. Only raw, honest emotion remained.

The simple question cut through her—through her excuses, her walls, her fear, all the years avoiding anything that would lead to a moment like this. And as she watched the emotion in Cassie's eyes, the beautiful specks of gold amidst the brown, a universe in a microcosm, everything seemed to fall away. It all seemed so clear to her now. No hesitation gripped her, only resolve.

She closed the gap between them. "What I should have done the other night."

As Cassie's eyes began to search hers, Drea took her in her arms, pulling her close as she kissed her so deeply that Cassie no longer had to ask any more questions. She would feel everything she needed to know.

Cassie wouldn't have been able to describe the short blocks

to Drea's apartment or, once inside, how exactly they moved through it. It was all a blur as they bumped into walls and tables, pausing at every surface to ravish each other, a flurry of hands and mouths battling to reach deeper. When she felt the press of the kitchen counter behind her, she shifted her focus to the wet clothes clinging to Drea's body, making her even sexier than usual. She yanked Drea's coat off her shoulders and Drea wriggled out of it as it dropped to the floor. Then she slid the charcoal gray suit jacket off to reveal a navy-blue dress shirt glued to her lithe frame. Her eyes dropped to the open buttons along her chest and the sultry expanse of silky olive skin. She paused at the sight, but Drea smashed her mouth to hers, the tempo unyielding. Drea made quick work of undoing the buttons down Cassie's coat and tossing it aside. Cassie felt her belt give way, quickly followed by the clasp at the back of her neck before Drea raised her dress up, pausing briefly for Cassie to raise her arms as she lifted it over her head. Drea stilled for a moment, her eyes raking over Cassie's body, lingering on her bright purple lingerie as a smile played on her lips. She took Cassie's hand and sat her on the arm of the sofa, kissing her as she knelt to the ground and started untying her laces and . . . kept untying her laces.

Cassie's giggle broke their kiss.

Drea looked down at the boots and laughed. "They're not exactly easy access are they?" She yanked at a few more laces and slid the first boot off, quickly followed by the second.

Cassie stood with her, needing to feel her mouth again. She took Drea's mouth in hers, lingering in the sweet deliciousness before kissing down her neck as she unbuttoned the soaked shirt, sliding it off to reveal the softest, sexiest skin she had ever felt. Drea wrapped her arms around her, pulling her close, as Cassie luxuriated in the sensation of their skin commingling. She had imagined what this might feel like, but nothing came close to the reality.

Drea kissed along her shoulder and up her neck, igniting

butterflies in Cassie's stomach; then she leaned back, lust swirling in her rich blue eyes. She ran her hand through Cassie's hair, pushing the wet strands out of her eye.

"You're so beautiful," Drea whispered.

Cassie stared deep into those eyes that had gripped her for so long. "So are you."

Drea ran her thumb along Cassie's bottom lip, and Cassie watched as her eyes grew darker. In a heartbeat, their mouths crashed together once more, their bodies following in a frenzy, as they whirled their way to the bed, bras tossed aside in the torrent. Drea laid her gently on the bed, and as she lowered her body, Cassie reveled in the magnificent weight of her, the melding of their bodies as one. Drea took her time kissing up to her ear, the tickle of her breath sending further jolts of arousal through Cassie's body. She kissed her way down Cassie's neck and chest before taking her nipple in her mouth, the glorious ache ripping a gasp from Cassie's lips. Cassie watched Drea paint a masterpiece across her skin, tangling her fingers in Drea's wild curls as she explored Cassie's body and brought her to the brink, and when she didn't think she could wait any longer, Drea moved her tongue lower, a visceral front-row seat to a repertoire of moves that took Cassie to the precipice and over, again and again, until she lay breathless and depleted, thoroughly consumed by the woman with the sexy grin climbing up beside her with an ocean of blue in those sparkling eyes.

"Hi," Drea's grin broke wide as she propped herself on her elbow.

Cassie shook her head and laughed. "Hello. You, um, definitely have some skills down there."

Drea trailed her finger along Cassie's chest as she held her gaze, and Cassie was struck by the enormity of her beauty. "Well, thank you." The southern drawl dripping from her words took the sexiness factor to another ridiculous level.

Cassie rolled onto her side, resting her cheek against her

wrist, so she could see Drea more fully. The sight of Drea's breasts quickly extinguished any exhaustion she felt, and as her eyes dropped lower, she frowned at the sight of Drea's pants.

"What's wrong?" Drea asked.

She tugged at Drea's waistband. "This." Before Drea could respond, Cassie closed the gap between them, taking Drea's mouth in hers. Drea wrapped her arms around Cassie, pulling her on top, the sensation of their breasts and hot skin together making Cassie wet again. Drea sucked on her lip and explored her mouth in ways that made Cassie feel like she had never been kissed before this day. They kissed and ground their bodies against each other until Cassie feared she might come again before exploring the beautiful woman beneath her. As if reading her mind, Drea slid her hand between them and ran her fingers in slow, luxurious circles around Cassie's clit until Cassie ripped her mouth from Drea's and buried it in her neck, fisting the covers on the verge of losing it.

"Stay with me," Drea whispered.

"I don't think I can take any more."

Drea kissed her cheek and urged her forward as she slid lower, Cassie's breath hitching as she looked down at Drea's gorgeous face between her hips. Drea locked eyes with her with one of the sexiest expressions Cassie had ever seen before taking her in her mouth. Cassie slammed her eyes shut and cried out as the sensation surged through her. Drea moved slowly and gently at first, taking her time exploring Cassie and watching her react, Cassie's hips rocking along with her rhythm. As Drea slid her fingers inside Cassie and reached up to take her breast in her other hand, Cassie slumped for a moment as sensations hit her from every erogenous zone. Drea's motions willed her back into a rhythm and Cassie rode her like that, holding her gaze as she rocked against her mouth. As Drea's tongue and fingers increased speed, the sensations climbed steeply to a crescendo until Cassie yelled out Drea's name and collapsed into a puddle.

She sat there for a moment as waves of pleasure continued to roll through her, then slid down and took Drea's head in her hands, touching her forehead to hers and kissing her cheek as she settled next to her.

She wrapped her arm around Drea's stomach and nuzzled into her neck. "You're fucking incredible. You know that, right?"

Drea's soft laughter was the only response. She put her arm around Cassie and placed a kiss on her forehead.

A while later, Cassie finally got the chance to return the favor, several times, and they rode that wave until light peaked out from behind the darkness.

Cassie woke to soft but sure fingers tracing shapes on her upper back as she lay on her stomach. She didn't move as memories from the night and morning returned and the corners of her mouth turned upward into a smile. Drea's fingers followed the lines along her back so delicately that she could feel the reverence in her touch. There was something so intimate in it that a tightness formed in her throat and she had to swallow down the intense sadness that gripped her.

This was Drea. The beautiful, charming, enigmatic woman who never went on a second date with anyone. Cassie could feel the pain of the realization in her chest as if she had been punched. She closed her eyes, willing herself to acknowledge the desire for more but accepting the beauty in this moment. This would be all there was and that would have to be enough. She would make it be enough.

She opened her eyes once more and took in everything. The morning light streaming into the bedroom, lazily waking the shadows on the bed. The openness of the loft and the high ceiling above her. The softness of the pillow against her cheek and the sheets resting haphazardly across one leg, the remains of a frenzied night with the woman who had so easily captured her heart.

And that touch. That light, steady, tantalizing yet torturous finger against her skin tracing the closest approximation to Cassie's actual heart and soul. Drea's finger extended to Cassie's shoulder and along her upper arm, taking her time exploring the intricacies of the design just as she had taken her time in the hours before. Honoring her body, her passion, and their time together. Making it count. Cassie could see why women never got mad at Drea after only one night together. It wasn't quick and cheap. It wasn't a transaction. There was intimacy and beauty there, and definitely appreciation. There just wasn't anything more. It was a one-time thing and expecting anything more than that would only lead to heartache.

Cassie was over heartache. She had experienced enough for two lifetimes as far as she was concerned. There was no contract for life, of course. No quota of how much trauma and grief one person had to endure before only good stuff came, but some people seemed to be dealt an unfortunately large share compared to others. Cassie had done enough soul-searching and personal growth to know she was in charge of her own thoughts. The choice was hers. And she chose to take this moment for what it was. Temporary. Expectations were where people got themselves into trouble.

She felt the mattress dip before Drea's lips were on her earlobe, her breath sending Cassie's heart racing.

"This is beautiful," Drea whispered as her finger dragged along the design on Cassie's skin.

Cassie turned her head to meet Drea's eyes, seeing the question there. She wanted to tell her what the tattoo meant, to open that part of herself to Drea, but she also knew this would probably be the only time they'd be like this, together. Her eyes searched Drea's, seeing only warmth and compassion, and she decided to take the risk, to stay in the moment and trust that feeling rather than all the others.

"Thanks," Cassie whispered, afraid to break the magic of the moment.

"When did you get it?"

"In college." If she was going to do this, she had to go all in, which meant putting herself out there, even knowing it might be futile, and so she did. "The reality was hitting hard that the ballet dream wasn't going to work out, but I kept pushing, forcing myself to fit the mold, and making myself sick doing it."

Drea's fingers continued running over the design as she listened, the steady pressure calming Cassie, along with the sincerity in her eyes.

"I eventually hit bottom, becoming someone I never wanted to be." She paused, remembering the emptiness she had felt during that time in her life. "It was Janay who picked me up and kept me going. She gave me a home and a family and eventually taught me to love dance again. And after a while, I got back to a good place." She clasped her hands together and slid them underneath her chin. "I decided to get that to honor those childhood dreams, and to let them go, to make room for the new me."

Drea leaned down and kissed her upper back. As her lips traversed the space, Cassie envisioned the designs she was seeing, from the ballerina below her shoulder blade to where it morphed into a butterfly flying away by her shoulder. The gentleness of her kiss and the intimacy of the moment brought a tear to Cassie's eye that she blinked away.

Drea ran her hand to Cassie's lower back and Cassie rolled over to face her fully. She searched Drea's eyes, wishing this could be more, that they could keep having moments like this forever, but knowing it was a foolish thought. So instead, she reached for her and pulled her into a kiss. If this was all there would ever be between them, she would let her heart dance with Drea's in the only way it ever could.

Cassie paced through her kitchen. Thirty minutes had passed since she got home and she still had no solid answer to the question. *What in the actual fuck?*

Except for a time or two in college, Cassie was not a one-night stand kind of girl. Not that anything was wrong with one-night stands. They just weren't for her. The intimacy of a night of sex had to come with a connection, with vulnerability. And definitely none of the excuses that accompanied her early twenties.

So how could she explain having a one-night stand? And not any one-night stand. This was Drea, for fuck's sake, a woman she happened to work with and thus could absolutely not escape. And not even really a woman but, like, a force of nature wrapped up in the sexiest body on the planet. A force of nature named Drea. Damn. Even her name was sexy.

Cassie felt a pang of arousal just thinking about her. The night and the early morning had been incredible. That was undeniable. And even waking up to Drea and opening up to her had been pretty great, but there was no way this was anything other than the aftermath of an emotion-filled romantic moment. It was probably the rain. If it hadn't rained, the romantic factor would have gone down by a hundred at least. It was a mistake and Drea was too kind or Southern or whatever to say so. It would be fine. She had gotten caught up in the moment, the beautiful, sensual, crazy, sex storm of a moment, but she was an adult. A professional. A professional adult. And she would go to work and be that, damn it. Yep, this would all be okay. So fucking okay.

Drea fell back on her bed, physically exhausted in the best way possible, and stared at the ceiling as images from the past day and night with Cassie floated through her mind. They all distilled into one singular thought. She had met her match. Cassie lifted her spirits with her brightness and how she saw things in Drea that most people never could or would, and the way she called her out on the sidewalk last night, breaking through something deep inside her, something she never knew she could traverse. It was unexpected. Everything about Cassie had been unexpected. Drea had torn through her in a frenzy of lust like never before. Gone were the light, fun times with all the others. Something had burned deep, a desire that she couldn't quench no matter how many times she tried. There was always more. And Cassie had matched her, every touch, every kiss, every orgasm, pushing her and them for more.

Normally after a night with a woman Drea would be glad to have her solitude back, in the one place where she could be herself, alone with no one watching or criticizing or being disappointed because their version of her was an illusion, one that she would never live up to, and would never want to. But she had learned to give them what they wanted. It was easier than actually investing, putting herself out there only to falter when they saw something that didn't match their fantasy. She would have gone on like that forever. There was no plan for a future or a happily ever after. She had scoffed at the ridiculousness of the premise, having let go of those silly notions long ago. Until one vibrant, intriguing girl drifted into her world and somehow managed to slip past all of the shadows within her and find a place to nestle inside her heart, warming it by merely existing.

She let out a slow breath, in awe at the wonder of this woman. She stretched out her arm, running her hand along the soft sheets, the scent of lavender still hanging in the air. For the first time ever, she wasn't relieved to have her companion leave. Instead, she found herself missing Cassie's bold lips, the depths in her majestic eyes, the warmth of her laughter, and the way she could make her feel seen and challenged at the same time. This thoughtful, strong, compassionate, beautiful woman. She groaned at the number Cassie had done on her, as Pickles leapt up on the bed with a meow.

All she knew was that for the first time in a very, very long time, she wanted to try for something more. With the woman who made her feel like there was a more to have.

Pickles stared down at her and meowed again.

"Hey, it could happen," she said, wanting to convince herself as much as him.

Chapter 17

Cassie steeled herself for Monday morning. She and Drea had been on an emotional roller coaster for weeks. Every time she thought they were growing close, Drea would pull back or evade, either verbally or emotionally, or sometimes both. But after this weekend, they had reached the peak, and the only place left to go was down. So Cassie had given herself a pep talk on the ride to work and entered the office expecting distance from Drea, the realization that she had made a mistake and now they would be stuck in a polite zone to suffer through work together.

But that's not what happened.

Drea caught her eye during the morning meeting and the expression she found there was not one of guilt or regret. It was something entirely different, lust. She nearly spit out her coffee, pausing to do the mental calculation: one player plus one non-player, plus one night of earth-shattering sex equals . . . nope. No part of that equation added up to a second date or more earth-shattering, life-altering, scream-from-the-rooftop . . . Cassie mentally shook herself. No. Drea didn't do relationships or even date. She had a very robust reputation for it in fact. Drea was a good-time girl and Cassie had definitely, abso-freaking-lutely, without question, had a good time. Her body still ached from the extent of the good time. But she would have bet a million dollars that Drea would not want more. It wasn't in her nature, and if tons and tons and tons—Cassie took another sip of coffee, letting the hot liquid coursing down her throat dislodge her from her mental hamster wheel—of women had not changed Drea's viewpoint on relationships, she doubted anything she could have done would result in anything different. Besides, Drea was amazing, in every way really. She constantly surprised Cassie with her zest and talent and thoughtfulness, but Cassie would never want to change her or trap her. Some people were meant to be free, and Drea seemed like one of those people.

So she played it off in the meeting and as Drea glanced her way later that morning. It wasn't until she went to refill her coffee that something shifted for her. And all it took, as Drea joined her in the break area, was the smallest touch of her hand, a stolen moment so sweet and intimate that it sent Cassie's thoughts crashing back to Drea's bedroom. She met Drea's gaze, and the wall she had prepared in herself that morning cracked open at the emotion she found there, her mind dizzy from the enormity of it. It took everything in her not to take that stunning face in her hands and kiss her until her lips gave out.

Drea's fingers grazed hers once more as she walked away, leaving Cassie's mind and hormones racing.

They made eyes at each other for the rest of the morning, ratcheting up the desire with each glance. Her body vibrated from the arousal surging through her. When she finally went to the bathroom to compose herself, she barely registered the door opening behind her before Drea pressed her against the wall with a passionate kiss. They held each other tight as the kiss deepened. Cassie couldn't get enough, wrapping her leg around Drea's hip, as Drea lifted her effortlessly, using her body to hold Cassie to the wall as she kissed her mouth and neck. Arousal shot through her with each touch and she ached for Drea's mouth on her, inside her, all of it.

Just as Cassie started envisioning moving things to a stall and going for more, office or no office, completely at the mercy of this woman who left her sanity hanging by a thread, Drea slowed and traced her tongue along Cassie's lips before placing a final kiss there and resting her forehead against Cassie's.

They stayed like that, against the wall, panting, as Cassie longed for more. "I want you so bad I can barely stand it," she finally managed, a rasp in her voice.

"I know. Me too." Drea lifted her head and ran her fingers along Cassie's cheek, her eyes brimming with emotion. "Come home with me tonight."

She didn't know what this was or where it would lead. But everything in that moment, the emotions, the desire, the connection, answered every question in her mind. She smiled at the striking woman before her who had captured her heart despite all of her resistance. "Try to keep me away."

"So, she's going to kill everyone?" Cassie asked, trying to comprehend the storyline and the situation on the TV screen.

"Probably." Drea grabbed a piece of popcorn from the bowl in Cassie's lap and tossed it into her mouth. "She's not a fan."

They had spent the majority of the past two nights in Drea's bed, only pausing when hunger got the best of them. And as much as Cassie enjoyed the bedroom activities, these quiet moments with Drea, curled up on the sofa together, half naked in the late hours of the night, pulled at her heart. It was what she had hoped a relationship with Drea could be.

"And Sam lets you watch this with Jake?" Cassie couldn't imagine how Sam would be okay with her six-year-old son watching something so violent.

Drea held her gaze and snuck another piece of popcorn.

"Did you just wink at me?"

"I don't know. Did I?" Drea put the popcorn in her mouth and chewed, but she couldn't hide the smirk on her lips.

"You did it again!"

Drea laughed. "I can't help it, the charm just oozes out of me sometimes."

Cassie laughed and shook her head, but her mind drifted back to a couple of months ago, when things were very different between them. "Not all the time."

Drea tilted her head with a curious expression. "No?"

"No, you weren't charming at all toward me in the beginning."

Drea frowned. "I'm sorry about that." She looked up at the ceiling as if searching for the words. "I've been kind of struggling with all of the changes with Sam and how I fit into her new life. So, seeing you two so close at work, it made me feel even farther from her in a way."

The admission clarified so much from those early days. It was about Sam, not Cassie. A sense of relief washed over her, finally having an explanation for Drea's early walls. She thought about how much it would hurt if Janay distanced herself or became close with someone else. "I'm sorry. You know that we're just coworkers though, right?"

Drea nodded. "Yeah. It wasn't about you, so I'm sorry I wasn't very friendly. I was dealing with a lot."

Cassie placed her hand on Drea's knee, wanting her to know she wasn't alone.

"But, it was only a matter of time." Drea sighed.

"Only a matter of time until what?"

"Until you hustled your way into my heart." Drea flashed her charming smile, all the more so because it was genuine.

"Hustled, huh?"

"Mmhmm . . . and with that bold lipstick, I had no chance." Her eyes danced with mischief.

"Oh, you like the lipstick?" Cassie could feel her smile take over her entire being.

In one effortless movement, Drea placed the popcorn bowl on the coffee table, then closed the gap between them. Cassie felt the air between them thicken, Drea's lips only millimeters away as she looked deep into Cassie's eyes.

"Mmhmm," Drea replied. She ran her thumb slowly over Cassie's lower lip, the heat in her eyes setting every neuron in Cassie's body on fire.

"We should go to bed," Cassie whispered in a rush, wanting to explore each other fully without the limitations of a sofa.

The sensuality and passion in Drea's eyes made Cassie dizzy. "Yeah," Drea replied. She pressed her forehead against Cassie's as they breathed each other's air, the intimacy of the moment threatening to overtake Cassie. Then Drea placed her hand against Cassie's cheek and kissed her so fully that Cassie forgot completely about moving anywhere.

Drea slid out of bed, leaving Cassie curled adorably in the covers, a shock of lilac hair sticking out. She grabbed her T-shirt off the floor, then sat on the stool and stared at the canvas before her, the soft light of her desk lamp illuminating the shadows along the water. She blended a spot and added a bit more depth underneath the steamboat. There was always more to do, more to create, and the hardest part, other than starting, was knowing when to stop, the finish line more a subjective resolution of good enough, often defined by a deadline, rather than the achievement of some artistic pinnacle. Tomorrow was her deadline, when Byron would decide if the work he had commissioned was sufficient and worthy of both display and further marketing endeavors, the idea of the latter still bringing a wave of nausea. He had seen her work at the wedding and had asked her for something similar, but there was still the possibility of rejection, that somehow she woud fall short of what he had envisioned.

But even if he was satisfied, then it meant her work would be out there, really out there in the city, and after so many years of trying to do that and falling short, the fear of victory was almost as overwhelming as the joy filling her the past few days.

It had been an exciting and unexpected whirlwind with Cassie. Thankfully, she had spent most of Sunday after Cassie left working on the painting or at least trying to while her mind kept drifting, because she had only been able to sneak in a few hours each night, either before Cassie came over or after she had fallen asleep in blissful exhaustion.

The sound of a soft snore interrupted Drea's thoughts. She turned on the stool and glanced at Cassie, who was lying peacefully with a small grin on her lips as she dozed, the tousled covers a remnant of their earlier escapades.

Not in her wildest imagination of how this could go had she come close to envisioning the thrill that Cassie brought to her life. There was an undeniable and insatiable chemistry between them for sure, and they had definitely devoted a sufficient amount of time to exploring that, but what she hadn't been prepared for were the emotions. The strength and softness Cassie exhibited pushed Drea to be better and to fall for her even harder than she thought possible. She had never wanted to make something work so deeply before. It seemed unsustainable, to feel so much for someone and have no control. To put her heart in Cassie's hands and hope she didn't break it.

She turned back to the painting, the steamboat reminding her of Nellie and Katherine's painting and the story of how they met that night on the water. There was so much hope in love. And despite her fears, she couldn't say no to Cassie. She couldn't not see what this could be. No one had ever affected her so completely. What did she know? Maybe she'd been wrong all this time and something amazing could last.

"Do you know how sexy you look right now?"

Drea smiled at the sound of Cassie's voice and turned to

see her lying on her stomach with her head propped on her hand, eyeing her from the end of the bed. Drea's eyes ran over the uninterrupted expanse of creamy smooth skin on top of the covers before settling on the delicious curve of her lips. "If it's half as sexy as you look right now, then lucky us."

"Come be with me." It wasn't a question or a command. Like everything else about this woman, it was a blend of extremes that resulted in the most wondrous soul she had ever met.

Drea placed her brush on the easel along with all the fears and doubts that could wait for tomorrow. "Yes, ma'am." Cassie sat up to meet her with a kiss, pausing only to lift her T-shirt off before pulling her deeper into the abyss. It would be a while before they both drifted back to sleep.

Drea woke with a start. She blinked as she adjusted to her surroundings, finding comfort in the darkness of her room. Her heart pounded in her ears and she breathed slowly, trying to calm herself from the nightmare, when a soft hand ran along her upper arm.

"Are you okay?"

She looked over to see Cassie lying beside her, watching her with an expression of concern.

"Yeah." The word was somewhere between a breath and a whisper. "Go back to sleep." She kissed her forehead and got out of bed, putting on her T-shirt and pajama pants as she headed to the kitchen. Moonlight seeped through the glass door to the balcony. She leaned on the counter and rested her forehead against her clasped hands, unable to determine what was more upsetting, the nightmare or waking up to someone who had witnessed it. A thought ran through her mind and as much as she tried to resist it, it rang louder until she couldn't ignore it anymore. This was why she needed to be alone. The truth of her, in all her brokenness, wasn't something that could be loved. She had hidden it for so many years, she almost forgot why, until she saw it in Cassie's expression. Sober concern where joy had been. She sighed, filled a glass with whiskey, and gulped it down, wanting to drown the memory.

"Cheers!" Cassie clinked her raspberry seltzer to Drea's margarita. "I told you he would love it. Get ready for the big time."

A flash of something dulled Drea's grin as she sipped her drink.

Cassie stared at Drea. There had been something off about her all day. Cassie hoped it was just nerves about the painting, but that had gone off without a hitch and still something lingered in Drea's eyes. Cassie wondered if it had something to do with this morning, but she had no idea how to ask Drea about it. She assumed it had been a nightmare, and Drea had removed herself from the room immediately, so she didn't seem to want to discuss it. Everything was so new between them, but she hoped Drea knew she'd be there for her, whatever it was. That she could talk to her. Maybe she should have followed her and comforted her, but she had been so alarmed herself. Drea's scream had ripped her awake and her heart had been racing so fast, she had to calm down a moment before she could see if Drea was okay. But it wasn't just a scream. She had yelled "no," which made Cassie think it wasn't something random. And then she was gone and Cassie didn't want to corner her if she didn't want to talk about it. But now she seemed distant and sad.

She sipped her seltzer, the tartness and bubbles lifting her spirit to proceed. "Hey, I actually have some news."

Caution passed through Drea's eyes, but curiosity won out. "Okay."

"A client is coming in tomorrow, and I may have mentioned

that you have some fresh takes on designs that might fit what they're looking for." She raised her eyebrows, hoping that Drea took it as good news. If Drea could see other people catching on, then maybe she'd believe in her art more.

Different emotions seemed to jockey for position on Drea's face, and Cassie started to think she'd made an error in judgment in setting up the meeting.

"Which client?"

"Pawper's Pups."

"I thought they wanted stuff months ago." Drea's brow furrowed, which at least wasn't an outright no.

"They did, but they had to postpone a few months. Something about a burst water line in the fall." She waited a moment before continuing. "Anyway, they are kind of artsy and fun, and I thought they might like doing something a little different." She pulled up their logo on her phone. "See." She held up the picture of an adorable West Highland white terrier in a polka-dot bow tie and a top hat so Drea could see. "Their mission is to bring classy pet toys and pet wear to people on every budget."

"All pets or just dogs?" The twinkle in Drea's eye returned. "I'd hate to think of all the cats and ferrets making it through this world without a top hat."

Cassie giggled. "All pets. Though I don't know that a snake would appreciate a top hat. The lack of external ears and all. And the bow tie would probably snag every stick and rock."

"Well, at least now I have a muse."

She could feel Drea's usual charm peeking through whatever had been on her mind all day and wished she could show Drea what was in her heart.

Cassie reached across the table and took her hand. "I think you're incredible."

Drea's shoulders relaxed and Cassie felt like they were finally connecting again.

"I just want others to see it too." She ran her thumb along Drea's hand. Drea seemed to warm to the touch, but there was still something distant in her eyes. And no matter what Cassie did, she felt like she was on the outside looking in. The distance stirred an uneasiness in the pit of her stomach that wouldn't go away.

"Yeah, I don't know about the style." Max, the coowner of Pawper's Pups, handed the mock-up Drea had sketched that morning to his wife and business partner, Amanda, and perused the watercolor from The Well campaign. They sat at the conference table across from Drea and Cassie, and despite all of Cassie's encouragement about today, Drea had guessed it might go something like this.

Amanda pointed at the smiling dog clad in upscale clothing that Drea had sketched. "Oh come on, that would look so great," she said. Though Max probably had some personality somewhere deep down, Amanda was clearly the bubbly and more optimistic of the two. "I can already picture Wiley . . ." She turned to Drea and Cassie. "That's our dog who inspired the company logo." They nodded as she turned back to her husband. "I can already picture him like this." She ran her finger along the image. "It's perfect."

Max stared at the mock-up in his wife's hands and then at the one he was holding. "I think we might have to chat about it and get back to you."

Drea knew what that meant. She had had many conversations like this before and while she appreciated Cassie setting this up, she wished she hadn't gotten her hopes up.

They said their goodbyes, and Drea went to get some coffee as Cassie walked them to the door.

"Hey," Cassie said as she joined her by the coffee maker and placed a hand on her back. "You okay?"

She sipped her coffee, letting it warm both the chill in the air and the one in her chest from the response to her work. "It's pretty much what I anticipated."

Cassie dropped her hand, taking a moment to brush the flop of lilac hair out of her eye. It was such a small gesture, but one Drea found ridiculously sexy—usually. "We don't know what they'll decide. Amanda loved it."

As much as Drea appreciated Cassie's positivity, she couldn't bring herself to match it. Another thing that swirled doubts in her mind. She wanted to tell her to just forget it and stick to the normal stuff people expected from their company, from every company. But she didn't want to hurt Cassie's feelings or seem ungrateful. Cassie hadn't done anything wrong. It just hadn't worked out, again. Max's lackluster response reminded her of all the rejection she'd experienced after art school and how at some point, she decided to let that dream go. She painted for herself now and tried to let it be enough.

"Drea, that was no reflection on you or your work. Seemed like a marital issue to me." A sly grin tugged at Cassie's lips. She placed her hand on Drea's arm, the steady pressure calming as Drea sorted through her feelings. "And whatever they decide doesn't mean we stop trying."

And there it was. The thing that had been percolating at the recesses of her mind, growing stronger each day. Cassie was so focused on getting her work out there that she wondered at the intention behind it. What if she continued as she was? Keeping her art for herself. Was that giving up to Cassie? Would it disappoint her? Was it not enough? Was she not enough? Now every time Cassie mentioned getting her work out there, it felt as if she was trying to fix something. But Drea would never be fixed. And the more she felt like that's what Cassie needed from her, the more she doubted whether this would ever work.

Chapter 18

"I like the lighting," Molly said as she walked through the rental's kitchen. She had let Cassie know the previous week that it was time for her to move forward with her life and that meant finding her own place.

It had stung at first, facing both the finality of the end of Molly and Eva and the end of their time together as well. She had enjoyed having Molly so close these past two months and though she wished it had been under happier circumstances, it had made their bond that much stronger.

Cassie ran her hands along the marble island. "I like the island." The thought of Drea's island came to mind and all of the delightful and sweet and wicked things that had happened around it, and on it, over the past week. And as much as she enjoyed being with her sister, she couldn't wait to be back with Drea again.

As they drove away from the apartment, the last of three for the day, Molly turned to her. "Is it time to give me the gory details?"

Cassie felt a wave of guilt. Though Molly had been happy to take care of Digit over the past week while Cassie stayed at Drea's apartment, she knew Molly was going to eventually want answers. Digit had voiced his disapproval by leaving a hairball in her second-favorite pair of shoes while she was gone. She flashed a guilty grin, but from the look in Molly's eyes, Molly already knew exactly where she had been.

"There's been a . . . development."

"I see. Sounds pretty serious." Molly took her attention off the road and asked her gently, "Is it? Serious?"

If she had asked Cassie that question on Wednesday, the answer would have been a resounding yes. But ever since the nightmare and the presentation to Byron, Drea had pulled away a bit. They were still intimate, but there was a distance to it. As much as she wanted to figure out a way to fix it, she was also afraid to ask because she could feel Drea slipping away, and it broke her heart a little more every day. Maybe there was nothing to fix. Maybe Drea's true nature, her resistance to commitment, was finally asserting itself.

"I think it's too early to tell." The fact that it was the truest thing she could say and that what she wanted to say might not be true anymore sent a ball of emotion to her throat. She looked out the passenger window, trying to breathe through any impending tears as a sense of dread for impending doom settled in her gut.

Molly took her hand and held it.

Cassie looked at her sister who had always had her back, who had never let her down even when her own life was falling apart, and squeezed her hand. No matter what happened, she knew she wouldn't have to face it alone.

They drove along Magazine Street, all of the shops adorned with garlands and bows, as people clad in scarves and winter coats scurried in and out of them trying to avoid the damp cold that was winter in New Orleans.

She pointed to one of her favorite local gift shops where everything was handmade. "Hey, can we stop here? We have a holiday party and gift exchange coming up at work. We all picked a name out of a hat, and I got Sam."

Molly's face lit up. "Ohh, what are you going to get her?"

"Some relaxing bath salts and a soothing candle. She works so hard all the time, I want her to have some spa time for herself."

Molly pulled into an empty spot along the street. "That sounds perfect."

Drea watched as Cassie closed her eyes in a moment of appreciation.

"This is so good," Cassie said as she took another bite of linguine.

The pleasure on her face warmed Drea as they sat next to each other at the kitchen island, casual and comfortable. In some ways, it felt like they had been together much longer than a week, and maybe they had if she counted all the time she had spent falling for her over the past couple of months. Though they had only been apart for a night, she had missed Cassie and looked forward to her coming for dinner this evening.

"If I had known you were this good in the kitchen, I would have ordered in a lot more this past week." Cassie's eyes sparkled with mischief.

Drea shrugged a shoulder, a bit proudly. "Well, you know," she gestured up and down her body, "Italian and all."

"All is right." Cassie leaned over and kissed her, the sweet taste of olive oil and butter on her lips.

They finished their pasta and Drea washed the dishes. It felt so domestic she almost didn't recognize herself. She grabbed her glass of wine and rejoined Cassie, her breath catching at the casual beauty emanating from her. If someone had asked her to explain the profound shift over the past few months, she wouldn't have been able to. It was something unexpected, and even miraculous, and as much as she wanted to believe it would last, enough doubt had crept into her mind over the past few days that she worried Cassie would be yet another person she disappointed.

"Hey, um." The hesitation in Cassie's voice caught her attention. So many things had gone unsaid, and she knew it was only a matter of time before it all caught up with them. But she had wanted to savor the good parts for as long as she could, knowing if this didn't work, it would be for the last time. "Listen, I wanted to apologize about yesterday."

She placed her hand on Cassie's knee. "You don't need to apologize."

"No, I do. I wanted to help you get your art seen, so people would realize how amazing you are, but maybe I overstepped."

She took her hand off Cassie's knee and placed it on her own. While Cassie probably meant it genuinely, Drea couldn't help but hear the subtext that had been playing in her mind the past forty-eight hours. "I know you were trying to help, but I've been through this many times before. It always ends the same."

"But it doesn't have to. Byron loved your work. So did Nellie and Katherine. So do I. I think it's just a matter of time until you find your audience."

"And what if it isn't? What if this is all there is?"

Cassie's brow furrowed. "Don't you want more?"

A piece of her heart broke, knowing where this was headed. "Do you want more?"

"Of course. I want so much for you."

"No, not that. If everything that I am is all I ever became, would that be enough or would you need more?"

They stared at each other, but Cassie said nothing.

She tried again. "Would you still think I was amazing if I never pursued my art further?"

Cassie shook her head. "But you're so good."

Her stomach roiled at the realization that this was all there could ever be. She swallowed the revulsion and plowed forward, knowing it had to be this way. "Cassie." Cassie's face stiffened at the word. "I don't think I can ever be what you really need." Cassie pulled back at the words, increasing the distance between them. "You're . . ." She shook her head. "Amazing and incredible don't come close to describing what you truly are. You light up a room with your vivaciousness and style. Even on my best day, I'm nowhere near as positive and joyful as you are. We operate at different frequencies, and mine will always be lower than yours, and I . . ." Emotion caught in her voice. "I couldn't live knowing that I dimmed your light."

"You don't," Cassie pleaded as a tear ran down her cheek.

"I will. I promise you I will. I'll bring you down and disappoint you. You want so much out of life and I can't be the person you want me to be. And I can't stand disappointing you every day when I try and fall short." She wiped at the tear welling in her eye.

"You don't disappoint me."

"I do and I'll continue to. I thought I could do this, but I was wrong. I can't change who I am, not even for you. It's not enough. I will never be enough. I'm sorry, but I can't do this anymore."

She wasn't sure what hurt more, the pain in Cassie's eyes or seeing the tears streaming down her face. It was all her fault. She wished she could go back in time and do it all differently, so she never would have hurt her.

Holiday lights and blow-up snowmen and Santas whizzed by as Cassie drove, the cheer of the season ricocheting off her broken heart. She couldn't make sense of what had happened. How did things go off the rails so quickly? She didn't agree with most of what Drea had said, but she also wondered if she had missed something. Something big.

She thought they were having a good time. It felt like they were actually being a real couple and not just sex-crazed teenagers, but the conversation had seemed to take on a life of its own. She had the sense that she was the only one it took by surprise. Something about what Drea had said seemed almost rehearsed or at least familiar to her. How long had she been thinking those things? They had had so little time together and yet so much had happened between them, but she didn't understand the leap between where they had been and where she found herself now, alone with a battered heart. Had it all gone so wrong that quickly? Or was it deeper than that?

When she got home, she found Molly and Digit on the sofa. Molly took one look at her and knew. Cassie could only shake her head as tears streamed down her face again. Molly reached up and hugged her as she sobbed over the best thing that barely happened. She lay down, resting her head on Molly's lap, and let Molly stroke her hair until she was out of tears.

Drea couldn't stay in her apartment any longer reliving Cassie crumpling before her as she broke her heart. She needed air and distance from it all, so she bundled up and wandered down the noisy streets, busy with laughter and music, an otherwise typical night in New Orleans. It always amazed Drea how alone she could feel in such a lively place. She wandered through the darkness, willing the cold to numb her memory of all of the amazing moments over the past months, especially the past week, and the horrible ones from the past few hours. After going down a few lesser-known roads, she found herself on the outskirts of the French Quarter, the smell of alcohol drifting through the air. A neon-green sign beckoned her with one word. "Bar." She pushed open the heavy wooden door, in search of a break from the pain coursing through her. The first thing she noticed was the darkness, a moody atmosphere as if she had entered a cave. But it wasn't depressing. A number of patrons were scattered throughout. A group of older men at a round table in the middle of the room, and several individuals hunched over the bar, staring into their drinks or at nothing at all. The sound of pool balls clacking and the low murmur of conversation brought some liveliness to the place, along with the uproar of the men at the table as a couple of them threw down the stack of cards in their hands while one grinned widely.

A few people lifted their heads as she sat on a plush stool at the bar. An older woman with deep lines at the corners of her eyes and around her mouth, and a white hand towel slung over her shoulder approached her from behind the bar. "What can I get you, hon?" There was something kind in her eyes, and her voice sounded much younger than Drea expected.

"I'll take a whiskey. Thanks."

She stayed there for a long while, sipping her drink, and willing the images in her mind to stop.

"Hey girl, it's going to be okay." Janay rubbed Cassie's back as she cried. Cassie still wore her pajamas from the night before, not able to summon the energy to change or do much but sit on the sofa and wallow.

"I don't know what happened." She sniffled.

"She didn't tell you why she wanted to break up?"

Cassie blew out a breath. "She kinda did, but I didn't really follow all of it."

"What did she say?" Janay asked gently.

"She said she didn't think she could be what I needed and she'd just disappoint me. And she said she can't change who she is for me, but I don't want her to change. She's all I need and want, and she's never disappointed me."

"Do you think it was a cop-out? Maybe she was in over her head and wanted out?"

Despite having wondered this herself more than a few times over the past eighteen hours, Cassie felt a flash of anger at Janay for voicing the thought. Being someone Drea needed to escape hit hard in her chest. "I thought it was real. The shortest relationship in history, but it felt real." Her mind wandered to when things had turned earlier in the week. "But some stuff did happen and she started pulling away a few days ago, so maybe. Maybe I was too wrapped up in her to see it wasn't what she needed." She shook her head, feeling stupid at her ignorance.

"What stuff?"

"She kinda shut down the day she presented her artwork to Byron, a client of ours. I thought she was just nervous, but it went really well, and she still felt off or distant, I'm not sure. Just different."

Janay's expression suggested it didn't make sense to her either. "Did anything else happen?"

The thing she had been replaying in her mind for days came to the forefront, and she grimaced.

"What?"

"Something weird happened the morning of the presentation and I think I handled it wrong. I think she had a nightmare or something and she yelled 'no,' which woke me up and scared the shit out of me. I asked if she was okay, but she played it off and left the room." Her voice got small. "I didn't follow her."

"You didn't talk about it again?"

She shook her head. "It didn't feel like she wanted to, but maybe I fucked up."

"You didn't know. You don't know what's going on in her world." Janay shrugged. "None of us ever fully know what's going on in someone else's life."

The words weren't as comforting as she probably meant them to be. Ever since yesterday, Cassie had a lingering feeling that there was a lot she didn't know.

"There was something else. Something I didn't follow. She said something about being on different frequencies and she didn't want to dim my light." She looked at Janay to see if any flicker of meaning resonated with her, but Janay just listened intently. "I have no idea what she meant by that."

Janay thought for a moment. "Did you ever feel like that was happening when y'all were together?"

Cassie hadn't actually considered it until Janay asked. "Not usually, except when she started pulling away. Then it felt like I couldn't reach her, but I wouldn't say it dimmed my light." She paused for a beat as a flash of anger hit that this was even happening. "She's definitely dimming it right now though."

Janay frowned and then shrugged, and it helped a little knowing she wasn't the only one who was stumped. But it didn't take any of the pain away.

"The thing is, when I was driving home, it didn't add up and I had this feeling that I missed something big. Like we were talking about different things, ya know, and we were missing what the other was saying or meaning, I don't know. It felt like she had made up her mind and I didn't have a say." She slumped back against the sofa, the emotions and the futility of it all swirling through her mind. Digit jumped up beside her and pushed her hand up with his nose, demanding affection.

"I know this sucks and it hurts, but it kind of was expected, right? I mean, Drea doesn't do relationships, and she actually tried with you. All the hearts across the city were breaking." There was a hint of humor in Janay's voice, but Cassie wasn't in the mood for levity yet and rolled her eyes. "The point is she cared enough about you to try something she has never done before, and we both know plenty of women who wish she had."

That last part twisted the knife already in her heart. She shot Janay a look to express how much it was not helping.

"Sorry." Janay grimaced. "All I'm saying is, maybe it was real and was even pretty huge for her. But . . .”

“But what?” Cassie asked, hoping Janay could offer something that would explain what happened.

Janay took a moment and Cassie could see her filtering, trying to find something that would hurt less to hear. “Some things aren’t meant to be.”

Cassie tilted her head. “What were you really going to say?”

Janay took a breath and exhaled. “That it wouldn’t have mattered what you did, it was never going to work out. That you shouldn’t take it personally because it was never about you. The ending I mean.”

Cassie grimaced at the brutal honesty.

Janay’s face softened at Cassie’s pained expression. “Yeah, that’s why I went with option B.”

She let the words marinate for a minute, but they didn’t seem to fit. It had only been a short time, but she saw how good they could be together and how much they both wanted it. And maybe it was just guilt or defeat, things she never accepted easily in her life, not without a fight at least, and yeah, maybe some of the stuff Drea said was coming from somewhere deeper than their relationship, but the ending had felt very personal to her. She didn’t believe that Drea was running because she was scared. Maybe a small piece of her, but deep down she knew Drea had ended it very much because of her.

Molly came into the living room, rushing to head to another holiday party she was working. She bent over and hugged Janay and Cassie.

As she let go of Cassie, she put a hand on her shoulder. “Are you going to be all right?”

Cassie nodded.

“I’m going to pick up some peppermint ice cream, and we can watch whatever movie you want when I get back.” She placed a quick kiss on Cassie’s cheek, said her goodbyes, and was gone. Cassie looked back at Janay and stroked Digit’s fur as he cuddled beside her. As much as she was hurting, she was so glad to be surrounded by family.

"What are you doing Thursday night?" Janay asked with a hint of mischief in her eye.

Cassie gestured around herself. "Probably this."

"Well, how would you like to meet me at Rosie's and have a little fun?"

The thought of dancing and being in a club did not ring true in her current state. "I'm not sure I'm up for that yet."

"Okay." Janay's voice was sure, but her eyes wandered along the floor.

"What is it?"

"I may have a date and I was thinking we could meet up after, especially in case it doesn't go well."

Cassie felt a wave of excitement for her friend. Janay hadn't been on a date in a year and a half. "Of course I'll be there for you."

Janay grinned. "Don't get your hopes up though. It's some friend of a friend of Renee's, so I'm hoping for just short of a disaster."

Cassie laughed, for the first time in a while. The realization made her miss Drea even more.

Chapter 19

Well, this sucked. Now Cassie remembered why she had tried so hard not to let anything happen between her and Drea. The past two days at work had been nothing short of miserable and so incredibly awkward. She had tried to be professional and civil, but her eyes seemed to wander to Drea on their own accord during the Monday morning meeting. Once or twice Drea caught her, and the way she had looked away without communicating anything between them felt like being broken up with all over again.

She cursed the fact that Drea's desk was in her sight line, something that had brought her great joy and other positive emotions only a week ago. Occasionally, Cassie would risk a glance, trying to get some glimpse into how Drea was feeling. Drea was quiet for sure, but Cassie wasn't sure if it was just due to the rush of projects before the holidays since everyone in the office was working nonstop it seemed. She was thankful for the busyness because it gave her some reprieve from her incessant thoughts. Beyond the quiet though, Cassie sensed an emptiness in Drea. Maybe she was grieving too? She didn't want Drea to be sad. She wanted to know she wasn't alone in caring about what happened. That it had mattered to Drea too.

As she started timing her trips to the break area and the bathroom so she wouldn't run into Drea, trying to decrease the chance of awkward encounters and more heartache, she chastised herself for getting into this position in the first place. She knew better. She knew this would happen all along. How could it not? And yet she still gave in, to Drea, to desire, to temptation. She sighed. To love. She swallowed the emotion in her throat and took a deep breath to temper the impending tears. No, she would not cry at work. She could break down again when she got home.

The office phone rang and she steeled herself. She could do this. It might take some time. She glanced at Drea, and her beauty and distance sent a shot of arousal quickly followed by pain through her body. Okay, maybe a lot of time. But she would get through this. The phone rang again and she grabbed it, willing her voice to match the normalcy she hoped she would eventually feel.

Drea smirked as the men at the poker table groaned.

"Damn it, she got us again," one of them said. Drea thought his name might have been Bill.

Drea corralled the one-dollar bills toward her.

"One more round?" another asked.

"Nah, this is enough to cover my tab," she said.

"Well, you didn't need to beat us in poker for that. George here woulda bought all the drinks you could want." The man speaking shoved his friend's arm. Drea glanced at George, the quiet one of the group. He was probably in his late sixties like the other guys, but there was a sadness in his eyes that she recognized. She had seen it in several of the other patrons at the bar as well, this place that seemed to be a hideaway for people struggling with grief and other turmoil.

She smiled and tilted her head toward the cards on the table. "This is more my style." She nodded at George and headed back to the bar.

"Want some coffee, hon?"

Drea raised her eyes to meet those of Cherie, the bartender and owner that she had grown to know over the past few nights as she avoided going home, her apartment just a sad and empty reminder that Cassie was gone. She glanced around the bar, seeing that only a few people remained. "That would be great."

Cherie poured a mug for Drea and herself and joined her at the bar. They had chatted a little about unimportant stuff and the weather over the past few nights, and Drea appreciated that she could come here and just be.

There was something special about the bar. It wasn't pretty or charming in any typical way. Maybe it was the low lighting or the other patrons who were going through the same stuff. Whatever it was, Drea had felt like she had found her place the moment she walked inside. She had felt like her life was spinning out of control and she wasn't sure exactly what she needed. And she still didn't know, but she felt safe here, like she didn't need to hide anymore. She could be herself, fucked up as she was.

Cherie was a big part of that feeling. It wasn't some seedy bar. It was a safe place for the downtrodden. Those that most people either ignored, avoided, or never saw in the first place. And in the short time she had gotten to know Cherie, it was clear she was an ever-present pillar of acceptance and love. That's what Drea saw and felt when she thought of this place. She had wondered why a woman like Cherie would ever spend her life running such a place though.

Drea sipped the black coffee, letting it push the sadness out of her mind. She took a long look at Cherie and gestured around them. "How do you do this every day?" she asked. "I mean, does it get to you?"

Cherie smiled, awaking the deep creases around her lips and eyes. "It's life. It's all around us wherever we go, maybe just a little more obvious in places like this. I wanted to make sure people had a safe place to go when they needed it." She raised her arms. "So here we are."

"Well, I appreciate it." Emotion tugged through the haze of alcohol and she sipped her coffee to curb it.

"You definitely learn to spot it after so many years here," Cherie said.

"Spot what?"

Cherie's warm eyes held hers. "Suffering."

Drea's eyes dropped to her mug, the recognition too direct. Cherie placed her hand over Drea's for a moment, and they stayed there together in silence.

Light music hummed in the background at Rosie's. Cassie took a seat across from Janay, eager to hear about her date. "So, how'd it go?"

"Girl, I don't know." Janay's dark hair was pulled back into a tight, high ponytail, and big silver hoops hung from her ears. A thin, tan sweater clung to her in all the right places, showing off the curves and fit body she normally hid under T-shirts and athletic gear, and accenting her flawless complexion perfectly. She was putting up her hard front, but Cassie could see the little grin behind it.

"You like her," she teased.

"She was all right, but damn if you think I'm gonna tell Renee that. I'd never hear the end of it."

Cassie laughed. Janay and Renee loved each other, that was clear, but they had a healthy dose of competition between them as well and had kept Cassie entertained over the years with their antics.

Janay started giving her the details of the date and it sounded promising.

"So did you ask to see her again?" Cassie asked, hoping her friend hadn't shut down a potentially good thing.

Janay pulled a small piece of paper from her pocket and waved it in the air. "Girl, you know I got the digits."

Cassie laughed. "Old school. I like it. I hope I get to meet her sometime."

"Well . . ." Janay's eyes danced. "How about Saturday? I asked her to meet me here, if you're free."

Cassie's jaw dropped. She was so proud of Janay for putting herself out there. She had been so focused on the step team that her personal life had become an afterthought. "I am now."

One of Cassie's favorite Robyn songs came on the speakers and for a moment, with her best friend happy and good music playing, things seemed to be okay.

"How are—ah shit." Janay stared off into the distance.

Cassie bristled at the change in tone and started to turn to see what Janay was looking at.

"Don't look, don't look. Okay, it's going to be okay." Janay patted her arm, but there was no calming the nervousness in Cassie at that moment. "Drea's here . . . and she's with someone."

Fuck. She had been worried they might run into her here, but she didn't have the heart to tell Janay no when she was excited about a date. And she knew she couldn't avoid her favorite places just because Drea liked them too. Maybe it wasn't what it seemed. "Like with someone or *with* someone?" she asked.

Janay looked off to assess the situation further and Cassie watched as her body language answered the question for her. Janay frowned and Cassie's heart dropped into her stomach. She wasn't sure what was worse, that Drea had moved on so quickly or the pity in Janay's eyes.

"You wanna get outta here?" Janay asked.

She nodded, not in the mood for anything anymore.

As she followed Janay toward the door, curiosity got the best of her and she glanced toward the dance floor. Some blonde girl was grinding against Drea, who was giving as good as she got, an easy smile on her face. Cassie's eyes dropped to the navy-blue dress shirt she had worn the first night they slept together as memories of that night sucker punched her. The blonde ran a hand through Drea's hair and Cassie had to look away.

When the morning sun stirred Cassie awake, she groaned as thoughts from last night seeped into her mind. She was generally pretty good at staying positive or at least getting back to a positive state after being derailed. Well, with most things. Though the situation with Molly had definitely thrown her. But Drea was an even bigger exception.

She had stayed up late, unable to keep her mind off Drea and the blonde. Her mind wandering to truly crappy places as she envisioned what Drea's night might have entailed after she left the club with that girl. She hoped she was wrong, but from the way they acted on the dance floor . . . a wave of nausea ran through her at the memory and she groaned and rolled over, eliciting a disgruntled meow from Digit, who had shifted his companionship from Molly back to Cassie given her current situation. "When will it stop hurting so much?" she asked him. He readjusted and slammed into her side on his way down. Cassie sighed at the unsupportive gesture.

By the time she made it to the office, with some strong coffee seeping into her veins and a little breakfast steadying her physical and mental energy, she had begun to think the negativity of the morning was behind her.

And then Drea walked in.

She was wearing the same navy-blue shirt from last night. Her curls a little more wild than the night before, the dark tint of smeared eyeliner making her eyes even more striking than usual. Of course she would look even hotter after a sleepless night. The stark realization that Drea had slept with the woman from last night hit her like a two-by-four, and this time she couldn't stop the tears from coming. She pushed her chair back and rushed to the bathroom.

Chapter 20

"Aunt D!" Jake ran down the sidewalk to meet Drea and wrapped his arms around her waist.

God, she had missed him. She bent down and wrapped her arms around him, feeling his warmth against the cold. "Hey bud, you ready for Christmas?"

"Yes." He jumped as he said it, and she wished she could bottle that kind of enthusiasm. Even when she was a kid, holidays had been tedious with her parents, not the fun they always seemed to show in movies.

"Hey, thanks for meeting us," Sam said as she joined them, and wrapped her arm around Drea's shoulders in a half-hug. They stepped to the side so they weren't blocking the sidewalk. With only a few days left before Christmas, the stores were packed with people trying to finish their holiday shopping.

"Of course. So what's the mission?" She rubbed her gloved hands together conspiratorially.

"First, I need to get a gift for the party. I was hoping you could help with that part. And then maybe you and Jake can hang out for a little bit while I have a chat with Santa?"

Jake's eyebrows raised like he had just heard a secret, the goofy expression pulling a laugh from her. She wished all of her relationships could be as easy as her and Jake's. They just got each other. She wasn't sure if that meant she had the emotional maturity of a six-year-old, even though he was a precocious kid, but she supposed there were worse things.

"Sounds good. Who'd you get?"

Sam took Jake's hand and headed for the first shop. "Cassie," she called over her shoulder.

Drea's steps faltered for a moment. Luckily Sam didn't notice.

"I know gift exchanges can be fun and silly items, but Cassie's done so much for me, for all of us, that I want to get her something special," Sam said as they perused the first shop, which specialized in hand-printed cards and gifts. "Since y'all have gotten close, I thought you might know what she likes."

Drea nodded, but didn't know how to begin to address that can of worms.

The next place had humorous and New Orleans-inspired kitchen accessories and home goods. Jake grabbed two plastic crawfish and made them dance on the display table. Drea chuckled at his silliness.

Sam held a tea towel up to Drea that said "There's probably cat fur on this." "That's kind of funny, right?"

Drea tilted her head from side to side. "Kind of, but I don't think that's the one."

"You're right. Looking for special, not funny."

By the third shop, Jake was starting to get antsy and so was Drea. Pine scent permeated the holiday-themed shop as a Christmas tree full of old-fashioned glass ornaments by the window caught her attention. She eyed a couple of typical holiday-themed pieces until she saw it. A vibrant blue, pink, and purple butterfly that reminded her of Cassie's tattoo. And since the tattoo had symbolized letting go of old dreams to let in new ones, something to celebrate the success of the company and Cassie's integral role in that success seemed perfect. She held it in her hands, admiring the craftsmanship.

Sam joined her. "That's beautiful."

Drea nodded. "This is the one."

Sam watched her for a moment, then nodded. "Okay, perfect."

Drea handed the ornament to Sam. "Mission accomplished. We are outta here." She took Jake's hand and they headed off in search of a sugar coma.

"So how do you know Renee?" Cassie yelled to Dasha, Janay's date, over the EDM blasting through Rosie's.

"Oh, we met at the gym. She's friends with a friend of mine."

Cassie nodded.

"Are you into step?"

"What?"

"Are you into step?" Cassie yelled louder. She gestured at Janay who was standing beside Dasha, both of them dressed up from their date, Dasha in a skintight black dress that fit right in at the club and Janay in a white dress shirt with an open vest and black wide-leg pants. "Janay runs a step team."

"Oh, no, I mean it's cool, but I'm not really into sports." Dasha sipped her amaretto sour through a straw and glanced around the room, looking bored.

This probably wasn't the best idea. She could barely hear Dasha, and she was nervous about possibly running into Drea again. Maybe she and Janay did need to expand their club scene. But Rosie's was the only dedicated queer club that focused on serving women, and she always felt out of place in straight clubs.

Cassie tried to make conversation with Dasha for a while longer as Janay kept being sidetracked by people coming to their table to talk to her. Then Janay excused Cassie and herself to get another round of drinks.

"So what do you think?" Janay asked as they waited in line at the bar.

"Yeah, I think she's cool. Um, I just . . . do you have much in common?"

"Apparently not. Maybe I didn't ask the right questions on our first date, but she seemed cool. But damn, you're taking one for the team trying to get info out of her tonight."

"Oh good, okay, phew. I was worried you didn't see it."

"It's as clear as a train wreck."

The group in front of them cleared out and they stepped to the bar.

"What can I get ya?" asked the bartender, an attractive androgynous person with a shaved head and cropped T-shirt hanging off one shoulder.

"Amaretto sour, a Pimm's, and an iced tea," Janay said.

"What are we going to do about Dasha?" Cassie asked.

"Let's have our drinks and dance. Might as well enjoy the night since we're here."

Janay was right. After another round, Dasha seemed to be as bored with the lack of connection as Janay. She said good night and Cassie and Janay headed to the dance floor.

After a couple of songs, Cassie took a break to get some water. But as she approached the bar, she saw Drea with a woman. A different one from the other night, of course. Cassie took the long way around, hoping Drea wouldn't see her, but snuck a glance while she waited in line. They were doing shots. Though the attractive brunette was flirting pretty heavily with her, Drea seemed kind of out of it. As she watched, recognition hit deep in her gut at the glazed look in Drea's eyes and the vacant grin.

She found Janay on the dance floor and pulled her aside. "Drea's here; she's drunk. Like, really drunk."

Janay's eyes widened. "Are you okay?"

Tears filled her eyes. "I can't do this, J."

Janay hugged her. "I know." She pulled out her phone and tapped the screen a few times. "Come on, a car's coming for ya."

They grabbed their coats, and Janay walked her outside and waited for the car to arrive. Cassie turned to her, concern pulsing through her body. "Can you keep an eye on her? Make sure she gets home okay?"

Janay nodded. "I got you."

Cassie hugged her tight. "Thank you."

"Hey Drea."

Drea turned toward the voice, taking in the woman standing next to her at the bar as a flicker of recognition hit. "Heeey, you're, uh, Cassie's friend."

She nodded. "Janay."

"Janay, right. How are ya?" Drea propped her elbow on the bar and leaned her cheek against her fist.

"Could we chat for a few minutes?"

Drea turned to Cammie or Kimmie or whatever her name was who was standing behind Drea with her hand on Drea's shoulder. "Could you give us a few minutes?"

She shrugged and walked off.

Janay signaled to the bartender. "Could I get a coffee?" The bartender glanced at Drea and nodded.

"How are ya doing, Drea?"

Drea shrugged. "Oh, you know."

"You know, Cassie's my best friend."

Drea nodded. "She's the best."

The bartender slid a mug of coffee her way.

Janay nodded at the drink. "Drink some of that, will ya?"

Drea grabbed the mug and took a sip, the caffeine warring with the alcohol subduing her. She wondered what Janay wanted.

The way she was standing there with a serious look on her face made Drea feel like she was in trouble.

"I know y'all broke up, but you care about her, right?"

The question struck her as odd. "Of course." She took another sip, feeling the need to be more clear-headed for this conversation, whatever it was.

"'Cause you're kinda hurting my girl."

Drea sat up straighter. "What? What are you talking about?" She tried to figure out what the hell Janay was hinting at despite her brain working a bit slower than normal, then glanced around. "She's here?"

"She was."

Drea continued to scan the room trying to find Cassie, a glimmer of hope at the idea of seeing her.

"She's gone now."

Drea exhaled, feeling smaller than before.

Janay continued. "I know things might be tough right now for both of you, but . . ." She gestured at the bar. "This is a little cruel, don't you think?"

Drea stared at her, the confusion and growing anger sobering her up. "Seriously, what the hell are you talking about?"

They locked eyes for a long moment until something changed in Janay's expression. "She didn't tell you, did she?"

Fear and hesitation gripped Drea. "Tell me what?"

Janay took a deep breath and blew it out, staring at the ground as if trying to figure out what to do.

"Please, Janay. What is it?"

Janay met her eyes and nodded, then took a seat next to Drea. "What did Cassie tell you about her parents?"

Drea thought hard, trying to remember it all. "A lot about her mom and how supportive she was with ballet. And that her parents passed away when she was eleven. I assumed it was a car accident or something."

Janay nodded. "It was. A single-car accident."

Drea took a moment with the comment before understanding hit.

"Cassie's dad was an abusive alcoholic. When I met her in college, she was in a bad place—feeling hopeless about her dancing career, drinking a lot, and still dealing with that loss. It took a while, but Molly and I helped her work through it."

Fuck. How did she not know any of this? "I knew she didn't drink, but we never talked about it."

"She's sober, Drea. And seeing you here tonight in this state…" She tilted her head at her. "You really hurt her. And you already broke her heart, so . . ."

Her entire body sagged at the weight of it all. "I didn't know." She shook her head. "Fuck. I didn't know." She had tried so hard to save Cassie from pain, not wanting to disappoint her or bring her any more sadness and, instead, she had ended up doing all those things and more. She didn't even need to be in a relationship to hurt people. Now, merely being in their lives at all was enough.

Chapter 21

Rays of light streamed through Drea's windows like ice picks to her brain. She groaned and rolled over, shielding her eyes from further assault. Pickles had other ideas, though, as he unleashed an energetic food march across her body, meowing incessantly until she finally caved.

"Alllll rriiiiggghhhhttttt already, Jesus."

He hopped to the floor and led her to the kitchen, meowing away.

She poured his food and started some coffee, then leaned over the island and rested her head in her hand as he munched away at his kibble.

Last night had been a blur until it wasn't. She had stayed up most of the night sorting through the conversation with Janay, trying to figure out how she had gotten to this moment in her life, and how, after months of conversations with Cassie, so much had been left unspoken. For most of her life she had prided herself on her ability to get others to talk. For one, it was interesting to hear people's stories, and also most people liked talking about themselves, and making sure women enjoyed themselves was kind of her forte. But the biggest reason was it kept the focus off of her, the queen of avoidance.

But everything had been different with Cassie. She knew that before they ever spent any time alone together. She thought it was jealousy over Cassie's bond with Sam, but what if her subconscious had known all along that this girl was different? Maybe that was the hesitation gnawing at the edges of her mind in the beginning, warning her to keep her distance. Not that it did much good, because little by little Cassie maneuvered into her heart and never left. Drea had spent tons of time with interesting, even incredible, women and she probably wouldn't ever be able to fully understand why Cassie shook her when no one else could. She just knew that she did. So many pieces caught her attention—her vibrancy, both in her style and her personality, her dedication, her strength and competitiveness, and all the moments, heartbreaking and cruel as many seemed to be, that had made her who she was today. But more than all of that was how *she* was with Cassie. Drea had opened up to her more than anyone else in her life, in some ways even more than Sam. In a life filled with surface-level encounters, Cassie had slipped past all of her walls without even trying and demanded more. And as much as she tried to resist it, it had almost felt inevitable.

So, had Cassie kept her talking, the student becoming the master? Had Drea become like so many others, grabbing the opportunity to talk and ignoring the person on the other end? No, there was plenty she hadn't told Cassie, and after last night, it was clear Cassie had done the same. Maybe despite being more vulnerable with Cassie than with anyone before, they both had kept a wall up. She knew where hers came from. *That* was inevitable. But maybe Cassie never fully trusted her either, not enough to let her guard down completely. She couldn't blame her. She knew her own reputation, and it wasn't based on a lie. It was all true, every scandalous, sexy detail. And in the end, after an amazing week together, she had proven Cassie right, ending things before Cassie could even have a say.

The coffee maker beeped, snatching her from her thoughts. She poured a cup, the sweet, nutty aroma chewing at the haze in her brain.

Pickles joined her as she nestled into the plush sofa and took a sip, the aftertaste lingering on her tongue, almost as bitter as what she must do next.

Last night had been a wake-up call, and now she had a choice to make. She could either continue down this path as she had always done, playing the role of what people expected from her, and continuing to hide her truth, gnarly and disturbing and even sometimes beautiful, until she no longer recognized herself. It was a comfortable route, though not painless. The fact that she couldn't walk it anymore without liquid courage was another warning bell. Things were turning dark fast, and right now she still had the wherewithal to choose, but if she went much further, even that would disappear. Or she could do what she had never done in her life, not fully anyway: the scary, terrifying, courageous thing of following her heart and doing what made her happy—no parents, no expectations, no lies. Of course that meant first finding out what the fuck that was.

She thought about Cherie and the bar, how easy it would be to go back there and settle into the shadows, and how much she wanted a drink right now. She thought of the haunted look in the eyes of the ones who had done that, and pain pricked in her chest at the thought of becoming something similar.

But then she thought of Cassie and the butterfly, and an idea started as a whisper that grew louder in her mind. What if? What if she tried? What if she dared to be the person she knew deep down she wanted to be? What if she still disappointed people occasionally but at least it was while trying to do the right thing, for her and not anyone else? What if she stopped avoiding it all and used all of the energy it took every day to hurt and run and hide to just fucking be herself?

She wiped at the tears falling off her jaw. Pickles rubbed

against her, settling on her lap as the rumbles of a purr soothed her. As she tried to imagine where she would even start, what really made her happy, an image popped into her mind, of a toothy grin and a giggle that always made her smile.

She grabbed her phone and started a search.

Cassie sat in the circle with her coworkers, trying to focus on Sam, who was unwrapping her gift, but so far it was one of the most painful holiday parties she had ever attended.

"Oh my gosh," Sam said as she unwrapped the lavender candle, then realized there was another gift in the bag and opened the matching bath salts. She scanned the people around her. "Who?"

Cassie forced a grin. "It was me."

"Thank you. This is perfect and much needed." Sam placed the bundle on the desk behind her. "Who's next? Tom?" She found the gift with his name on it. "Here ya go."

Tom leapt up from his chair and tore into the snowman wrapping paper.

Cassie tried to enjoy the moment with the community she had found working here, even Tom's youthful exuberance on display, but she couldn't help but sneak a few glances at Drea. The past two days had been trying to say the least. Seeing Drea so out of it on Saturday had hit her on so many levels, the guilt and concern that she was struggling and Cassie couldn't help her, the anger at her for getting drunk, and the pain from all the memories it brought up for her, both from her childhood and her own journey in college.

She had had no idea what to expect when she came to work today, worrying about the worst but hoping for something better for Drea. No matter what had happened between them, she cared about her, and hated seeing her like that. By some miracle

Drea seemed like herself, maybe even better than usual. The pang that realization caused surprised Cassie. She was delighted that Drea was okay, she hoped so at least. But if she was okay, then that meant that she really was . . . okay, and seeing her better than okay today meant she wasn't struggling over their breakup or the absence of Cassie in her life. Not like Cassie was. And that hurt, like everything about Drea seemed to lately. She wasn't sure how long she could last like this. Seeing Drea every day at work, having to pretend it didn't hurt. It hurt to see her happy, to see her sad, and just to see her. But this job wasn't only a job to Cassie. It was a home. She couldn't let her situation with Drea ruin that.

"This is so awesome! This had to be you, right?" Tom's words pulled Cassie from her thoughts as he pointed at Erin and waved some *Star Wars* figurine around. Cassie was thankful she didn't get Tom's name because she would have been lost in some far-off galaxy trying to find him a gift, or was that *Star Trek*, or maybe *Spaceballs?* Anyway.

Her eyes fell on Drea by accident, for what seemed like the thousandth time today. And as Drea met them, a small smile slipped from Cassie's lips before she could stop it. Seeing the small twinkle in Drea's eyes again made her so much happier than the last time she saw her. But there was something behind the twinkle as well and Drea looked away, leaving Cassie there as usual, alone, feeling like an idiot.

Thankfully, she only had to make it through today and then she'd have the rest of the week off for the holiday. It had been an odd day anyway. A few accounts needed some final details to be completed, but she and Sam had nailed those out by noon, so now it was just this party. Everyone was pretty checked out in that almost-vacation, delirious state that reminded her of senioritis back in high school. She checked the clock, willing it to tick faster.

"Cassie." She looked up to see Sam holding out a neatly

wrapped box. "It's your turn."

A small burst of excitement ran through her as she took it and slid her nail under an end flap, trying not to rip the paper. She lifted the lid of the forest-green box, and everything stopped as she gazed at the beautifully intricate ornament inside. She looked at Drea, searching her eyes, trying to understand why she would give her such an amazing and meaningful gift, especially now when it was too late. Drea held her gaze, and for a moment she felt the connection as emotion swirled between them.

"Do you like it?" Sam asked.

She turned to Sam, confused. "I love it," she said slowly.

"Oh good. I wasn't sure if you collected ornaments."

Embarrassment for being so dumb overtook her. She stared at the ornament, trying to hide the heat creeping up her neck. "It's great. Thank you."

After a few more gifts were opened, the party finally ended and she could pack up and go, and maybe never show her face again.

"Hey." Sam joined her on the way back to her desk. "You okay? You seemed a little upset earlier."

Cassie forced a smile. "Yeah, I uh, I was confused. I thought maybe Drea got the gift, but I was wrong. I love it, so thank you very much."

"Oh, well, Drea helped me pick it out. I wanted to get you something special for everything you've done over the past few months. We wouldn't be here without you. I wouldn't be here without you." Sam placed her hand on Cassie's arm.

"Oh." She tried to focus on the compliment and the kindness of the first boss who ever really appreciated her, but her mind swirled with confusion. Why would Drea do that? "Well, thank you. It's very meaningful to me."

Sam smiled, but a flash of something crossed her expression. "Have a wonderful holiday, Cassie. You deserve it." Sam squeezed her arm and headed to her desk.

Drea hadn't been sure what was up when Sam grabbed her after the party and strongly suggested they go to Charlie's immediately, but Cassie had crossed her mind as one of the possibilities.

"What happened?" Sam asked from across the table.

Drea scratched her neck. "Can you narrow that down a little?"

Sam sighed. "With Cassie. Something happened, didn't it?"

Drea grimaced and turned her face to avoid whatever might spew out of Sam as she nodded.

Sam's eyes widened as she gasped. "You slept with her?" It felt more like an accusation than a question, despite the weak inflection at the end.

Drea raised her hands. "In my defense, you never said that was a rule."

"Oh my god, Drea. Not Cassie. Why Cassie? You could sleep with anybody else, literally anybody. Why her?"

"We did sleep together," Drea said, trying not to focus on the rage in Sam's eyes before continuing. "We slept together a few times actually. More than a few times."

Sam's mouth tightened, about to launch into a tirade before the realization hit. "Wait, what?"

"We kinda dated." Drea held up her hands and wiggled them in the air. "Surprise."

Sam stared at her blankly, her mouth agape, and Drea wondered if she needed to plug her in.

The waitress came up to their table during the brief silence. "What can I get you ladies?"

Sam came alive again at the waitress's voice. "A margarita." She held up her hands and moved them apart from each other to indicate the size. "The big one."

"And for you?" Her voice dripped with sweetness as she

turned to Drea.

"Just a water for now, thanks." Drea passed her a warm smile.

"Alrighty."

Sam rubbed her forehead. "Okay, I'm going to need you to tell me what's going on here. You're not drinking and you're dating now? Did I die? Is this like a twisted version of heaven?" Her eyes widened. "Oh god, is this hell?"

"I hope hell has margaritas. That would be awesome."

Sam's concerned expression killed the laughter in Drea's voice. Drea thought for a moment, not really sure where to begin.

"So, remember when Cassie was really down at work?"

"Yes."

"Well, it's because her sister, Molly, had broken up with her partner. They'd been together like twenty years or something. And Molly moved in with Cassie and was really struggling so Cassie started helping her plan some weddings because that's what she does for a living."

Sam's brow furrowed as she tried to follow. "Okay."

"But Cassie was really sad, so I asked her what was up and she told me, blah blah blah, so I started helping her with the weddings."

Sam's brows raised in surprise. "You hate weddings."

"I know. And, you know—one thing led to another and I, um, kinda fell in love with her." She waved her hands in the air again. "Surprise."

Sam short-circuited again.

"Here you are." The waitress slid the massive margarita in front of Sam, whose eyes never left Drea's, then passed Drea a questioning look as she placed a glass of water in front of her. Drea gave a thumbs-up and the waitress nodded. "Let me know if you need anything else," she said as she headed toward the bar.

Drea moved the margarita closer to Sam. "Here, drink this."

Sam took a sip, seeming to take a moment with her words. "Drea, you haven't expressed real interest in anyone since . . . AJ."

Drea and Sam said the name at the same time.

It was funny how something so long ago could stick with somebody. But things that scar tend to have that effect. Drea remembered how hard she had fallen for the star soccer player in high school, how giddy she had felt back then, and how she had worked up the courage to tell her and come out at senior prom even though Sam had concerns. Sam had been humiliated by her crew of bullies that night and all Drea had told her after the anguish of that incident died down was that she had been right, AJ wasn't gay. Drea never mentioned the part where AJ and her friends had laughed at her. Or how her heart had been broken. She had vowed to herself then never to let anyone close enough to hurt her again. Of course, she heard that AJ did come out a few years later. Her gaydar always had been spot-on.

Drea shrugged. "I know. But don't worry. I ended it. It's a little raw right now, but she'll be okay."

"That explains earlier then," Sam said.

"Earlier?" Drea asked.

"Yeah, Cassie seemed upset after the party and the butterfly present." She shook her head with a solemn expression. "I didn't know there was more going on between you when I asked for your help finding her a gift."

Drea's heart sank. She hated that something she thought would bring joy to Cassie ended up upsetting her.

"And what about you?" Sam asked. "Will you be okay?" Sam's eyes held such sincerity it sent a ball of emotion to Drea's throat, but she shrugged it off.

"You know me," Drea said with a forced smile and took a sip of water to swallow down the emotion.

"Why did you end it?"

"I thought you'd be happy to hear that."

"No, I'd like to know."

"You know me." She tried to smile, but she couldn't do it. Not anymore. "I couldn't stand the thought of disappointing another person. I'm great for a short time. I can do the best impression of a happy, fun-loving person. But when someone sticks around, there's nowhere to hide the real me."

"You've never disappointed me, or Jake. I've stuck around a long time, and I think you're the most incredible person I've ever known."

"That's because you've always had this crazy idea that I'm great, and I've worked my ass off to keep it that way. There's stuff I've never told you because I don't want you to ever look at me the way my parents do. That would kill me."

"I'm sure there are things I don't know about you. That's true of everyone, no matter how close you are. But . . ." She laughed. "I don't think you're as good at hiding things as you think. I've known you since middle school."

"Sam, there's a darkness to me that you haven't seen."

She paused for a moment. "Well, I disagree. What about all those times after your parents came down on you and I had to build you up just to go outside and see the river with me, or after prom when you were so down and we ate ice cream and had a movie marathon all weekend?"

"We did that because you were so down after prom."

"Maybe the first day, but the second day was all you."

She stared at the table thinking through those times, realizing that Sam had always been there even when Drea thought she'd been masking her true feelings.

"And I've always thought you were great because you are great," Sam said. "You've been the best friend a girl could ever ask for. And you've put Jake above all else, always. You don't know what that means to me."

Drea smiled at the thought of Jake.

"So." Sam gestured to her water. "What's this about?"

Drea sighed, not wanting to talk about it, but knowing she had to. "I, um, started drinking a bit too much after the breakup. A lot too much actually. Things got out of hand." She scratched her neck, feeling a little too vulnerable. "But I'm working on it and taking it one day at a time."

Sam put her hand on Drea's arm. "I'm sorry." She glanced at her margarita. "Shit, I'm sorry." She moved her drink to the side of the table.

Drea shook her head. "You're fine." She knew it would be an adjustment before Sam got used to her not drinking.

"You know I'm always here for you, right?"

"Yeah." Drea glanced at the table, because the truth was she felt pretty alone nowadays. Even though they saw each other almost daily at work, it was different. She missed her friend, her family.

Sam continued. "I know things have been rough the past few months. I've been absent and I'm sorry. I'm trying to figure out how to juggle all of the things, but I love you and I would drop everything for you. I hope you know that."

"I do. I've just been struggling a bit with where I fit into your and Jake's life now. I'm glad you're happy with Ash, but I miss you sometimes."

Sam looked incredulous. "Drea, you're family. You always have been and you always will be . . . and, for what it's worth, I think Cassie's pretty great."

Drea nodded. "She is." The thought of Cassie's smile earlier warmed her, but the pain of knowing they weren't together anymore stilled her.

Sam met her eyes. "And so are you. I know your parents were really strict and your family dynamic was very different than mine growing up, but they didn't see you for who you are. And that's their loss."

Drea gave her a weak smile and Sam took her hand.

"You have so much to offer. I've just been waiting, hoping that one day you'd realize it. I've known you a long time, Drea, and I've never heard you talk about anyone the way you talked about Cassie tonight. It's your decision, but I don't think you should give up on her so quickly." She squeezed her hand. "Give her a chance. And give yourself one too."

Cassie groaned, and Digit nuzzled deeper against her on the sofa as if trying to offer more support. She had been trying unsuccessfully to zone out to some mindless TV, but her mind kept returning to the party that afternoon. How embarrassing. She felt so stupid for thinking Drea had given her the butterfly ornament. Helping Sam pick out something that she knew would mean so much to Cassie, that Cassie had shared with her and her alone, it felt . . . it felt . . . she didn't know how she felt. Her brain and thoughts were muddled, a million emotions surging through her and gripping her chest as tears started to form. No! She wasn't going to do this. She wasn't going to cry over Drea for weeks or months or any amount of time. It was over and the sooner she got out of this funk, the better. And only she could make that happen.

She grabbed the TV remote and clicked it off, then hopped up from the sofa and moved the coffee table out of the way. She needed her one true thing—her one safe haven. She grabbed her phone and selected a song.

As the hauntingly beautiful acoustic notes began, she put one foot en pointe, a position as familiar as breathing from her many years of ballet. She closed her eyes, feeling each note in her heart, and raised her arms slowly to arc above her head. As Taylor Swift began to sing the words to "Safe and Sound," the beauty and sadness in her light, breathy voice raised the hair on Cassie's arms.

She took a step forward and began to dance around her living room. The initial gentle and measured movements progressed to free-form as the lyrics progressed, and tears began to fall down her cheeks. But as the song picked up, Cassie burst forward, releasing everything, the hesitation in her movements and the thoughts swirling in her mind. She twirled and leapt and punched through the air as if nothing could ever hold her down.

And when the notes finally stilled, Cassie fell to her knees, panting, exhausted, and finally . . . free. She didn't know how long it would last, and it didn't matter, because in this moment it was enough.

Chapter 22

Mama J carried the cake to the table as they all sang, the multitude of voices canceling out the few off-pitch notes. As she placed the chocolate cake, adorned with "40" in white icing, on the table, the final line rang out. Cassie smiled across the table as Molly beamed in the candlelight.

"Happy birthday, sis," Cassie said as the table went silent.

"Thank you all." Molly grinned. She paused for a moment, then blew out the candles.

"Here, honey." Mama J handed her a knife and she started cutting slices for everyone.

Cassie looked on, taking in the moment. They had been coming here for Christmas Eve dinner since college, and though Molly's birthday was a few days away in the no man's land between Christmas and New Year's, Mama J had always made a point to celebrate it while they were all together. This was a big one, not just for the number, though the thought of her sister turning forty still felt surreal, but because so much had changed over the past year.

Even though it was their second holiday with the Jeffries family since Eva left, her absence still lingered at the table. Molly was embarking on a new chapter, one she never anticipated or hoped for, and trying to move forward. And though she rarely said so, Cassie knew how much she was still hurting just getting through every day. She felt it deeper than she could have expected now that she was navigating her own broken heart. But they had been through tough times together before, and as she looked around the room at all the faces of those who had wrapped them in love and acceptance since the moment they stepped through that front door so many years ago, she knew they'd be okay again. One day.

After they had all stuffed themselves further with cake, Janay caught Cassie's eye and tilted her head toward her old bedroom where they snuck away to chat. When Janay closed the door and filled Cassie in on the conversation she'd had with Drea a few days ago, Cassie glared at her.

"You told her what?" Cassie could feel a tinge of anger creep into her voice.

To her credit, Janay looked remorseful. "I know. It wasn't my place, but I kinda came down hard on her thinking she was being kinda shitty given your past, and then it became clear she didn't know about your past." She pointed to the ceiling and arched a brow at Cassie. "We'll get to that in a minute."

Cassie ducked her chin regretfully, not looking forward to explaining why she hadn't told Drea about her past.

"Look, she was struggling, and when her eyes lit up thinking you were there and then got sad again when I said you'd left, I don't know, I felt like I had just kicked a puppy or something."

Cassie got stuck on the part about Drea's eyes lighting up thinking she was there.

"I'm sorry," Janay said. "But more importantly, why was I the one telling her all that new information?"

Cassie sighed and looked away, rubbing her hand on the yellow comforter as if it would save her from this conversation. It wasn't like she told everyone the first moment she met them that she had a problem with alcohol and now was sober. Most people were chill enough that when she said she didn't drink, they didn't push for answers. And she definitely didn't go into the details of how she lost her parents. Despite working through that grief for many years, it was still hard to say it out loud. And did it matter? They were gone. That's what mattered. Why bring up all the sordid details?

She wanted her mom's memory to be of the amazing, caring woman who raised her, not how she was ripped from the world too soon. And her dad, well, she didn't think much about him at all anymore. She had spent too many years hating him for what he did, to all of them, but it only drove her to the bottom. No, she had made the choice not to let that event dictate the rest of her life, not anymore. And it had all seemed behind her until this moment as she grappled with why she hadn't told the person she was dating two crucial parts of her backstory.

She turned back to Janay who was watching her, waiting patiently as usual. "It's hard to talk about."

"Well, yeah. But I thought y'all were getting serious. I mean, how could you get serious with someone who doesn't know some of the biggest things about you?" There was no judgment in her voice, only the obvious question that now seemed so simple.

Cassie bit her lip. "You can't." And for the first time, she realized it wasn't just Drea alone who had pushed her away. She had kept one foot out the door as well. Sure, they had discussed some important things, but apparently only the stuff that didn't cut too deep. If she was being honest with herself, she knew the reason she hadn't opened up fully to Drea. And it had nothing to do with Drea's reputation or how new it had been or even how deliciously unstable she felt when those devastating blue eyes searched hers.

"She's not over you, you know. And you're not over her. Maybe y'all should talk, for real though."

Cassie held her gaze for a moment, trying to decide if it was really that simple, that all of the anguish might be resolved by simply communicating. That maybe they could resolve this. She blew out a breath and nodded, then looked at her watch. It wasn't even seven yet. She had to at least try.

"Here ya go, bud." Drea held out the misshapen gift to Jake, who leapt up from his spot on the floor, mid-LEGO construction, to grab it. Drea, Sam, and Ash all laughed as he tore open the dragon wrapping paper.

He pulled out a small plastic container with a blue top, followed by a red one, then green, and finally yellow, placing each on the coffee table as he went.

"Oh, I remember those," Ash said.

Jake's face was full of wonder as he looked at Drea. "What are they?"

Drea grinned. "Finger paint."

"Awesome!" Jake grabbed the green one and started to open it.

Sam raised her hands in the air. "Whoa, whoa, whoa. Hang on, I'll help with that. This stuff will go everywhere." She shot Drea a pointed look. "Thanks, Drea."

Drea ignored the sarcasm in her voice. "You're welcome, Sam." Then she pulled out a thin package hidden beside her on the sofa and handed it to Jake. "You'll need this too."

He ripped it open with equal fervor to the first one, jumping up and down when he unveiled the glossy white paper. "Mom, can we paint! Please?" He dragged out the word for maximum effect.

"What do you say?" Sam said.

"Thanks, Aunt D." Jake ran over and wrapped his little arms around her neck. She hugged him back, relishing in the moment, hoping he never became too old for hugs.

"Okay, go put on some play clothes first. I'll get the kitchen set up," Sam said.

"Okay." The word was barely out of his mouth before Jake bolted from the room.

Sam turned to Ash. "Babe, do you mind helping him? Find the green ones. Not the neon-green ones, the other ones, with the dinosaur on them."

"Got it." Ash set her hot chocolate on the coffee table, then kissed Sam before heading in Jake's direction.

This had been their holiday tradition the past few years, getting together the evening of Christmas Eve and Jake getting to open his gift from Drea. Drea had worried that things might be different this year, with Ash and everything. But it felt like normal, except Sam seemed more content now that she had found Ash. Drea was happy she and Sam had hashed things out the other night at Charlie's. She felt as if she were back with her real family, back home.

"Well, now we get to wrap the kitchen in newspaper." Sam grabbed the remains of the wrapping paper off the floor and pointed at Drea. "And you're going to help."

"No problem." Drea grabbed her hot chocolate and stood up.

"So why finger paint?" Sam asked over her shoulder as Drea followed her to the kitchen.

"I actually started volunteering with kids at an art space downtown."

Sam tossed the wrapping paper in the trash and turned to her. "You did?"

Drea shrugged. "Yeah, it's only been a couple of times, but it's been cool. We were working with finger paint the first day and I thought Jake might enjoy it."

"That's really great. I'm proud of you."

Drea set her hot chocolate down on the counter and grabbed a cookie from the pile sitting there, her chewing stopping abruptly as something off hit her taste buds.

"Oh, don't eat those. I made them," Sam said, but it was too late.

Drea winced, then grabbed a napkin and spit it out, chugging hot chocolate to kill the acrid aftertaste.

"Sorry." Sam held out a platter of cookies. "Jake and Ash made these. They're safe." Sam grabbed a pile of newspaper and watched her for a moment. "Have you talked to Cassie at all?"

Drea had thought of nothing else since admitting to Sam how serious it had been. But she couldn't bring herself to make the call. She finished chewing the reindeer sugar cookie that was redeeming cookies single-handedly. "No."

Sam waited.

"I don't know what to say and I doubt she wants to talk to me ever again."

"Well, you work together, so you're going to have to talk at some point."

Drea frowned. "I know."

"And going by her reaction to the butterfly ornament, she very much still has feelings for you." Sam grabbed a bell-shaped cookie and took a bite.

Drea felt a prick of hope, but when she thought more about Cassie, she couldn't imagine Cassie forgiving her for how she had treated her. She was glad the ornament had meant something to Cassie, but Cassie deserved more than she could give her.

Sam shrugged and pointed her cookie at Drea. "Up to you, but this *is* the season of miracles." She gave her a goofy grin and Drea rolled her eyes.

After Jake wore himself out with finger paint, Drea headed home for the night. Seeing Sam and Ash so happy, and driving past all the homes lit up with families inside spending quality time together made her feel more alone than ever. Her thoughts kept returning to Cassie, and as she imagined driving to her house and making up and a future of bliss, her mind went back to all the things Cassie had kept from her. She hadn't trusted her, and if she didn't trust Drea then, she definitely wouldn't now.

No, she had fucked up and hurt Cassie, in ways she hadn't even known at the time. There was no coming back from that. No matter how much she felt for her, she had to let it go. They'd go back to being coworkers and that had to be enough. She could build a life that made her happy, even without Cassie in it. And maybe if she kept telling herself that, one day she might believe it.

"Merry Christmas, Miss Cassie," Earl said from his station in the lobby. Even in the short time Cassie had known him, she had developed an affection for him, and seemingly most of the people who lived in the building felt the same way.

"Merry Christmas, Earl. I was hoping to talk to Drea."

Earl rubbed at the gray stubble on his chin. "I'm sorry, but she's not in right now."

"Oh." She'd come straight here from Janay's, intent on finally having a conversation. A real conversation. She had been so focused on what she would say and how Drea might react that it hadn't occurred to her that Drea might not be home. Of course she wouldn't. She had a life and it was Christmas Eve night. She was probably with family—or not family. She felt deflated at the idea.

"Do you want me to tell her you stopped by?"

She contemplated the question for a moment, then smiled at him. "No, that's all right. Thank you. Merry Christmas." A blast of cold air slammed into her as she pushed the door open, and she tightened her scarf as she rushed to get out of there. She felt so stupid. What had she been thinking?

"Cassie?"

The sound of that voice saying her name stopped her, as memories of better times flooded her brain. She turned around to see Drea shrouded in a dark coat with a white scarf around her neck, a streetlamp illuminating her wild hair against the night sky. Cassie watched as Drea closed the gap between them.

"What are you doing here?" White puffs of cold air trailed Drea's breath as she spoke. The sight of her up close, so exquisitely beautiful, hit Cassie in the chest and she resisted the urge to place her hand on Drea's cheek to make sure she was real.

Suddenly the words seemed silly and she feared she had miscalculated the situation, but something in Drea's eyes gave her the courage to press on. "Can we talk?"

The inside of Drea's apartment brought a rush of memories, mostly good, except that last one. She wondered where this one would fall. Drea gestured to the sofa and grabbed two waters as Cassie sat.

Her eyes were earnest when she joined Cassie. "How are you?"

A small laugh slipped out at the question. She tilted her head from side to side. "I've been better. What about you?"

"Same."

She glanced around the room. "I hope I didn't interrupt anything."

Drea's brow furrowed.

"I mean, I hope I'm not keeping you from anyone." She quickly added, "Or anything."

A twinkle entered Drea's eyes. "I'm not seeing anyone if that's what you're referring to."

She shrugged. "I wasn't sure after the other night."

"The other night?"

"Yeah, the blonde on the dance floor." Cassie felt dumb even bringing it up. This wasn't how the conversation was supposed to go. She wasn't here to check up on Drea.

Drea's eyes fell to the sofa as she seemed to think through something. "I've gone out a few times, but that's all."

Cassie nodded, realizing this might be futile if Drea wasn't going to be honest.

Drea seemed to notice her dissatisfaction with the response. "What is it?"

"This is awkward, but I saw you out one night and then you were wearing the same thing at work the next morning, so yeah."

"I didn't sleep with her, Cassie." Drea rubbed her forehead and blew out a breath. "We danced, but then I went out alone to another bar . . . to drink." She stared at the sofa. "It was starting to become an issue, but I've got it under control now."

"I'm sorry."

Drea raised her eyes. "Why?"

"That you went through that."

"I'm the one who's sorry. I didn't know about your past and Janay said you saw me drunk." Drea shook her head as her voice cracked. "I never meant to hurt you."

"I know." Cassie wanted to reach out and comfort Drea, but she needed to focus on saying what she came here to say, and she knew if she touched Drea, it would jumble her senses the way it always did.

"I wish you had told me that stuff. That you had trusted me enough to tell me, but I know I didn't give you much reason to."

"That's not true." Cassie sighed. "I think we both could have done a better job of communicating."

Drea nodded.

"That's why I came here tonight. There's so much I should have told you and I have questions too. So I was wondering, would you be up for having an honest conversation?"

Drea's eyes brightened. "Okay."

And they did. They talked about all of it. Their childhoods and Cassie's journey to sobriety. Drea's nightmares, issues with depression, and use of alcohol and one-night stands to avoid rejection. Why Drea had ended things and how she decided to turn things around and start working with kids at the art center. The more they talked, the more they discovered in common and the deeper Cassie's feelings grew. She had never been so fully open with anyone in her life, but Drea had no judgment of anything she shared, only acceptance and understanding. As dawn broke through the sky, Cassie felt a lightness she had never felt before, a massive weight having lifted from her soul, and she knew that she had never loved anyone more than she loved Drea, in all her imperfections and beautiful flaws.

"I never wanted anything other than for you to be yourself," Cassie said.

"And I wanted you to love me for who I am, but you also made me want to be a better person, not just for you, but for me too."

"What if we didn't have to be this *or* that?" Cassie asked. "What if we focused on the *and*—sober *and* happy, depressed *and* creative?"

"Sexy *and* hot?" Drea added with a sly grin.

"Kinda." Cassie laughed. "We're all so many things. It seems so incredibly reductive to feel shame and guilt about some parts and good about others. We're so much more complicated than that."

"Beautiful disasters," Drea said.

"Exactly."

They sat in the quiet of the early morning for a few moments before Cassie spoke again. "I guess we should have said all of that a while ago."

Drea nodded. "Probably, but better late than never?"

"For sure. And just so you know, I didn't keep any of that from you because I didn't trust you before." Anxiety started to grip Cassie's chest. She held her wrist, took a deep breath, and blew it out, steadying herself.

Drea put her hand on Cassie's knee, trying to comfort her. "It's okay."

Cassie nodded and took another breath, needing to say what

was in her heart. "I was in love with you and afraid that I'd lose you."

Drea held her gaze. "Was as in past tense?"

She bit her lip for a moment. "Am . . . head over heels."

Drea closed the distance between them, an ocean of emotions in those blue eyes, and ran her hand along Cassie's cheek. "I'm in love with you too." And when Drea kissed her, Cassie felt all of the passion from before, but this time it was so much deeper than she ever imagined.

When Drea woke a few hours later, she smiled at the woman sleeping peacefully beside her. She leaned over, kissing along her back and up to her neck as Cassie squirmed and let out a happy sound.

"Merry Christmas," Drea whispered.

Cassie turned over to face her. "Merry Christmas," she said with a satisfied grin.

Drea propped herself on her elbow. "What would you like to do today? I was thinking—"

Cassie interrupted her with a kiss that lingered for several long moments until Drea had forgotten what she was saying.

"This." Cassie motioned between them. "This is what I want. To be here with you and do everything and nothing together, forever."

Drea looked at the easy smile on her face and those brown eyes that had captured her heart what felt like ages ago. She had never felt so happy and at peace before. There was nothing to hide or be ashamed of or make excuses for. She was herself and Cassie loved her all the more for it. And she did too.

Chapter 23

Cassie curled up next to Drea on the sofa in Drea's apartment as she listened to Janay and Molly talking. Sam, Ash, and Jody sat at the kitchen island, snacking on cheese and crackers as they chatted about New Year's resolutions while the New Year's Eve celebration played on the TV in the background.

"So Molly, when do you move into your new apartment?" Janay asked.

"I can start tomorrow in case you're free." Molly grinned.

Janay pretended to look at her watch. "I think I have a thing at that time." She flashed a smile. "I'm kidding. Of course I'll help you."

Cassie laughed, then caught Jody's eye in the kitchen and nodded. "And we'll be there to help as well," Cassie said to Molly. She intertwined her fingers with Drea's, still amazed at how good everything felt with this woman. "To start the new year off right."

"We can help," Ash said.

"Jake will be happy to help too," Sam added, smiling.

"Well, I think it calls for a celebration," Jody said as she carried the cake into the living room and set it on the coffee table.

Ash and Sam followed Jody with plates and forks, and they all gathered around the cake, peering at the intricate piping on top, and oohed and aahed.

"Raspberry chocolate," Jody said. "Happy birthday, Molly."

"Oh my gosh, this is for me?" Molly asked.

"Well, forty's a big deal, so we figured why not have two parties," Cassie said. "Besides, you deserve it."

Jody cut everyone a slice and the room fell silent as they ate, punctuated by the clinking of forks on plates and low sighs of pleasure as they tasted the interplay of tart raspberries against the rich chocolate.

"Oh my god, Jody, this might be the best cake I've ever had," Sam said. "You're hired for every birthday party in my house. I don't have any baking skills."

Cassie watched as Ash's eyes went wide and she shook her head at the others.

"Hey." Sam slapped her leg. "I have other skills."

Cassie and the others chuckled.

"You do." Ash kissed her. "Just none in the kitchen."

Sam nodded. "That's true."

"It's getting close to that time," Drea said as the countdown on the TV showed only a few more minutes.

Cassie followed Drea to the kitchen, sliding an arm around her waist as Drea peered into the fridge. "What can I help with?" she asked.

Drea wrapped her arms around her. "You being here is everything I need." She gave her a lingering kiss then pulled away to grab the bottles out of the fridge.

Cassie pulled out enough glasses for everyone and placed them on the island for Drea. Then she bent down to pet Pickles, who was meowing for attention.

She helped Drea carry glasses of champagne to everyone. Then Drea handed her a glass of sparkling grape juice. "These are for us," Drea said and clinked it with her own.

They all counted down as the ball on the TV started to drop.

"Four . . . three . . . two . . . one . . . Happy New Year!" They all shouted in unison and went around the room hugging each other. As Cassie hugged each person who had become part of her inner circle over weeks, months, years, and even a lifetime, she was overwhelmed by the love she felt for them and how lucky she felt to call them family.

They bundled up and went out on the balcony to watch as fireworks erupted over the river, a vast array of shapes and colors lighting up the sky before disappearing into the water.

Drea held her close, keeping her warm. Cassie wasn't sure what was more intoxicating, Drea's white musk perfume or the feeling of Drea holding her tight. "Do you have a New Year's resolution?" Drea asked.

"Hmm." Cassie thought for a moment. "You know, I feel like everything I've ever wanted and even the stuff I never dared to ask for is all right here. I couldn't ask for more than this. And normally it would make me scared to say that, but it doesn't. I feel . . ."

Drea tightened her arms around Cassie's waist. "Full," she said.

Cassie nodded. "Exactly. What about you?"

"Well, there is one thing," Drea said in a serious tone.

"What?" A flash of panic gripped Cassie. The last week had been the best of her life, but fears about the future couldn't help but wriggle through.

"Do you think Digit could teach Pickles how to be a baller?" Drea's face lit up like a little kid's, making her as adorable as she was sexy.

Cassie laughed, falling even more for this woman as the worry left her body. She was learning to trust and would eventually learn to trust completely. "I can have my people talk to his people, but I have a good feeling that can be arranged."

"Cool," Drea said. "I mean it would be good for them to

have a thing since they're gonna be brothers and all." Cassie felt her heart swell at the sweet sentiment and the idea of finally having a family of her own.

As if hearing his fate, Pickles slammed his outstretched paws against the other side of the glass door and let out a loud meow.

"See," Drea said. "He can't wait."

Acknowledgments

As some of you may know, I was diagnosed with breast cancer a little over a year ago. It's definitely been a challenging year, but there's been a lot of beauty amidst the trying times. Times like these can clarify who's in your corner, and I feel very fortunate and grateful to have an incredible group of friends and family who I know I can count on. So many people, some I know, some I will never know, made an impact on me this year, in small and big ways, and I'll never be able to list each one, but just know you are appreciated.

It is because of a team of amazing doctors, nurses, specialists, and support personnel that I made it through this year. The number of providers and caregivers that have been involved in my journey has been eye-opening and I want to thank all of you from the bottom of my heart, not just for what you did for me, but for what you do every day for others. There is a stigma that surrounds cancer, and a lot of people try to steer very clear of it. But you show up and live in the hard part, trying to bring some healing and peace, and even a little joy, to those going through one of the toughest times in their life, and it's not without its toll. So, thank you . . . for all that you do.

To Lisa, John, Nancy, and Josh, I have no idea what I would have done without you this year. Words can't express how much your support and friendship has meant to me. My only hope is that I can be there for you as much as you have been there for me.

Janeen, Millie, Cindy, Kim, and Jaycie, thanks for your constant support and many kindnesses. I feel very grateful to know I have such great friends despite the geography between us.

Thanks to Rey for your support throughout this year. And thanks to Kris Bryant for always leading with kindness. It's more appreciated than you'll ever know.

As hard as a serious health diagnosis is on an individual, I think it can be even harder on their family. I've always been a pretty independent person, but this year gave me the opportunity to spend more quality time with family than we've had together in many years. And while we all wished it was under different circumstances, it meant a lot to share those moments with the people who matter most to me. Thank you to my family for rallying around me and supporting me in ways I'll never fully know.

Speaking of the people who matter most to me, Sevvie and Stripe may technically be dogs, but they're still my favorite people. In all honesty, they had to navigate a lot of change this year as well and though they had many reasons to never bark at me again, they stayed by my side throughout this journey, truly exemplifying unconditional love.

Despite the curveball this year has been, it was important to me to finish Drea's story and publish the follow-up to *Other Girls*. Thanks to Finnian Burnett for providing feedback on the first draft of the manuscript. You're an incredibly talented writer and I feel grateful to call you my friend.

Thanks also to the entire team at Bywater Books. In particular, thanks to Salem West, my publisher, for being so supportive of my situation and making the publishing process a smooth ride. Thanks to Fay Jacobs, Penny Mickelbury, Nancy Squires, and Elizabeth Andersen for your expertise and helpful feedback. And thanks to Ann McMan for another incredible cover. I feel very lucky to work with such a talented group of people.

Lastly, thank you to the readers. Your support and kind words mean so much. And to those who read *Other Girls* when it first came out, thank you for your patience. I promise not to take so long next time.

About the Author

Avery Brooks grew up on the East Coast and has spent the years since gradually moving west. She has a Ph.D. in evolutionary biology and has spent much of her life studying dominance, climate change, social justice issues, and human rights atrocities. While conducting postdoctoral research in New Orleans, she fell in love with the city, which has featured prominently in her writing. She has taught at multiple universities, but her most rewarding experiences involved teaching interdisciplinary courses on dominance, climate change, and LGBTQ studies.

Avery is a graduate of the 2018 Golden Crown Literary Society's Writing Academy. When she's not busy reading and writing fiction, she serves as a freelance copy editor for other authors and uses her free time to advocate for social justice issues, women's empowerment, and animal conservation in the face of a rapidly changing climate. She lives in Colorado, where she enjoys hiking with her two dogs, trying different microbrews, and rooting for the Saints.

You can connect with her at www.averybrooksauthor.com.

Bywater Books believes that all people have the right to read or not read what they want—and that we are all entitled to make those choices ourselves. But to ensure these freedoms, books and information must remain accessible. Any effort to eliminate or restrict these rights stands in opposition to freedom of choice.

Please join with us by opposing book bans and censorship of the LGBTQ+ and BIPOC communities.

At Bywater Books, we are all stories.

For more information about Bywater Books, our publishing mission, authors, and our titles, please visit our website.

https://bywaterbooks.com

www.ingramcontent.com/pod-product-compliance
Lightning Source LLC
Chambersburg PA
CBHW020412110726
47899CB00006B/1951